Torn Sky

Torn Sky

by

Kathleen Keating

Visit Our Website!
www.countingcouppress.com

Published by Counting Coup Press, Inc.
PO Box 352
Ainsworth, NE 69210

This edition published 2002
by Counting Coup Press, Inc.

ISBN 0-9708598-1-3

Printed in the United States of America

For Our Lady of Mount Carmel

Chapter One

Michael Cross veered into the passing lane on the crowded mountain highway, desperate to get around the slower moving traffic. He glanced at the yellow sky that looked like cloudy urine in a specimen jar. Something strange had come over the earth. His thoughts raced ahead of the Thunderbird convertible as he pushed the accelerator to the floor. An oncoming semi barreled at him bringing him back to reality. Cross swerved back to the right and crammed on his brakes to avoid hitting a military transport.

The traffic ahead slowed to a crawl. Although it was barely spring, the temperature soared over 100 degrees. Cars overheated on the steep grade of Cheyenne Mountain littering the narrow road. Cross weaved in an out of the stalled cars like a mouse in a maze after being fed crack.

As he passed some of the stranded drivers, he noticed they were all looking into the sky. Cross looked up to see what had caught their attention, but clipped the side of the mountain with the front bumper. He slammed on his brakes and was nearly rear-ended by a van. The driver behind him flipped him off as Cross got out of the car.

Drenched in perspiration, Cross wiped his face on his shirt and then stared at the sky. He held his hand over his eyes to block out the tremendous glare that proved too

much for his Ray Bans. Cross felt his heart stop and then it
began racing with his fear. Two suns beat down on the
parched mountain. The already brown pine trees appeared
on the verge of combustion.

Michael Cross jumped back in his car and raced up the
mountain. He pushed the buttons on his car radio hoping to
hear some news. All he got was static. Fumbling for his cell
phone, Cross managed to punch in some numbers. It was
dead. Furious, he flung the phone out of the car window.

Frantically he drove to the guardhouse at the base and
flashed his credentials. Immediately, he was waved through
the gate. A siren blasted everyone outside and red lights
flashed all around the perimeter. The giant blast doors
started to close. Cross recklessly parked his car and ran
with military personnel through the doors before they
slammed shut. The enormous thud of the doors echoed
inside the cavernous tunnel.

Two giant security officers spotted Cross in the
congestion and grabbed him by his arms. They pulled him
to the side and checked his credentials. Lieutenant Stone
leaned over and got in Cross' face.

"What are you doing here, Mr. Cross," Stone asked,
breathing his anchovy pizza breath into Cross' face.

"Easy, boy. I've got an appointment with the old man."

"This isn't a good time," Stone snapped.

"I can see you guys are busy. Got anything to do with
what's going on in the sky?"

"Wait here with Sergeant O'Reilly, wise guy, and stay
the hell outta trouble."

Stone walked quickly to the Situation Room. It was like
traversing New York City at noon. Personnel were hurrying
in every direction. Stone arrived outside the Situation
Room and ran his ID card through the scanner. The door
buzzed and then opened.

Inside the room, personnel hurried to computer consoles and to telephones. Some officers were watching the enormous screen on the wall, which displayed a world map. Orbits of satellites were monitored along with an unknown object that lit up the massive display.

General Wolfe paced nervously around the consoles. He clenched a long cigar between his crooked teeth.

"Come on, people. Give me some input," he said.

Lieutenant Stone caught up with Wolfe by the Defense console.

"General, we have a problem," Stone gushed.

General Wolfe reeled on his heels and took the cigar out of his mouth.

"Brilliant, Lieutenant. I can see that."

Stone's face flushed. "Yes, sir. I don't mean that, sir. I mean that reporter, Michael Cross, is here."

Annoyed, Wolfe snapped, "Now? Double-Cross is here now? Get rid of him."

"Yes, sir."

"Excuse me, General. Hang on a second, Stone," interrupted Major Purvis.

"With all due respect, General, I don't think that's a good idea. If we send Cross home, he could get the word out that something is wrong," Purvis continued. He had promised Cross this interview and did not want to look like a fool.

General Wolfe threw his cigar to the floor and squashed it.

"Hell, in a few days, the whole freaking world is gonna know about it, Major," Wolfe growled. "But you're right, Major. Bring in Cross."

One Week Earlier - Lourdes Garden At The Vatican

The evening sky was glowing from the fires burning throughout Rome. Church bells cut the sultry air, calling the faithful. Two cardinals, impervious to the ringing, strolled cautiously through the garden. A bear of a man, Mikhail Makarov, joined them.

Damian Cardinal Cantore wiped his hands with a handkerchief and then blew his nose as he listened to his colleagues. He was miserable in the heat. Cantore's cassock irritated him greatly, not so much the tight fit around the middle, but what it represented.

Unlike Cantore, John Cardinal Truman, from Chicago, was fit for his fifty years. His overly large head sweat like a Roman fountain. Truman wiped it occasionally and tugged at his constricting collar.

The trio stopped near a statue of Our Lady of Lourdes, whose serene face made Truman uncomfortable. Glancing over his shoulder at the statue, Truman said, "Let's keep walking, shall we?"

Makarov was amused at the cardinal's paranoia. He took out a cigarette from a gold case and offered them to the cardinals. They declined. Makarov lit his cigarette and swallowed the smoke.

"I trust your group is prepared to remove pope from his throne," Makarov exhaled.

Cantore became somewhat breathless and said, "Certainly. We have been waiting for this moment for over thirty years."

Truman patted Cantore on the shoulder.

"You must excuse Damian's excitement. We will have no trouble installing our mutual friend as the new pope. He'll be elected in the first round."

Makarov grinned exposing his tar stained teeth.

"Excellent. We are also ready to make move. Then there are no problems to eliminate," Makarov inquired.

"Maybe one," Truman offered. He looked around and lowered his voice.

"Michael Cross. He's pushing for a private audience with the pope. Our sources are saying he's trying to pass information to the old fool about our plans," Truman added.

"Sounds like he is more than problem," Makarov grumbled.

Cantore wiped his hands a little harder and then stuffed his handkerchief in his cassock.

"He was not always so on top of things. Monsignor Getty knew him as a lapsed parishioner more interested in liquor than news," Cantore said.

1971- Madison Square Garden

A horrible din inundated the Gardens as barking dogs; grouchy dog handlers and a bombastic PA system collided, assaulting the hung over Michael Cross. He tried to track down the woman he was supposed to interview for The Times. The Best in Show competition was scheduled to start and he wanted to finish the painful mandatory assignment.

The disheveled Cross stumbled over grooming tables in the prep area looking for the snooty owner of Alexander the Great, the Best of Breed in the Working Class. Not seeing her, Cross propped himself up against a pillar and pulled out a flask of fortification. He took a healthy swig and slid down the pillar, sitting in a pile of warm manure.

Cross ran his hand underneath him and retrieved an odiferous mess. Looking around to see if anyone was watching, he wiped the residue on his trench coat. Spying Alexander's owner, Cross took another drink and then recklessly navigated his way to the dog's kennel.

"Excuse me, madam. I'm Michael Cross from The Times."

Mrs. Walter Throckmorton III gave him a hard look from under her Arden painted face. Her nostrils curled ever so slightly from the tossed salad of odors emanating from Cross. She wasn't sure which smell made her more nauseous, the booze, the manure or the clothes that hung on his emaciated body. She put on her glasses almost afraid of getting a better look. Resting the glasses at the tip of her long nose, she searched his once famous face for any sign of familiarity.

"I really doubt that you are Michael Cross, young man. You aren't fit to walk his dog."

Anesthetized beyond caring, he didn't take exception to her comment right away.

"No, really. I am Cross."

Mrs. Throckmorton ripped her glasses from her nose.

"Now why would they send an investigative reporter to cover the dog show? You're obviously a fraud."

Anesthetized or not, Cross visibly winced. He grabbed her glasses that hung by a chain around her sizable rich neck and pulled them off.

"Look, madam. I am Michael Cross and we are going to do this damn interview."

He roughly handed the glasses back to Mrs. Throckmorton. Startled, she starting screaming, "Security! Security!"

She ran off looking for someone to help her, leaving Cross by her dog's kennel. The Great Dane eyed him curiously, and whined a bit. Taking out his flask, Cross took two more swallows of vodka. He looked around and saw Mrs. Throckmorton with two security officers. Quickly turning his back, he emptied the flask into the dog's water bowl. Cross leaned over and whispered to the friendly giant.

"With all the bitches in this show, it's too bad you got stuck with that one to go home with."

A few minutes later, the excited crowd in the arena buzzed with anticipation over the final competition. Several dogs lined up with their handlers to enter the ring. Final touches were added to the well-groomed dogs and small treats were parceled out to the more anxious ones. The announcer boomed out his call.

"Will all the handlers and their dogs for the Best in Show competition report to the ring? This is the final call."

Back in the prepping area, Alexander the Great was on his back in his crate. His large pink tongue hung limply out of his mouth. Alexander had conquered all of his pre-show jitters. Mrs. Throckmorton tried to get the mammoth dog on his feet, but the dog couldn't support himself on his floppy legs.

"Police! Police! Someone get me the police!"

Chapter Two

Sol Abrams pulled down the blinds in his glass office, hoping his argument with Michael Cross would be more private. The whole floor could hear the stout man scream. Each time he pulled a blind down, his temper escalated. Cross sat unperturbed with his feet on Abrams' desk.

"Of all the sorry ass things to do. Do you know who Mrs. Walter Throckmorton III is?"

Cross lit a cigarette and exhaled in Abrams' reddened face.

"The third what? Third bitch from hell," Cross said, pleased with himself.

"Don't you give me any crap over this, Cross. She's the sister of the owner of this paper."

Cross examined the ash on the end of his cigarette. "He has my condolences."

Abrams slammed his fat fist into his hand and leaned into Cross.

"I outta fire your drunken ass right now. If it weren't for Joey, you'd be history, ya jerk."

Michael Cross sat straight up and bored a hole through his boss.

"Leave my son outta this."

Abrams thumped Cross on the shoulder and leaned even closer.

"You're the one leaving him out. Do you think you've been any kinda father to the kid?"

Cross came out of his chair and grabbed Abrams by the throat, slamming him against the wall. Some of the pictures and awards came to the floor with a crash. Outside the office, startled staff writers stopped their persistent typing, and wondered about calling the cops when they heard Cross screaming at Abrams.

"Shut the hell up. Ya hear me?"

Cross suspended Abrams in his grip for another moment. Abrams' face was bright red and saliva escaped from the corners of his mouth, covering his chin. Coming to his senses, Cross released him. He lit another cigarette with his shaking hand and inhaled deeply. Knowing he went too far, he did not want to think of the consequences, not now.

"Sorry, Solly. Ya finished? I gotta go." Cross avoided making eye contact. He felt tears welling up and bit his tongue to keep from breaking down. Abrams loosened his tie, rubbed his neck, and then wiped his face with his handkerchief.

"God knows the chief will want your head for that stunt with his sister. Jesus Christ. You're a Pulitzer Prize winner. You were a decorated fighter pilot for crying out loud. You were somebody. Now look at you. Listen, Mike. This is your last chance. The only story I got left to cover is a schlock story that no one else wants."

Cross did not like the sound of that. He stiffened, "Sorry, Sol. I don't take charity."

Abrams started to wind up again, but thought about it first.

"And I ain't givin' it. 'Sides, got any better offers? Anyway, this woman says she's been seeing the Virgin Mary. Ain't that a hoot? The Virgin Mary is coming to see this old frump of a housewife. Take it or leave it."

He did not need to think about it. "I'm leaving it."

Cross snuffed out his cigarette as he glared at Abrams, and then left the office slamming the door behind him. His jolted co-workers tried to busy themselves. Cross flung papers from desks as he walked by.

"Waddya all staring at, you sorry excuses?"

On his way home that night, Cross stopped in every bar along the way and decided to head home only after his money ran out. He knew he couldn't face his wife, not after what he did to Sol. Cross hoped she would be asleep, as he put the key in the lock of his front door. After shooting some breath freshener into his mouth, he carefully opened the door and took off his shoes. He nearly fell over trying to get his left loafer off. Glancing to see if Annie was up, Cross shut the door behind him. He tried to make his way through the darkened living room.

The small balloon lamp in Joey's room lit the narrow hallway as Cross headed to check on his son. He stood briefly outside the room and looked at the stuffed animals that stood guard over the sleeping boy. As he entered, Cross tripped over the oak rocker on his way to Joey's crib. He grabbed the rocker and put his finger up to his lips, shushing the toys scattered about the room. Joey remained asleep. His breathing made Cross feel better, safer. He stood over his son and stroked the boy's blonde curls, then leaned over and kissed him. Tears formed in his eyes. Taking a ragged breath, Cross sighed and slumped into the chair. A large Mickey Mouse doll stared back at him with a wide-eyed grin. Cross picked up the toy and clutched it to his chest. He started to cry harder and buried his face into the softness of the toy.

Annie Cross watched him from the hallway and her heart sank.

"Sweetie, is something wrong with Joey?"

Cross shook his head as Annie joined him.

Relieved, she focused on her husband. She had never seen him like this.

"Mike, what is it? You're worrying me."

Afraid he couldn't get the words out of his mouth, he took a deep breath, and then quickly spit them out.

"I quit my job."

Annie stood up, obviously upset. She raked her fingers through her blonde hair, but she would have rather raked him over the coals.

"Have you lost your mind," she raised her voice and caught herself. Annie glanced into the crib to make sure she hadn't wakened her son.

"Joey's gotta have surgery to get the rest of that tumor."

She did not need to tell Cross that. He lived with that prospect every moment.

"I know. It'll be all right. I've got friends at The Journal."

Cross felt confident that would placate his wife.

"Who are you kidding? They haven't spoken to you in years. Have you looked in the mirror lately?"

He knew he hadn't taken a good look at himself in months. Facing that reality was something he wanted to put off indefinitely.

Joey stirred in the crib. Uncomfortable and in pain, he started to cry. Annie gently scooped him up before Cross could get to him.

"Now look what you've done."

The little boy turned to his father and even Cross could see the grimace on his beautiful face.

"Daddy, my head hurts."

"I'll take him," Cross said. He put out his hands.

Annie turned away from him.

"Don't you touch him."

Joey started to scream. Annie cradled him as best she could, but she couldn't comfort him.

"Michael, get the pain syrup. Hurry."

Cross left the room; glad he could finally be of help. Distraught, he searched through the medicine cabinet until he found the brown bottle. He rushed to the kitchen to get a spoon before going back to Joey's room. The child's cries cut through his parent's anger.

"Joey, it'll be okay, buddy," said Cross, as he shakily tried to open the bottle.

"Here let me do it."

Annie jerked the bottle from Cross and then handed Joey to him; half afraid he would drop him. The bottle was nearly empty, but she managed to get one remaining spoonful. Joey didn't put up a fight in taking the medicine.

"While you're out talking to your rich friends, see if you can't get Rockefeller to give you a loan for more medicine."

It would have been easier for Cross to be shot in the heart. The pain would have been less. Dejected, he left the bedroom with a glance over his shoulder and shut the door.

The next morning, Michael Cross was cleaned up, sober and out of the house early. He had an appointment with Veronica Lueken in Queens. As he approached her house, he saw three cops in an intense struggle with an ordinary looking man wielding a butcher knife. Cross thought about helping out the cops, but they knocked the knife out of the perp's hand and subdued him. The fight was over. The largest cop, Mallory, slapped handcuffs on the guy and roughly placed him in the back of his squad car. Mallory slammed the car door shut and noticed Cross.

"Hey, Mikey. Ya lost? That is you, Mikey, right? I didn't recognize yous all dressed up. What's the occasion?"

Cross did not hesitate. "I'm gonna go see your wife. What the hell is going on?"

Mallory walked over to Cross and offered him a cigarette. Cross gladly took it.

"Some slime ball wanted to take this lady outta the game."

Cross paused before lighting his cigarette.

"Veronica Lueken?"

Mallory lit Cross' cigarette and then his own. "Yeah. So what are you doing here?"

"Got an interview."

"Ain't you got nuttin' better to do?"

Cross smirked, then headed up the stairs and rang the doorbell. As he waited, he watched the squad car pull away. The perp banged his head against the window all the way down the street. Cross shook his head. He laid into the doorbell again. His patience was thinner than he was. A pretty middle-aged woman cautiously answered the door. Cross dropped his cigarette and brushed back his hair. Veronica smiled at him. He smiled back reluctantly. She spoke through the screen door.

"Yes?"

"Mrs. Lueken, I'm Michael Cross."

"Oh, I thought you were with the police. Come in."

She unlocked the screen and opened the door. Cross noticed she had rosary beads strung through her fingers. The living room of the modest house was filled with religious statues and pictures. Candles were lit by some of the statues on a small table.

Michael Cross studied Veronica, who was visibly shaken.

"Please have a seat, Mr. Cross. May I get you anything?"

Not only was he unaccustomed to this beat, but he wasn't used to people being so kind.

"No, thanks. Listen, Mrs. Lueken, if this is a bad time for you, we can just forget...I mean, you must be upset by what just happened."

He was hoping she didn't want to do the interview at all. That would have been fine with him. He could still draw a paycheck and keep Sol Abrams off his case.

"This isn't the first time someone has tried to kill me and it won't be the last."

Cross took out his notebook. Veronica intrigued him with her response.

"Why would someone want to kill you? You seem like a nice enough lady to me."

Veronica sat in a chair next to the couch and let out a big sigh. "They don't want me to tell the world about the messages I'm getting from the Blessed Mother."

She could see he was getting uncomfortable with the subject. Cross did not bother to hide his suspicions.

"Why is that," he asked half-heartedly.

"The messages are very serious and detailed about what's going to happen to us if we don't change."

Cross closed his notebook and put the cap on his fountain pen. He figured she was nuts and the lack of nicotine was driving him crazy.

"Mind if I smoke? Ya mean the end of the world stuff?"

"Yes, but it's more than that."

Cross knew it had to be. There was always something more.

Veronica calmly continued, "The messages reveal information about people who are selling out our country, even the world. So you see, I've got to get these messages out."

"Wait a minute, Mrs. Lueken."

"Veronica, please."

"Okay, Veronica. First, I didn't say I would print any of this yet. I'm just here to get some idea about what's going on with you and now you're saying some people are involved in what? A conspiracy? All I know for sure is that the cops hauled away a would-be killer."

She smiled, but it didn't disarm him. "Then something must be going on. You don't have to be some reporter to see that. If you want more information, why don't you come to the prayer vigil on Thursday."

Cross quickly put his pen and notebook away. He hadn't seen the inside of a church in years and the thought of attending a prayer vigil made him want a drink, a tall one at that.

"Will the Blessed Mother be there," he asked snidely.

"Oh, yes. Yes, she will. Jesus might even come with her."

Cross looked like a rocket had just launched him off the couch. He hurried to the door.

"Wait a minute, Mr. Cross. Why don't you take a few of these tapes with you?"

"Tapes?"

Veronica went to the dining room table and retrieved a handful of cassettes. She placed the stack in his hands.

"A friend of mine records my visits with the Blessed Mother."

"And her voice is on the tapes," he asked, thinking he should call Bellevue to see if they had an available room.

"I repeat her words out loud," she answered confidently.

"Uh-huh. Well, I've gotta go. Thanks for your time."

Veronica showed him to the door and he rushed to get out. Once outside, he shoved the tapes into his jacket pocket and lit another cigarette. He looked back at the house and shook his head. Cross climbed into his red '64 Chevy Impala convertible and drove away.

Thinking the tapes would prove there was no story with Mrs. Lueken, Cross flipped on the radio. The bad news about Viet Nam was all over the dial. The light turned red and he turned off the radio. Glancing over at the newspaper stand on the corner, a headline on a tabloid paper caught his eye: *UFO Spotted In Michigan.* He laughed out loud.

"Jesus. The Virgin Mary or UFO's. I guess it could be worse."

Cross looked around and in his rear view mirror before taking a quick swig from his flask. The light turned green and the guy behind him in a delivery van pounded on his horn.

Outside Exeter, New Hampshire

On a New England evening, Ray Inman walked home after football practice. He made his way down the gravel road about a mile from his home, when he suddenly became engulfed in a bright white light shining down in the field. Squinting into the light, he tried to see if it was the local news chopper, but inside he knew it couldn't be. He couldn't hear a sound in the still night air. The intense beam narrowed, giving him a better view.

Ray couldn't move now if he tried. The mammoth black ship hovered over him in terrifying stillness. Bright red and blue lights on the belly of the craft lit Ray's horrified face.

As the ship descended to five feet above the corn rows, Ray's hopes descended with it. He no longer thought UFO's were cool and he had absolutely no desire for contact. Of course, he would change his story when he talked about it with his friends at school, if he made it out alive. His heart looked like it would break loose from his chest. Ray held his breath and prayed the ship wouldn't touch down.

Suddenly, the menacing craft was drenched in an orange glow, as though it had been swallowed by something twice its size. It vanished, seemingly disappearing into thin air. Ray ran the rest of the way home, never once looking back.

Mrs. Inman busied herself in the kitchen waiting for her son to come home for supper. Steam rose from the pans on the stove, as the lids rattled the news that dinner was just about ready. The windows in the small kitchen were steamed over obscuring Mrs. Inman's view of the road. With a final stir, she turned off the burners and reached for a serving bowl, as Ray shot through the door.

"Ray, for heaven's sake, you scared me. Look what you made me do."

He paid no attention to his mother or the floor now covered in sweet potatoes. Ray knocked down a kitchen chair, as he hurried to the phone.

"What's the matter, Ray?"

He gasped for breath, while he dialed the phone. His hand shook as he wrestled with the rotary dial.

"Hullo? Give me the sheriff."

Mrs. Inman stopped cleaning the stove and hurried over to Ray.

"What on earth is wrong? Why do you need to talk to the sheriff?"

Ray turned his back to her. "This is Ray Inman. I'd like to report a UFO."

"A what," answered the sheriff. Ray's mother worried her pink and white apron as she listened.

"A UFO not more than five minutes ago was smack dab over old man Toomey's farm."

Mrs. Inman ran to the window and rubbed off the steam so she could look out.

The sheriff said, "We'll send somebody out there. Will you meet 'em where you saw the damn thing?"

"Yeah, I'll be there." Ray hung up the phone and grabbed the car keys.

"Come on, Ma. Let's go."

The Pentagon, Washington D.C.

Captain Wolfe got out of his chauffeured limo and headed for the main entrance. He ran his way through dozens of military personnel looking like he did on the Airforce Academy's football field. He showed his ID to security and was escorted into the bowels of the complex by three men in suits and an armed Marine. They took an elevator six floors below ground to the Operation Blue Beam Unit. One of the men punched in an access code on the keypad next to the door. He glared at the Marine making sure the young sergeant kept his eyes forward. The buzzer sounded and the door popped open.

As they entered the darkened room, the men spotted George Hawthorne sitting behind an impressive desk. A cloud of smoke circled the strange man's head, as he vigorously puffed on his pipe.

Captain Wolfe slowly approached the desk trying to see through the blue haze that surrounded Hawthorne. The other men stayed near the door, forming a barricade.

"Sit down, Captain," Hawthorne offered. Wolfe nervously obliged him.

Hawthorne slid a file across the desk and flipped on a light over Wolfe's head.

"Read that."

Studying the file as Hawthorne studied him, Wolfe became excited over the file's contents.

"Then they do exist. We saw two of them flying near our transport on the way back from Nam."

Hawthorne tried another draw on his pipe, but the tobacco had ceased to burn.

"We know all about that," he said, as he tapped on the pipe. "That's one of the reasons you were chosen to join Project Blue Beam."

Wolfe sat forward a little. "Blue Beam, sir?"

The men near the door looked at one another without trying to be obvious. Hawthorne still noticed them. He took out a penknife and cleaned out his pipe.

"It's the ultra top secret program that is run by our elite group, Captain. It was formed to defend the world from an alien threat."

Captain Wolfe uncrossed his legs and put the file back on Hawthorne's desk.

"So all these sightings are real?"

"Not all. It is our goal to keep the lid on this thing. Naturally, we don't want to panic people, at least not yet," Hawthorne warned.

"Of course not," Wolfe said. He knew he couldn't contain his excitement, but he tried.

"How can I help?"

Wolfe had his career to think about and this stellar assignment was just the vehicle he wanted.

"At some of our missile stations, we have had a security problem. Apparently, when these bastards hover over the bases, we lose our ability to launch any defense. Entire grids go down." Hawthorne got the reaction he sought from Wolfe, who pushed the no-nonsense button.

"How long does it take before they get back online?"

Hawthorne smiled slightly, "When these mothers fly off, everything returns to normal."

Wolfe raised his eyebrows over his hazel eyes. "That means they render the United States totally helpless," Wolfe said, not liking the sound of his own words.

"Exactly. With enough ships at various bases, they completely destroy our capability of launching counter measures. As I mentioned, Captain, this is ultra top secret."

Wolfe sat back in his chair a moment, gathering his thoughts. Hawthorne tamped down new tobacco in his pipe and lit it, giving Wolfe some time.

"Is the president up to speed on this," Wolfe had to know.

Hawthorne puffed slowly on his pipe and looked over his glasses at Wolfe.

"Only what he needs to know," replied Hawthorne.

Wolfe was somewhat surprised by that answer, but not alarmed. He did some fast calculations in his head, wondering what his chances would be working for Hawthorne. Wolfe cleared his throat.

"And, uh, if this mission is not for me?"

Hawthorne put his pipe in the ashtray and stood up. "There's only one way you can leave this room alive, Captain Wolfe."

The young captain could feel three pairs of eyes trained on the back of his head. He took Hawthorne's threat seriously. Hawthorne was ready to set the hook. He poured a glass of water and drank it down. Wolfe tried to anticipate his next move.

"This whole thing could work out nicely for you, Wolfe. We know you're ambitious. There's a project we have going in Colorado that you could be a part of, if you join the team. And if not ..."

"I'm dead." Wolfe was ashamed at how weak his voice sounded.

A Villa Outside Rome

Storm clouds gathered over the ancient villa of Giovanni Cardinal Martinelli. Lightening ripped through the sky briefly illuminating the cars parked in the driveway. Martinelli stood by the window in his library and drew strength from the growing turbulence. His small stature belied his great power. Walls of books surrounded the cardinal. Spaced between the shelves, Davincis and Rembrandts looked down on the prelate adding color to the dark room. Across from him hung an oil painting of Pope

Paul VI. He was never fond of that picture, but displayed it more out of necessity rather than loyalty to the aging pontiff.

Martinelli was soon joined by two of his colleagues, Cardinal Billot, an angular, scrawny Frenchman and Cardinal Cantore, a robust man with a matching personality. Martinelli fixed some drinks for his friends and hurriedly went to the intercom.

"Dr. Vento. We are ready for you."

Cardinal Billot quickly downed his drink. "I cannot wait to see the results."

"I agree," said Cantore. "I have waited for this for a very long time."

"The reward of patience is patience, my friends," answered Martinelli with a chuckle.

Dr. Vento knocked lightly on the door and opened it. He entered with Luciano Riccelli, an elderly actor of little fame. Riccelli's entire face was bandaged except for the small slits for his eyes, nose and mouth. Vento guided the man to a chair beneath the picture of the pope.

"Sit down, Luciano," Martinelli said. Let us look."

Dr. Vento took out a pair of bandage scissors and carefully cut through the gauze. The three cardinals closed in on the poor man, as Vento gently peeled away the final layers. The prelates looked like red ants on sugar.

Martinelli lit a cigarette. "Luciano," he exhaled. "This will be your greatest role ever."

Vento stood back and looked at his handiwork, and then turned to the cardinals.

"Well, your eminences. What do you think?"

Although Luciano's face was still somewhat bruised, he bore a striking resemblance to the Pope's picture.

"Magnificent. Multi bene," Cantore shouted.

"A triumphant procedure, Doctor Vento," Martinelli said. He went to the picture behind Luciano and took it down.

Chapter Three

Sunlight streamed through the stained glass windows of Holy Name Cathedral, home to the archbishop of Chicago. Father Hunter entered the cathedral and looked around the lavish structure. An old lady lit a candle, knelt by one of the side altars, and then said a prayer. There was a homeless man in a pew near the front. The old man stared blankly at the altar before him. Father Hunter could barely stand the smell as he passed the man on his way to the confessional. He looked over his shoulder before entering the dark booth.

Hunter knelt and the priest slid back the partition.

"The meeting is set for midnight at Cardinal Truman's residence."

The priest quietly shut the partition and Hunter left.

That evening, twelve priests joined Cardinal Truman in the basement of his home. A few of the men were nervous about the meeting. Father Hunter poured cognac into Waterford snifters for the guests clad in long black robes. The hoods of the robes were down, wrapping the shoulders and backs of the priests like thick moss. Each man grabbed a glass, and then took his respective place in the circle. Father Hunter, Cardinal Truman's aide, raised his glass.

"A toast then to his eminence. To the new cardinal of Chicago and our ranking knight."

The men dutifully raised their glasses. "Your eminence," the men said in unison.

"Thank you. And now a toast to our plans: Gentlemen, may we take over the Church by the end of the century."

They downed the cognac and threw the glasses into the fireplace. Cardinal Truman pulled his hood over his head and the rest of the men followed. Father Hunter lit the black candles atop an altar, highlighting the upside down crucifix at its center.

Although the fireplace blazed, the room got strangely cold. Some of the priests were noticeably chilled. Father Hunter placed an ornate chalice on the altar along with a golden dagger. Cardinal Truman nodded to Hunter.

"Please bring in our guest."

Hunter bowed slightly and left the room. The men gathered around the altar as anticipation and impatience filled the room. Truman lit some incense and handed the incense burner to one of the men, who immediately blessed each man with the sweet smoke and then the altar. Hunter returned with a squirming bundle in his arms. He laid down the tightly wrapped bundle on the altar. Truman quickly opened up the black blanket, revealing a newborn baby.

The Bayside Shrine

Cross arrived late at the shrine. He had trouble finding a place to park. Everybody in Queens must have decided to show up. Finding a parking space five blocks away, Cross grudgingly walked to the shrine. He felt like he would rather walk to the gallows. In the distance, he could hear people saying the rosary. Many people brushed by him in an effort to get a good seat.

"Suckers," he groused.

He arrived at the gathering and immediately was surrounded by people, all hoping to get a glimpse of the Virgin Mary. Looking around the crowd, Cross spotted

Veronica Lueken seated in the front row. She was saying her rosary. Making his way through the crowd, Cross noticed the faces of the people. Most showed signs of excitement and peace. Even the people in wheelchairs seemed to be awaiting something spectacular. Their faces were oddly happy, exhibiting no indication of their afflictions. Everyone in the crowd, except for Cross, had their eyes on the statue of the Blessed Mother. Cross did not know if the crowd expected the statue to suddenly come to life or not.

Cross lit a cigarette, but felt awkward smoking it. His discomfort grew as he caught the eye of a middle-aged man who approached him. He stepped on the cigarette when the man offered Cross his hand.

"Mr. Cross? I'm Art Lueken, Veronica's husband."

Cross firmly shook Lueken's hand.

"Got quite a crowd, Mr. Lueken. Hope they won't be disappointed."

"In what," replied Lueken, somewhat amazed by Cross' statement.

"In case the Virgin Mary doesn't show."

Lueken smiled. "She'll show. Have a little faith." Lueken winked at him.

"Say, have you met Monsignor Getty? I'll introduce you." Before Cross could say no, Lueken took him by the arm and walked him over to the somber priest, who stared at the crowd. The young cleric's mouth turned down slightly, almost in disapproval.

"Monsignor, I would like to introduce…"

"Michael Cross. We've met," Getty responded.

Cross went blank. He searched his brain, but he couldn't place the priest.

"Monsignor, I'm sorry. I don't recall meeting you."

"Probably not. You passed out in my confessional. I checked your ID and sent you home in a cab once you were able to walk."

Cross didn't know what to do or say and stared at his shoes.

"Sorry, Monsignor. Uh, you must be here to see the Blessed Mother?"

"Just checking things out, same as you."

Cross detected some acid in the Monsignor's words, but didn't want to engage the priest further. He turned to Arthur Lueken impatiently.

"So, when is she supposed to arrive? I've got plans," he said, checking his watch.

"She arrives at the same time at every visit," Lueken answered. "We have about fifteen minutes, Mr. Cross. By the way, did you listen to those tapes Veronica gave you?"

"Uh, no. I, well, I've been busy." He didn't think he was lying exactly.

Monsignor Getty vaguely smirked and then excused himself. Cross watched him walk away into the crowd and wished he could leave. His need for mass quantities of booze settled in hard and his hands began to shake a little. He checked his watch again, knowing he could have been well into his second fifth for the day. Cross mumbled something incoherent to Arthur Lueken and walked around the growing crowd. Suddenly, a wave of antipathy washed over Cross.

As the crowd started to sing a hymn, Cross had to escape. He headed for his car. Behind him, two lights appeared through the trees above the statue of the Blessed Mother. A great gasp from the crowd stopped Cross in his tracks. He turned around and saw the brilliant lights coming through the branches of the trees. Slight breezes seemed to be blowing at treetop level and suddenly increased with a dramatic swoosh.

Cross noticed every eye focused on the beautiful beams. Thinking it was the lack of alcohol; he took out his flask and finished the contents. A pale pink light caught his attention. Suddenly, a strange feeling coursed through him that caused him alarm. He knew it wasn't the vodka.

"Aw, forget this crap."

Disturbed, he left the grounds in a hurry.

The Times

Cross arrived at the office on the verge of being drunk. Most of the lights were off on the floor with only an occasional desk lamp brightly breaking the darkness. A lone reporter worried over his overdue piece. Nick Peters looked up from his work to see Cross stagger through the aisles. He made it to his desk and turned on the desk lamp. A large box sat on his blotter.

"What's this?"

Peters stood up and stretched. "A guy named Lueken left it for ya. Something about tapes."

"Christ."

Searching through his desk for some gum, Peters did not know if he should ask Cross about his assignment. He had seen Cross come unglued for less. Finding a stale piece of gum, Peters unwrapped it, folded it, and then shoved it into his mouth.

"So, did the Virgin Mary show up," Peters risked it.

"Dunno. I left early."

Peters sat down hard in his chair. "Jesus, Mikey. You got a make an effort. Abrams will have your stinking ass for sure."

Cross knew it too. He didn't even bristle at Peters' words. He and Nick went way back and there wasn't much they couldn't say to one another.

"It's just a tough story to cover," Cross said, knowing the story was impossible.

"Nobody sees her 'cept this lady."

Peters thought a minute and spit out his gum into the wastebasket.

"Yeah. Not like Zeitun."

"Huh?"

Cross reached into his desk for his bottle of aspirin.

"Zeitun, Egypt. They actually got video of the Blessed Mother several times and ran it on Egyptian TV."

"Serious?"

"As alimony to two ex's. I think one of the news stations showed it here a while back.

Cross popped the top off the aspirin bottle and shook the last three tablets into his hand. He grabbed the remains of a bottle of vodka from his lower desk drawer and washed the pills down his throat with the dregs, and then threw the bottle in the trash. Peters took out a bottle of Smirnoff and peeled the label off the cap. Cross was magnetically drawn to Peters' desk. Grabbing the bottle to read the label, he sat down. Spotting two pictures of UFO's on Peters' desk and copies of top-secret documents, Cross forgot about the vodka. He reached for an official looking piece of paper, but Peters snatched it.

"What are you working on?"

Peters tidied up the papers and guarded them like a private prize.

"It's no big deal, Mike."

"Those docs say otherwise, Nicky."

"I'm working on a government cover-up."

"On UFO's? C'mon."

"No kidding. Look at this stuff. And it's not just UFO's. They're only part of the puzzle.

Peters handed Cross a fistful of photos. Cross thumbed through them, not sure what to make of them. Peters was one of the best investigators in the world, but Cross did not want to admit the UFO's were real. Perhaps it scared him a little. Growing up in the fifties and sixties, some of the scariest movies were about UFO's landing in backyards. Strange aliens would kidnap the occupants of the house and implant devices in their heads, controlling them forever.

"Some amateur photographer's pulling your fat leg, Nick," Cross hoped.

"Oh, yeah? Those shots came from a military informant."

Peters' phone rang. It was his wife and he quickly turned his back on him. Cross was happy about the interruption. It gave him time to flip through the evidence on Peters' desk. He knew his friend would forget about everything but his wife. It was one of those marriages that clicked in a big way. Peters' got more into the conversation and didn't see him take two photos, some documents and the bottle of vodka. Cross managed to leave the office undetected.

The following day, Michael Cross held his head as Sol Abrams went on a tirade. Cringing, he would have done anything for a little quiet. As Abrams continued, Cross went to the water cooler in the corner of the office and got a glass of water. The large gurgling bubble that rose was almost too much for his pounding head to handle. He briefly put his finger in his ear. Trying to pry open a tin of aspirin seemed futile, so he used his teeth. Finally getting the tin to open, he dumped five or six aspirin down his throat and chased them with water. He gingerly walked back to his chair and carefully sat down, not wanting to antagonize the blood vessels in his head anymore than he already had. Sol Abrams' fury grew and so did the decibels. Cross covered his ears.

"Where in the hell were you last night?"

"Can you keep it down, Solly?" Cross started to rub his temples.

Abrams walked around his desk and leaned over next to Cross' left ear.

"Where the hell were you last night," Abrams screamed. Cross came right out of his chair, but Abrams continued.

"You were supposed to go to that shrine!"

"I went to the shrine," Cross screamed, but his words were too loud for his headache.

"A woman was healed last night."

"Where?"

"The shrine! Haven't you been listening? So, did you see it? Did you get her name?"

Cross hunched over in his chair.

"No," he said softly.

That was not the answer Sol Abrams wanted to hear. His porcine body tensed and his upper lip curled down. He got so angry that his upper plate dislodged, but he didn't care.

"Why the hell not," yelled Abrams, as he shoved the denture back in place. "The Post had it all over the damn front page."

Cross did not know what to say. He wasn't sure he cared, but he did care about Joey. That was the one thing he knew.

"I guess I left too early."

Abrams went crazy. He cared for Cross, almost as if he were his brother. Motivating his one-time star reporter was always a challenge, but he didn't know the man anymore.

"Ya, guess? Guess this. Get an article on my desk by 10:00 p.m. or you're history. And I want names, details, the whole bit. Ya got that?"

Cross did not care if he made the deadline. "Sol, I don't think this is my kinda story. Really. There's not enough action."

"How 'bout the freakin' action in the unemployment line?"

Abrams meant it this time and Cross knew it.

"Ten o'clock," Cross mumbled and walked out of the office. Abrams went to the doorway to deliver another dig. "Not one second later," he hollered at the back of Cross' head. Abrams slammed his office door so hard that he broke the glass into hundreds of pieces.

"Oh, shit."

Cross looked back, grinned and then headed for Flannery's. He considered it his second office and so did his friends. The dark paneled bar had framed front pages from most of the papers in town. Many of the yellowed pages told of one kind of disaster or another. Some covered corruption in the city government; others hailed baseball's best. The headlines spanned more than a century.

Cross sat in a booth at the back of the bar. It was his favorite location. Usually he came to Flannery's for two things: serious drinking followed by some serious work. According to Cross, he could not have one without the other. He tried. It never worked.

With his headphones on he couldn't hear the commotion about the bartender and his lotto winnings, nor did he care about some poor sap's good luck. Right now he had to get into those tapes of Veronica Lueken's whether he liked it or not. Two empty glasses marked the time he'd been sitting there along with an empty pack of cigarettes. Cross tried to take notes, but the dim lamp on the table was not cooperating or perhaps it was his eyes. He preferred to think it was the lamp.

Nick Peters walked in and spotted him. Peters was exhausted and somewhat frazzled. He took his time to get to Cross. The bartender saw Peters and left two hot numbers to fill a glass of beer. He slid it down to him.

Peters drank half the glass before the bartender returned to his stimulating conversation.

He pushed his large stomach into the table across from Cross.

"How's it hangin', Mikey?"

Cross took off his headset and shot Peters the look. Peters knew it would cost him.

"You're just in time to buy me some lunch."

"Glad to see you're hungry. What'll you have," Peters asked, as he polished off his beer.

"Vodka. Double."

"I shoulda known. The old Double Cross."

Peters put two flabby fingers into his mouth and let go with a terrible whistle. He waved two empty glasses over his head.

"Hey, Jerry, two more of the same."

Peters started to tidy up the table. He put the filled ashtray on a nearby table and grabbed a clean one. Cross was waiting with a freshly lit cigarette. Peters unwrapped a Cuban cigar, which Cross lit for him.

"Come to your senses and started workin' on that story, huh?"

Cross did not answer. He exhaled into Peters' face.

Peters shrugged it off. "I can't work at the office neither."

"How's your UFO piece? The Enquirer wantcha yet?"

The bartender shoved two drinks at the friends and ran a damp cloth over the table.

"Jesus, Mikey. This is some serious shit here. Keep it down, will ya? I'm trying to get in touch with my government guy. There's been a rash of UFO activity. He has this file he's gonna slip me."

Cross put a huge dent in his drink.

"Careful with those pricks. Are you sure this guy's on the level?"

"True blue, Mikey." Peters let go with an awful belch.

"Watch your back. If any of that shit is true, those mothers will be playing for keeps."

Cross finished his drink and gathered up his cigarettes and tape recorder.

"Where ya goin'?"

"Gotta go see somebody about a wheelchair."

He left the bar and thought about whether or not he should drive out to Long Island to see Mary McLaughlin. The thought of being too drunk to drive didn't occur to him. He still hadn't had a fifth, so he figured he was legal.

The drive seemed to clear his mind, which angered him. The tight lines around his eyes gathered as he thought about the supposed miraculous healing from the previous night. More snake oil he thought.

Pulling into the long circular driveway of the McLaughlin estate, his stomach lurched. He felt even more the failure. Thoughts of Joey and Annie tormented him as he stepped on the brake. Cross took out his notebook and headed for the door.

He was quickly shown into a cavern of a living room with a black grand piano in the center. The big bay window exposed a garden beyond anything Cross had ever seen. Terribly uncomfortable, he paced nervously. A grandfather clocked chimed and echoed in the luxurious room. A wheelchair was folded and propped against the wall just to the right of the monstrous clock.

Mary McLaughlin entered through butter yellow French doors and sprightly walked towards Michael Cross.

"Mr. Cross, how do you do?"

"Mrs. McLaughlin." He didn't know what to make of this older woman. She was beautiful and didn't seem challenged in the least.

"Isn't it a magnificent day?"

"Hadn't noticed."

"Where are my manners? Please have a seat."

She was positively glowing and Cross thought she had to have been Veronica Lueken's shill, right down to the folded wheelchair.

"I got your name from Veronica Lueken. So is the story true?" Cross usually cut to the chase, especially when something was painful and this was definitely worse than death.

"You saw me walk across the room. How did I do?"

"Remarkably." There was no denying it. "How long were you in the wheelchair?"

"Over twenty years." Her smile was beautiful. "All of my money couldn't free me from that hideous contraption."

"Why do you still have it out? Worried you'll have a relapse?" Cross tried to blame her cure on her hysteria.

"It serves as a reminder of the great blessing the Blessed Mother gave me." She was confident of that fact and didn't try to convince him. He admired that.

"How do you know it wasn't a spontaneous or psychological healing?"

Mrs. McLaughlin's face brightened and a look in her eyes captured Cross without a fight.

"Because of the miraculous warm feeling that ran up and down my spine, and because Father Ed told me the Blessed Mother was going to heal me last night. He gave me this statue."

She leapt out of her chair and retrieved a foot tall statue of the Blessed Virgin.

"How did he know? You just believed him?"

Cross could not figure it out. She seemed like an honest woman.

"I'm living proof. I'm walking aren't I?"

"Sure, I guess."

"You don't sound convinced, Mr. Cross. Afraid I'm lying?"

"Not exactly."

She got up and went over to an antique desk and wrote something down on a vellum note card.

"Here, Mr. Cross. That's the name of my doctor. I will call him and tell him that you will be contacting him about my case and that he has my permission to discuss it with you."

He thought that sounded quite fair. Cross glanced at the name and saw that it was one of the best neurologists in the country. His theory about a con game started to disintegrate

"Permit me to ask you a question."

Mrs. McLaughlin snapped him back into the moment.

"Tell me, do you believe in God?"

Chapter Four

The newsroom was in an uproar. Reporters made last minute changes to their stories and the keystrokes grew deafening as the deadline approached. Even the well-seasoned reporters joined their younger colleagues in furtive glances at the large clock outside Sol Abrams' office. Phones rang incessantly. As Cross entered the newsroom, he grimaced at the intensity of the fluorescent lights and the din that had taken over the room. He shielded his bloodshot eyes with sunglasses. One or two reporters hollered to him as he entered Sol's office. As he closed the office door, the racket mercifully subsided. Abrams had his pocket watch in hand, winding it.

"Not a second to waste."

"Here's your damned story."

"Better be your damned story, and it better be damned good."

Cross toasted Abrams with his flask. He took a drink and left, slamming the door. He was disappointed he didn't break the glass. That would have been too much to expect. Cross walked to his desk and read his phone messages. The phone on Nick Peters' desk rang insistently, driving Cross out of his skin. Not seeing Peters on the floor, Cross picked up his phone.

"Times. Cross."

Nick's wife was on the phone and she seemed upset.

"Mike, is Nick there?"

"I dunno, Maggie. Hang on."

Cross put the call on hold and looked around the office one more time before letting go with a bellow.

"Any of you guys seen Nick?"

Several reporters shook their heads not taking their eyes off of their work.

"Nobody's seen him. Guess he stepped out."

"I'm worried about him, Mike. He was supposed to be home two hours ago."

Nick Peters had many faults, but he never lied to his wife and was rarely late. The last time he was late was in the third grade. Cross remembered the story. Peters had been caught in the zipper of his uniform pants at Holy Face School. He'd turn up, just as he did back then, only this time he wouldn't have to answer to Sister Theresine. Even Maggie couldn't be that tough.

"Don't worry. I'll track him down."

Cross got off the phone and decided to check out the john just in case history repeated itself. It hadn't. Cross decided to stop by some old haunts to see if Nick was anywhere to be found. He exited the building and took a deep breath. For once, the city smelled decently. He stopped by the alley to light a cigarette, but a man came running out, knocking him down.

"Hey, watch it, you bastard."

His cigarette was broken in half, which made Cross madder than his skinned hand. He reached into his coat to get another cigarette and lit it, curious about the guy who ran into him. Cross entered the poorly lit alley. He saw a large clump of garbage at the other end. Slowly, he realized it was a body. As he got closer, he recognized Peters' checked sport coat. He ran to his friend and carefully turned him over. Peters was badly beaten and bleeding profusely from a stomach wound.

"Aw, Jesus, Nick. I'll get help."

Peters grabbed Michael Cross with a bloody hand, startling him.

"Mike, no. Wait."

Cross did not want to hear what was coming next.

"You'll be all right. I'll go get help, Nicky."

He tried to pry Nick's hand from his jacket.

"My shoe. There's a key."

He wasn't sure if Peters was coherent or not.

"What?"

"My shoe."

Peters tightened his grip on Cross and then suddenly let go. He started to gurgle. Rivers of blood streamed down his chin from his mouth. Trying to breathe, death caught him before he could exhale.

"Nick? God, no!"

Tears streamed down Cross' face. He didn't know what to tell Maggie. He didn't know why anyone would want to kill Nick. There wasn't anyone in the world that didn't like Nick Peters. After a few moments, Cross composed himself and thought about why Peters was in the alley.

"What in the hell were you saying about your stupid shoe?"

Cross straightened Peters' limp right leg and removed the bloodstained wingtip. Not seeing anything, he ran his hand in the shoe and felt something under the shoe insert. Hurriedly, Cross ripped it out and found a key. He grabbed it and went to call the police.

By the time he was able to get home, it had been forty-eight hours since he had seen his family. With his last ounce of energy, Cross unlocked the front door and dragged himself into the living room. The house seemed strangely quiet. He looked around and called to his wife.

"Annie, I'm home." Cross went from room to room. "Annie? Joey?"

Not seeing anyone, he shrugged and headed to the kitchen. Dirty dishes were piled precariously in the sink and on the kitchen table. The smell of bacon grease hung heavily in the bright yellow kitchen. Cross went to the refrigerator and pulled out a carton of milk. Shutting the door with his foot, he opened the carton and took a drink. Cross spotted a note stuck to the fridge by a giant magnet. As he read it, the milk carton came of his hand and exploded on the floor. Cross ran out of the house and jumped in his car. The mid-morning traffic held Bellevue Hospital at arms length. No matter what route Cross took, the streets were jammed.

He finally parked his car and ran the rest of the way to the hospital. His years of smoking took a toll as he pushed himself as far as he could. Cross was not tired now. His steel blue eyes started to tear as he made his way between the blocked cars. Briefly, stopping to catch his breath, Cross did not know what to feel. He was scared for Joey, but he was more scared of failing his family one more time. He wiped the perspiration from his face and sprinted the rest of the way to the hospital.

The emergency room was packed. He couldn't see Annie, so he ran down the corridors looking in every treatment room. Not seeing his wife or his son, Cross began to panic. He ran to the nurse's station and asked if Joey was being treated.

A long-nosed nurse gruffly looked through the charts as Cross felt himself coming unglued. She went through each file much too slowly for Cross' liking. He understood why she had such an interesting bump on the bridge of her nose. Someone got fed up with her.

"Please, will ya just hurry up?"

"Let me check the computer. What did you say your son's name was?"

"Cross. Michael Joseph Cross. C'mon, lady."

The nurse shot a killer of a look over her glasses and finished typing in the name.

"Well?"

"It's still searching. These terminals are so slow."

Cross ran his fingers through his hair and thought about pulling the nurse over the counter.

"He is in intensive care," she finally said.

Those words hit Cross hard and he knew his heart missed a couple of beats.

"Where's that?"

"Take the elevator to seven."

He ran to the elevators and pushed all the up buttons. The wait seemed interminable. Frustrated, he ran to the stairwell, nearly knocking down everyone in his path. The smells of the wards started to turn his stomach. They reminded him of his dad's prolonged battle with cancer, but he quickly pushed it out of his mind. Cross did not want Joey to end up like his dad, not if he could help it.

Cross burst through the doors to the intensive care unit and ran to the nurse's station. A middle-aged roller derby queen in white was busy charting her medications.

"I'm looking for my son. His name is Joey Cross."

He started to cough deeply. Then he almost gagged.

"Mr. Cross, doctor's been trying to reach you."

"Where the hell is he," snapped Cross.

"Doctor Jarvis should be out of…"

"Not the damned doctor, you idiot. My son. Where is my son, for Christ sake?"

The roller derby queen looked like she was ready to break away from the pack.

"I'm afraid you can't see him," she said, pushing up her sleeves.

"Waddya mean? The hell I can't. Where is he?"

He grabbed a patient list from the desk, but the unintimidated nurse grabbed it right back. Doctor Jarvis walked up to the station.

"Michael, come with me."

Jarvis was a short man, but long on talent. His bald head gleamed in the hall lights. All the nurses thought he buffed his pink scalp every morning before surgery.

Doctor Jarvis took Cross to a small lounge. He walked over to the enormous coffee maker and poured two cups of coffee. Handing one to Cross, he shoveled sugar into his cup and stirred.

"Sit down, Michael."

"I want to know about Joey. Where is he?"

"He's here in ICU." Jarvis took a protracted sip of his coffee.

"Michael." Jarvis stared into his cup.

Cross did not like the look on Jarvis' face. The doctor's shaggy eyebrows joined, curling over his small glasses.

"I want to see him. Now."

"After we talk. Michael, Joey is going downhill. Apparently the tumor has grown since his last CT scan."

"So, you'll have to operate sooner is all."

That's all Joey needed. He tried to convince himself of that.

"I'm afraid not. The cancer has spread to the entire brain."

Cross felt like running, but he knew he could not move.

"You said he was better. Damn you."

It was true that was what Jarvis thought, but Joey's condition rapidly deteriorated and he knew the little boy had little resiliency left.

"I can't explain it, Michael."

"There must be something you can do. Tell me there's something you can do for him. Please."

Jarvis looked into Cross' eyes and set his jaw.

"I can't. We can keep him comfortable. That's all we can do."

Cross threw his coffee across the room and in a rage turned over the coffee maker. He pounded his fists repeatedly into the table until he couldn't throw another punch. Fighting back tears, Cross turned to Jarvis, who patiently waited for him to take the next step.

"How long?"

Jarvis was glad that Cross could ask that question. He seemed more sober than Jarvis ever remembered him and he hoped he would stay that way for his family's sake.

"No more than six months. Maybe a lot less."

"I want to take him home."

Jarvis nodded. "He should be stabilized by the end of the week. Pull yourself together and I'll take you to his room."

Cross and Jarvis walked down the hall together in silence. Things seemed distorted to Cross, as he passed people and gurneys in the hall. The beeping of the monitors at the nurse's station pierced his eardrums. Panic started to build. Outside Joey's room, Cross saw his wife through the glass in the door. She was hunched over in her chair, holding Joey's hand. Now the panic jumped sideways down his throat and stuck. He vomited reactively and bolted out of the hospital and into the arms of a torrential downpour.

He was impervious to the horrible weather. Soaked to the skin, Cross ended up outside St. Patrick's Cathedral. Pacing by the main entrance, he took out a cigarette. Pulling his suit coat over his head, he tried to protect the cigarette from the rain, but it absorbed the water like a dry creek bed.

Cross looked at some of the people going into the church. Some had serene looks in their eyes, at peace with themselves. Others seemed at loose ends, distraught, like him. Shivering, Cross waged a brief debate with himself. He lost and went inside.

Several people were in the church, most lost in their prayers. Cross was just lost. He searched for a quiet corner and knelt before a statue of the Blessed Virgin. Rows of votive candles lit his well-worn face, but yet exposing the face of a bewildered little boy. Shakily, he lit a candle and made the sign of the cross, surprised he remembered how to do it.

He buried his face in his hands and started to sob softly. After a few minutes, Cross raised his head and looked into the statue's compassionate eyes. A small smile crossed his lips.

"I guess you know why I'm here. It's not for me. I don't even know why you'd listen to me. But see, my son, he's done nothing wrong. He's just a little boy. I'm the problem. Please, I'm begging you. You gotta help him."

Chapter Five

Sunlight bounced off the reflective windows of the Hilton Hotel in downtown Toronto, making the massive structure glow. Heavy security was posted all around the building and across the street. Guards at every door were checking ID's of anyone who entered. The hotel was closed to regular guests to accommodate the convention of the world's elite. Long black limos waited to unload their prestigious passengers. Oddly, no press was seen anywhere near the complex. Presidents and prime ministers walked without fear of media scrutiny.

In the Grand Ballroom, princes, would-be presidents, presidents and has-beens joined bankers and power brokers. The small flags in front of each guest heralded their origins, not that countries really mattered to these leaders. Some people took notes as they listened to Paul Gold, president of this secret Who's Who, while others snacked from the copious plates in front of them, filled with every kind of pastry and fruit imaginable.

Paul Gold was in his early sixties, but looked like he stepped out of the pre-World War Two era. His hair was parted just to the left of center and greased back with a little too much pomade. The bow tie that tickled his double chin was smartly tied, but did nothing for the navy blue suit

Gold wore. A three-pointed white handkerchief peeked just above his breast pocket like pristine sails against the midnight sky. The black horned-rimmed glasses that crept towards the end of Gold's nose were more for appearance's sake than necessity.

"The standard of living of the average American has got to decline," said Gold.

Harvey Killian, the Secretary of State from the United States listened intently to Gold, as he bit into a sizable chunk of pastry. He agreed with Gold's assessment and stared briefly at the teeth marks he left in his chocolate éclair. His bite was nearly perfect.

"The wealth of the average American must be depleted to the point that it equalizes them with the rest of the world's inhabitants," Gold continued.

Killian passed the pastry plate to Graham Katz, owner of The Times and then to Shoji Yashiro, president of Japan Motors. Both men declined to indulge. Killian wished he had grabbed just one more cake. Yashiro looked around the room at the security guards posted at every exit. He watched the guards as they gave the waiters and the trays they carried careful scrutiny.

Gold cleared his throat before continuing with his speech, capturing Yashiro's attention.

"Religion especially must be undermined. Without concrete morals, the people will capitulate. Then, and only then, will they tolerate global authority. As it stands now, the average American is far too independent to go along with our plans and too religious for their own good."

Graham Katz could attest to that. He hated the very notion of religion thanks to his father. So what if he hadn't wanted to become a rabbi?

Gold glanced over his glasses at the gathering and cleared his throat again. "If you'll look at the supporting documents you have in front of you, I am sure you will concur with the proposition that will level the situation."

Harvey Killian thumbed through some of the pages.

"So, by these figures, you're estimating that within 25 to 30 years, Americans will be reliant on so many foreign countries for their goods and by reducing their take home dollar, you can ultimately install a global authority?" Killian thought he cut through the meat with adeptness.

"That's right, Harvey," Gold withheld his annoyance.

"Whether it be farming out manufacturing to third world countries, castrating the American worker or manipulating the stock market and federal legislation, or even taking over the Vatican, we can make it impossible for small to medium sized companies to afford to stay in the United States."

Yashiro liked the sound of that. "Then, are you meaning that technical jobs will decline in the United States as well?" Yashiro was busy calculating the profits Japan would see.

"The abundance of workers in the United States, after 30 years, will be service workers with no skills. Burger flippers," Gold sneered.

"And this would be done by what means, please," asked Yashiro.

"For starters, no one will become president without our blessing. In fact, at least someone on the ticket will be one of our members. Mr. Katz will continue with the news blackout and not print anything related to our plans or members."

"That's correct," Katz nodded in agreement.

Paul Gold took a drink of water. "We are grateful to The Post, and The Times, the major magazines and so on, whose directors have attended our meetings and respected their promises for discretion nearly forty years now. It would have been impossible for us to develop our plans for the world, if we had been subjected to the light of publicity during that time." Gold thought about his reporter-wife. He had her right where he needed her.

"But, the world is more sophisticated and prepared to march towards a world government. The supernatural sovereignty of an intellectual elite and world bankers are surely preferable to the national auto-determination practiced in past centuries."

"Whatever," Killian whispered to himself, as he grabbed a cannoli.

Katz figured it was time to speak up. He was getting sick of watching Killian make a fool of himself.

"I've got the rest of the print and electronic media with me on this. So, we can continue to dominate and influence the world situation the way we want, insuring more wealth for our members," Katz commented.

Yashiro put down his glass of water. "But Americans won't tolerate being taken over by force."

Killian wiped his lips and his hands then folded his napkin. "Today, Americans would be furious if U.N. troops entered Los Angeles; tomorrow they would be thankful. This is especially true if they were told there was an outside threat, whether real or promulgated, that threatened our very existence. It is also possible that a nuclear attack, arranged and agreed upon by our members, could throw the country into chaos. Martial law would be necessary. It is then that all peoples of the world will pledge with world leaders to deliver them from the future."

Killian pushed his tongue between his teeth trying to dislodge a wedge of food. He quickly took a drink before he continued.

"The one thing every man fears is the unknown. When presented with this scenario, individual rights will be willingly relinquished for the guarantee of well-being granted to them by their world government."

Graham Katz smiled broadly and then quickly became sober. "This is like playin' God or something." Perhaps there was a hint of a wannabe rabbi in Katz.

"Eventually, we will control the globe, the people, the money, everything. We won't play God, we will be God," added Gold.

New York City

"God! I can't believe this," griped Cross, as he went over stacks of paper deposited on his dining room table. "No wonder they got to Nick."

Annie thought she heard him say something while she was doing the dishes. She peeked into the dining room.

"Did you say something?"

"Huh? Uh, just talking to myself again."

Annie joined him and put her arms around his neck.

"Joey okay?" Cross hated to ask.

She smiled faintly and started to rub the back of his neck.

"He's sleeping. What are you doing," Annie asked, hoping whatever it was would be a temporary distraction.

"Working on a story." Cross noticed she had on the blue sweater he had given her. It was the first thing he'd noticed in months.

"This stuff keeps me from going crazy over Joey." Annie thought the work must be extremely interesting and welcomed an escape from her worry.

"Can I see?" Annie started to go through the papers, but Cross got defensive.

"It's nothin'."

She knew better and he knew he hadn't fooled her.

"Are you still working on that story about that Veronica woman?"

"I'm seeing her tomorrow. Why?" Cross looked at his wife carefully. It had been too long since he really looked at her. She appeared worn out. Her blue eyes had lost their luster and he noticed her hair was graying at the temples. At the mention of Veronica, her eyes took on a glimmer. There was light bouncing off the warm color of her eyes. Cross remembered that was why he had gotten her that sweater.

"If there is something to what she is saying, maybe Joey could be healed." Annie watched his eyes as he pulled her onto his lap. He anticipated what she had on her mind, and he was a little frightened of it, not at the prospect of a healing, but over the chance of failure.

"Baby, there is nothing I want more. But we gotta face facts." Cross could not bear to see her grasp at false hope.

"Like that lady who walked out of her wheelchair? C'mon, Michael."

There was that supposed healing he had tried to dismiss. He knew he couldn't explain how it happened, but believing in miracles wasn't something that fit well into an investigative journalist's work. Cross could hear Sol Abrams if he had given in to the belief, something about losing his objectivity. Yet, a healing was what he'd prayed for, what he wanted more than anything.

"I dunno, Annie," he mumbled. He suddenly got irritated. "What's God done for us lately? Isn't Joey's illness proof of that? Just give it a rest. Now let me finish what I'm doing here."

Annie quickly stood and thought about getting angry, but decided against it. She didn't have the energy. She went back to the kitchen, back to the dishes and her worries. Annie hoped her problems could be scraped away and run through the garbage disposal.

Cross lit a badly needed cigarette and worked through the night and part of the morning. By noon, he couldn't focus on the documents, no matter how fascinating they were. He finished what was left of his second pack of cigarettes, then tried to get some sleep.

He listened to Annie reading stories to Joey. The pain of Joey dying cut him like jagged metal. He pulled his foam pillow over his head to block out the noise, to mute reality, but his mind wouldn't shut off. Out of cigarettes, Cross decided to shower and then head for Queens to see Veronica Lueken. He knew there was a convenience store on the way where he could load up on smokes and some beer.

Cross was one of the first to arrive at the shrine. He surprised himself that he hadn't touched the beer yet, but he knew it would be waiting for him like a patient mistress.

Veronica Lueken arrived by car shortly after Cross got there. Her husband, Art, dropped her off and went to find a place to park. As she walked over to the statue of the Blessed Mother, she clutched a large crucifix and a rosary in her hands, her weapons and her comfort.

Cross could not believe he was hurrying to see her, and he hoped that no one recognized him.

"Hi, Veronica."

"Michael, did you talk with Mrs. McLaughlin?" Veronica looked at him sweetly.

Cross thought about a nasty comeback. For some reason, Veronica disarmed him.

"Yeah. Seems something happened to her," he reluctantly admitted. "Expecting another miracle tonight?" Cross almost sounded excited about it. Veronica detected the enthusiasm, however weak it was.

"That's up to the Blessed Mother." At first he thought her answer was pure baloney. Yet something made him tone down his skepticism a notch.

"There may be a healing or another miraculous photo taken." Now she did it. He couldn't let this one go.

"What kinda photos?"

"Lots of unexplained photos have been taken here with only a supernatural explanation for them."

Cross thought those photos would help her case in the believability department. He also thought it was strange she had never mentioned photos before now.

"With all respect, photos can be retouched or faked." He felt that these so-called photos might prove Veronica to be nothing more than a fraud.

"That's why Our Lady insisted that only Polaroid's be used so scientists couldn't dispute the pictures." If there were Polaroid's, legitimate shots, she just might be legit. For some reason, he was also amazed that Our Lady would have suggested Polaroid's.

"She sounds like a hip lady," Cross said politely, thinking that the Polaroid idea was someone's earthly invention.

"She's more than that," Veronica answered, glancing at her watch. "Please excuse me. I want to start the prayers.

Cross looked around and then sat behind Veronica. She kissed the crucifix on her rosary and made the sign of the cross. As she knelt, most of the crowd joined her. Cross remained seated. He looked up at the statue of Mary and noticed she wore a crown of fresh cut roses, deep red roses and baby's breath. Someone had placed a blue velvet cape over her shoulders fastened by a gold braided chain.

A man with a microphone knelt next to Veronica. Her warm voice filled the speakers located around the grounds. She continued with the rosary.

"Hail Mary, full of grace. Oh! Oh! I see her," she beamed.

Cross looked hard, but couldn't see anything. He turned to a woman next to him. She seemed fixated on something.

"Do you see her? Where is she?"

"Shh," she said softly, not turning her head. "Be patient."

He'd never been good at waiting. As a little boy, he would find his mother's favorite hiding place filled with Christmas presents and neatly unwrap the ends of the packages just to get a peek. As a child, he hated to wait, even if the element of surprise vanished. Cross had not changed.

He looked at the man next to him, whose Polaroid camera was trained on the statue. Cross shrugged and strained his eyes to see.

Veronica began to speak and the entire crowd held its collective breath.

"Directly at the center of this light, which seems to be circular, at this time, Our Lady is coming forward."

"What light," Cross whispered. No one heard him.

"She's dressed so beautifully. It makes you feel as though you're in a garden of flowers." Veronica paused for a moment and then continued.

"There is no way you can explain the impact of the feeling when you see Our Lady coming forward through the sky. So absolutely beautiful."

Cross leaned forward to look at Veronica. Her face had taken on a surreal beauty and there was an unmistakable peace about her. He could almost feel it, but he fought those feelings the best he could.

"Our Lady is touching her finger to her lips. She's going to say something and she wants me to repeat it." Cross thought this was an act, that the smoke and mirrors were about to be utilized, but he could not nurture the thought the way he had hoped.

Veronica grew silent, as she appeared to listen intently. Then she repeated the words, "My child, you must pray more, do much penance, for the warning is coming upon mankind. There will be a tremendous explosion and the sky shall roll back like a scroll." No one made a sound; Cross swore he could hear his heart beat.

"This force shall go within the very core of the human. He will understand his offenses to his God. However, this warning will be of short duration, and man shall continue upon their road to perdition, so hard are the hearts."

Cross glanced around at the faces in the crowd. They had become quite somber. People leaned forward trying to hear Veronica. He also noticed Veronica's face, which had grown very pale. Her eyes were fixated at a point about twenty feet above her.

She then spoke softly and deliberately. "Our Lady is looking over the crowd now. She seems so sad. Now she wants me to listen and to repeat her words." Veronica appeared to listen for a moment. Cross thought that she was either a talented actor or really was listening to someone. Then Veronica spoke.

"You have had two reprieves in the past, My children. The third reprieve shall not be given. I give you one indication in regard to the warning that the time is ripe when you see, when you feel the revolution in Rome, when you see the Holy Father fleeing, seeking refuge in another land, know that the time is ripe."

Michael Cross started to shift in his seat. An intense heat radiated through him and settled in the center of his chest.

"Man has reached to the stars for power, self-gratification, glory, money - for what? They are but a shell that one day must be destroyed. You must now live each day as though you were to go over the veil tomorrow, for as suddenly will many be taken from the earth."

Cross shifted again. He was uncomfortable with the severity of the message. Folding his arms in front of him, he watched Veronica, who was totally oblivious to her surroundings.

"Our Lady said, 'Earthquakes in your country, the United States, extending up through Canada, earthquakes in places never before known to exist. And they will know it comes but from the hand of God. Famine, starvation, your crops will rot. The heat will burn, your cattle will starve. And why? Because you refuse to turn back, complacent in your arrogance.'"

Veronica took a noticeable breath and said, "The Blessed Mother said that we should continue to pray for our country. Pictures can now be taken."

Camera motors whirred all over the grounds and flash bulbs popped like electric popcorn. Cross looked at the man on his right who was waiting for a snapshot to dry.

"You don't believe all that shit, do ya? How do you know something, anything, is going on here?"

The man blew lightly on the snapshot and waved it in the air a few times. Then he gave the photo to Cross.

"Take a look at this photo and you tell me."

Cross thought he was being a wise guy. Carefully, he took the photo from the man and looked at it in amazement. The picture revealed the statue of the Blessed Mother, but written above it in white cursive was 'Jacinta 1972'. Cross was too shocked to answer.

Chapter Six

Michael Cross sat on the couch in his smoked filled living room listening to Veronica's tapes. On the coffee table was an old hubcap filled with cigarette butts. A light blue haze hung over the mahogany antique, camouflaging dozens of tapes. He found a section on of the tapes that interested him. Cross rewound the tape a bit, hit play and lit another cigarette. A raspy cough had become a constant companion.

"There is now a conspiracy of evil in your country, the United States. Recognize the meaning of the Illuminati. It is Satan who guides them, they are dead bodies and souls."

Cross turned up the volume and started to take notes.

"They are now performing wonders to confuse and capture the mind. You call one of them UFO's. They are supernatural manifestations from hell. They are created in the minds of some by the demons, who are capable, because of great power upon the earth, to control now the elements, nature."

Cross coughed so deeply that it sounded like a hairball was going to pop out of his mouth. He stopped the tape and rewound it again. Annie shuffled into the living room half asleep. She waved her arms trying to disperse the smoke, as she made her way over to the couch.

"Mike, what are you doing still up?" Annie curled up on the couch next to him and yawned.

"I can't sleep. The prayer vigil has my mind going, ya know?"

"Why? What happened," she yawned again. Annie stretched out her long legs over his lap.

"Here. Look at this." Cross pulled out the Jacinta photo and waited for her reaction.

"A guy took that picture tonight. I asked him to take a shot of the original for me."

Annie pulled back her hair and looked at the photo.

"Jacinta-1972. Wasn't she one of the girls from Fatima? So this was written on a banner there?"

Cross sat up with excitement. "That's just it. This guy took a photo of the statue and this is what came out of his camera."

"What do you make of it?" Annie was still somewhat in a fog.

"I dunno," Cross began to yawn. "It's driving me nuts. I deal in black and white, but there is something there. I'm just not sure what. It's late. Let's go to bed."

Cross turned out the lights and they headed to Joey's room. They tucked Joey in and picked up a stuffed bear from the floor and placed it in the crib.

"You go on. I'll be there in a minute," Cross said softly. He kissed Annie and she headed for bed. Cross stared at his son a moment. Joey seemed so peaceful. He patted the boy's cheek, and then kissed him. He sat down and pulled the photo from his shirt pocket. Straining to see it under the light of the balloon lamp, he thought about the possibilities.

Rome

Caught in hideous traffic, Cardinals Martinelli and Cantore sat in the back seat of a limo and headed towards the papal apartments. Wedged in between an old truck and a VW bus, the cardinals scarcely noticed the traffic. They were engaged in another one of their infamous discussions.

"Too many people are paying far too much attention to all of these visionaries," Cantore offered.

"First, you had those girls at Garabandal back in the 1960's. Then a Japanese nun started to rock the boat. Now there is this anomaly coming out of New York. We have managed to keep the Third Secret of Fatima under wraps, but it seems that these modern visionaries are circumventing that secret with their messages," Cantore said.

He was visibly upset, but Cardinal Martinelli paid no attention. The cardinal focused on his fingernails.

"True. Some of the latest ones surely seem as though the visionaries have read that secret themselves. But how could they," Martinelli asked.

Cantore flushed, "You do not suppose then that…"

"Nonsense," Martinelli snapped, waving him off. "But we will have to have the pope silence them just the same."

"Ah. But Pope Paul seems to find Garabandal and the New York situation interesting enough not to have released a statement in the past, despite what the Secretary of State tried to do."

"Well, we must see that is changed."

Cantore pursed his lips in a strange way, showing his indignation. Martinelli knew they were taking their plans to new heights and he hoped his comrades were prepared.

The limo pulled up in front of the papal apartments. The sun beat down on the clerics as they entered the building. Just like the day, Martinelli felt things would heat up.

The cardinals were shown to the pontiff's bedroom. They entered to find a frail pope seated in a chair. His hands and feet were tied. A nurse was busy preparing an injection, but stopped briefly to acknowledge the cardinals with a short bow.

"I do not think this pope will be issuing any statements soon," smiled Cantore.

He patted the hunched back of the pope, who was barely aware of the cardinals. Cantore would have preferred to chop off his head.

"It is time to use Luciano," Martinelli said.

The nurse injected the pope's arm with a heavy sedative and then left the room.

Cardinal Cantore took out a handkerchief and blew his nose. He walked over to the window and looked at the people below the apartments.

"And what will become of our ill-fated pontiff," asked Cantore, keeping his back to Martinelli. A scantily clad young woman on the street had captured his attention.

"His sacrifice will please the World Teacher." Martinelli also knew it would solidify his position as well.

For a brief moment, the pontiff appeared to have regained lucidity, but the medication overwhelmed him. His bony hand gripped his chair and then relaxed. The pope fell unconscious.

Montana

On a deserted highway in big sky country, a black sedan sped through the night. Captain Wolfe was in the back seat smoking a cigar, his eyes boring a hole through the back of Lieutenant Teller's head. The young officer had been assigned to Wolfe's top-secret program, but lately he had been having difficulty keeping his mouth shut.

Teller had financial problems trying to keep up with his kleptomaniac wife. He couldn't bear to send her away for treatment, so he paid off the department stores that fell victim to his wife's substantial character flaw.

Captain Wolfe thought about how Mrs. Teller would get along with her old man's life insurance, not that it really mattered. Perhaps he could stop by and fill in the void on occasion, to assist her in her times of need, but the larceny was something he wouldn't cover. Wolfe was furious with Teller for selling classified information about UFO's to the tabloids. To Wolfe, national security was breached and now Teller had to die. It really wasn't personal. He was just following orders.

Wolfe puffed on his cigar one last time before throwing it out the window. His driver glanced in the rear view mirror and saw Wolfe take out a cord. He wrapped the ends around both hands. The driver stared at the road ahead, as Wolfe tightened the cord around Teller's neck.

Teller was not an easy kill. The driver's stomach felt as though he had swallowed acid instead of the two beers he had with dinner. Wolfe's fingers blanched with the pressure of the cord. Finally, Teller died.

"Stop the car, Sergeant."

Wolfe put the cord into his jacket and got out of the car. He opened the passenger door and dumped Teller's body by the side of the road. The captain emptied Teller's wallet and kicked the body. Teller was long past feeling the kick or the contempt that drove it, but Wolfe somehow felt better. Suddenly, headlights appeared on the horizon. Wolfe jumped back in the car and they sped away.

The driver outran the car and the two men relaxed a bit.

"Do you think he knew why you killed him, Captain?"

"Who cares? His body will be a reminder to anyone else interested in leaking information to the press."

As the driver crossed the Wyoming state line, he thought about his long-term career plans. Wolfe only thought about lighting another cigar.

In New York, Sol Abrams chewed on his fat cigar and thought about the evidence Michael Cross had brought in on UFO's and what seemed to be a growing government cover-up.

Abrams put his hands behind his round head and propped his stubby feet on his desk.

"So, you're telling me you got all that stuff from Nick and it proves what?"

Cross knew he had to win this one. He had to see this story to its conclusion. Briefly, he looked over Sol's head, as if he found something to tell his boss written on the wall behind him. Sol thought he looked like a small boy trying to pull a story out of thin air, something about why he got into his mother's purse and took her money.

"Well, there are people high up in the government who are selling us out. Solly, you gotta let me run with this. I'm telling you I could get back on top and perhaps even put a stop to this crap."

Cross meant what he said. However, Abrams was not going to let Cross off that easily.

"And I suppose you want me to take you off the visionary story, even after you finally turned in a decent piece?"

Abrams was ready for Cross, but got a surprise.

"If it's all the same, I want to do both."

Abrams restrained from reacting and grabbed for a danish, shoving half of it into his mouth.

"Mbbmmph…" he mumbled.

"What?"

Abrams rolled the danish around in his mouth until he could speak.

"That's fine for now," he said before cramming the other half into his mouth.

Cross jumped out of his chair and shook Abrams' sticky hand.

"Thanks, Solly. By the way, those things will kill you."

Abrams took a gulp of coffee to wash down the remains

of the lethal dose. "Not a chance. You'll be listed on my autopsy report as the cause of death."

Cross left quickly. Abrams smiled to himself and then spilled his coffee on his already stained tie, burning his formidable gut.

Hurrying out of the office, Cross took a file and headed for the men's room. A man slowly followed him down the hall and into the bathroom. Cross made a frenzied dash for the urinal. He put the file between his teeth and unzipped his pants, heaving a huge sigh of relief. The man went up to the urinal next to Cross, whose eyes immediately hit the ceiling.

Tossing a cigarette into the urinal, the man relieved himself, while engaging a flustered Cross in conversation.

"Hey, aren't you Michael Cross?"

"Yeah," Cross answered through clenched teeth. He swore to himself that this guy had better not ask for his autograph.

"You're a friend of Nick Peters."

Cross zipped his pants and flushed.

"What's it to ya," asked Cross, already irritated. He went to wash his hands.

The man zipped his pants and walked over to Cross.

"I was just wondering if you'll be working on any of his stuff now that he's dead." Cross had the funny feeling the guy already had the answer.

"What if I am?"

The man grabbed Cross and kneed him in the groin. Doubling over, Cross fell to the floor.

The strange man put his foot on Cross' chest and ground his boot into him. "My advice to you is don't or you'll get hurt. Maybe dead."

It took Cross several minutes to escape the pain before he could stand. He finally pulled himself up by hanging on to the lavatory. Splashing cold water on his face, he took a quick look in the mirror. Not liking what he saw, he gingerly left the building.

A black BMW shadowed Cross on his way out of Manhattan. He headed for the Bayside Shrine. Finally noticing the car behind him Cross moved into another lane. The car followed him, sped up and nudged the Impala's bumper. Cross sped up and veered across three lanes causing minor fender benders. The BMW stuck with him. Seeing the La Guardia exit, Cross swerved across the entire expressway. A honking and screeching party ensued as the BMW tailed Cross.

Flooring it as he entered the GCI, Cross checked his rear view mirror repeatedly. He was glad he'd taken good care of his car, better care than he had taken of himself. The palpitations in his chest unnerved him almost as much as the guy in the car behind him. Quickly he dumped that concern and replayed the scene from the restroom. He knew he was getting to someone and just like the old days, someone was trying to get to him, a watershed mark of his worth. It had been a long time since he raised this much angst, except from Annie.

Cross suddenly switched lanes and the car's left front hubcap peeled off, rolling into oncoming traffic. In a lane with no place to go, he slammed on his brakes causing the black sedan to smash into the rear of his classic. He didn't even think about getting out of the car and pulling the driver out of the sedan. Instead, he stepped on it. Catching sight of the Shea Stadium exit, he got off the expressway and headed for the World's Fair marina.

The sedan's crumpled front end was obscured by white billowing smoke. It limped along for another block before it stalled. Cross made a u-turn onto the stadium road. He drove a couple of blocks. Once he realized he lost the sedan, he stopped. Taking out his last cigarette, he lit it, throwing the empty package out of the window. He took out his flask and poured the booze down his throat.

After swallowing the last of his liquid strength, Cross drove the rest of the way to the shrine. Still somewhat shaken, he got out to inspect the damage to his first love. Two taillights were smashed and the trunk was slightly dented. With some effort, he opened the trunk and took out his camera bag. The trunk would not close completely, so Cross used his tie to secure the lid and went to find Veronica.

The vigil was just getting started. Not able to find a seat, Cross stood near the front where he could easily see Veronica. As he adjusted the lens on his Yashica, he studied the visionary's face. She smiled and pointed to the sky above the statue of the Blessed Mother. Veronica never blinked and the lines in her face completely disappeared.

A man placed a microphone near her as she apparently went into ecstasy.

Cross thought she looked fifteen years younger. He snapped a couple of shots. The flash from the camera went unnoticed by her.

Totally focused on something, Veronica started to speak.

"My child, the picture Jacinta must be read by all of earth's children. You will read the wording Jacinta and search the lines and figures and numbers. Within the miraculous picture is given the date by God the Father for the Chastisement."

Cross wasted no time in taking out his copy of the photo. Turning the picture sideways and upside down, he tried to find the date.

Veronica continued with the message she received. "You cannot count time, My child and My children, for your earth time is not akin to the counting of time in

Heaven. So do not speculate on dates, but be prepared for it will come upon you fast, without any knowledge to many."

Cross watched as tears formed in Veronica's eyes. "Our Lady looks sad," she said. Veronica's face grew serious. "Our Lady said a coalition of evil is being formed in the Eternal City, My child. You must pray for Cardinals Billot and Martinelli, Giovanni Martinelli."

Surprised with the explicit nature of the message, Cross took out his notebook and jotted down some notes.

"My child, you must tell them by letter that their actions are not hidden to the Eternal Father. He has looked upon them and found them wanting. Come out of the darkness now or you will be cast into the Abyss!"

Our Lady continued through Veronica, her voice box.

"Pray much for your great Pastor in Rome, the Holy Father, your Vicar, the Pope."

Cross' pen ran out of ink and he searched his pockets for another. An older man next to him gave him a fountain pen.

"He suffers much at the hands of his enemies. He is but a prisoner in the Eternal City. The forces of evil are working to remove him, My child."

The fountain pen ran out of ink and Cross returned it with a smile. He decided to ask Veronica for a copy of the tape.

"Now there is one ruling in his place, an Impostor created from the minds of the agents of Satan. Plastic surgery, My child, the best surgeons were used to create this Impostor. He must be exposed and removed. Pray children."

Cross walked back to the car, stunned by the flood of information. He got in and sat for a moment before turning on the ignition. His mind raced as he turned the key, revved the engine and headed back downtown to work.

Cross flipped on his desk lamp and it blinded him. He quickly pushed the shade down. No one was left on the floor except for a cleaning lady who was busy emptying trashcans and dusting around the desks. He noticed the woman wore huge Bugs Bunny slippers.

"Love the footwear, Gladys," Cross smiled.

"Don't you give me none of your lip, Mr. Cross. They're comfortable." She shook a crooked finger at him.

"Whatever you say, Glad. How's Tyrone?"

The woman's face came to life. "He's graduating college next spring."

"No kidding? That's really great, Glad."

He got on the phone and called the research department. While waiting for someone to pick up, Cross combed through his desk drawers for some smokes. Gladys waited for him to light up and then started to cough. He got the hint and put out his cigarette.

"C'mon, Teri. Pick up."

Frustrated, he hung up and punched the numbers again.

"Research."

"About freaking time, Teri. This is Mike Cross. I need everything you got on the pope, pictures, clips, the works."

Teri sounded bothered. "Yeah, if you really need 'em."

"I love ya, Teri. Hey."

"Yeah," she snapped.

"Can you get me a list of members on the Trilateral Commission?"

"It'd be easier to get you an audience with the pope. When do you need it?" Teri's boyfriend was waiting for her and she wasn't in the mood for more work.

"Yesterday."

Cross put the phone down before she could object, and it rang immediately.

"Yeah, Teri."

"Michael, come home," Annie's voice shook. "It's Joey."

Chapter Seven

By the time Cross made it home, he found Doctor Jarvis examining Joey. The doctor had flashed a penlight into Joey's eyes, but his pupils were unresponsive. Annie had a death grip on the rails of the crib. Cross was not sure if Joey was alive or dead. The child just lay there. His father was afraid to say anything for fear he would disintegrate. So he paced and chewed his nails.

"Well, doctor," injected Annie. Cross was grateful she said something.

Jarvis put his penlight in his pocket and put his arm around her. Cross did not like the looks of that.

"Let's go to the living room."

Cross paused to kiss Joey and followed them into the living room on rubber legs. He joined Annie on the couch and took her hand. It was trembling and moist. She welcomed his hand, feeling a little safer. They listened to Jarvis as a heavy rainstorm opened the first act. The rain beat hard against the windows, almost as hard as Cross' heartbeat. Annie could feel the strong pulse of his heart through his fingers.

"I can't say this wasn't expected," Jarvis said softly. Cross did not know what to think, but he was miffed with the doctor. It wasn't that Jarvis hadn't done everything he could. Perhaps that was at the core of it all.

"Can he see anything at all," asked Annie.

"No." Jarvis' face appeared to have turned to stone. "The tumor seems to have taken over."

Cross never had much hope for him, but he always had hope where Annie and Joey were concerned.

"So, what are we looking at here, doc," Cross finally spoke past his cigarette.

Jarvis looked at him and then Annie, formulating his best answer. "Maybe as little as two weeks."

Annie burst into tears and dissolved into Cross. He held her tight and searched Jarvis' face for any sign that there was a chance for his son. Jarvis walked away and gathered his things. Annie pulled away from Cross and ran to the bedroom. Cross cleared his throat and swiped at his eyes. He went to the bay window and watched the rain.

"I'll let myself out," Jarvis said.

Cross barely heard him. A bolt of lightening ripped through the blackness and briefly lit Cross' face. Tears streamed from his tired eyes as he watched the street fill with water in the downpour. It swirled and grew until it overwhelmed the storm drains. A deafening clap of thunder shook the house and the already shaken Michael Cross.

Manhattan

The intense lightning illuminated the United Nations building, which was mostly dark. A few office lights were on, beating back the night.

George Hawthorne stood at the window observing the skyline in the deluge. He listened to Mikhail Makarov, the Secretary of Agriculture from the Soviet Union.

"I tell you this, my friend. If we are cautious, and if we plant correct seeds, turmoil we spread will eventually play right into our hands." Makarov really despised Hawthorne, but he had to befriend him to a degree. They were the first string players on a global team that would not accept defeat.

"Risky business, Makarov. Risky business," Hawthorne replied, looking at the portly Russian.

"Da, but worth it."

Hawthorne knew Makarov was ambitious and untrustworthy in most things. However, he was useful and essential to their overall plans.

"Yes, Makarov. Ultimately, it is worth it."

"Americans have been weakened by Viet Nam. This unrest at home is proof your country will be reluctant for more conflict."

Yes, it was Hawthorne's country. He fought for it in his youth before he began to fight sovereign barriers.

"We'll be very careful about getting involved in skirmishes far from home," Hawthorne added. He knew that there were some skirmishes that could not be avoided, that had to be fought as part of the overall scheme.

"The cuts in our military will make any intervention too big of a gamble. We'll see to it, Makarov.

"Keep on schedule," Makarov said.

Rome

Cardinals Truman and Martinelli enjoyed breakfast out on the terrace of Truman's apartment. Every kind of flower decorated the terra cotta, but their beauty was lost with Truman.

"Giovanni, we have to move Catholics and the Protestants towards each other. A melding of beliefs, if you will, accenting the similarities, especially in the United States."

Martinelli seemed pleased. "I agree. Making the separate faiths more alike in appearance will make our efforts easier."

Truman knew Martinelli understood the direction the church, their church, had to go.

"Perhaps we could work at getting the kneelers removed and eventually the statues and even the tabernacles. It is so distasteful to see parishioners kneel."

Cardinal Truman liked the idea of doing away with anything Catholic, any reverence or ritual that gave honor to the wrong God.

"I will see the pope and see that he signs the necessary papers. We also are planning on enhancing our actions regarding certain apparition sites and becoming harsh with the visionaries, especially at the diocesan level." His antipathy was hard to hide.

"Excellent. I'm glad you said that, Giovanni. I know that Lueken woman is undermining our efforts."

"She will be taken care of. We already have people infiltrating her support staff. We will make her out to be a total imbecile."

Truman knew that Martinelli was extremely proficient when it came to creating imbeciles.

Queens, New York

It was a warm fall day. Leaves had just started to turn into a delightful autumn palette. Cross made his way to Veronica Lueken's home and haphazardly parked in front of her house, too tired to care about parallel parking or the car that had followed him there. Wearily, he got out of his car and slowly climbed the Lueken stoop. As he knocked on the door, three of the Lueken children ran outside. Veronica followed behind to open the door for Cross who managed a smile. He followed her into the living room and saw she had company.

Declan Cavanaugh, a white-haired man in his fifties, stood when Cross entered the room. Cavanaugh had a kind face and bright piercing eyes that seemed to catch Cross off guard.

"I guess I shoulda called first," Cross apologized. He felt awkward and Veronica immediately came to his rescue.

"Nonsense. Let me introduce you to Father Declan Cavanaugh. This is Michael Cross."

"Father," Cross said, extending a hand.

"Michael. I've enjoyed your work. You're a fine writer."

"Thanks, Father. Veronica, I don't mean to interrupt, but I really need to speak with you alone, if I could."

"That's okay, Michael. I was just leaving." Cavanaugh patted Cross on the back. The priest smiled at Cross and it seemed to put him at ease.

"I don't want you to run off, Father."

"Don't be silly. I have Mass to say."

Cavanaugh excused himself and Veronica walked him to the door. Cross did not know whether to sit or to stand. Nervously, he did both, neither for very long.

"Michael, what is it," asked Veronica. It was obvious he was upset.

"It's my son. He's, well, he's got this brain tumor," he blurted out.

Veronica's eyes grew concerned and for a moment, she reminded Cross of his mother.

"Joey's awful bad. He's blind now and he's only three. He's run outta time."

Veronica hugged him and then took his face in her hands.

"Michael, there's always hope."

Cross needed more than platitudes. The doctors were past that point and Joey certainly was.

"No. The doctors have given up."

"God doesn't give up, Michael. You've got to have faith."

"You don't understand. The freaking tumor is all over his brain." Cross lost it and buried his head into Veronica's shoulder. She patiently held him, quietly praying until he calmed down.

"Sit down, Michael. I want to get you something."

Veronica went to an antique bureau and pulled out the top drawer. Carefully, she pulled out a rose petal.

"Hold out your hand."

"What is this," Cross asked, wiping his eyes.

"It's a rose petal blessed by Jesus and Our Lady. When Joey goes to sleep tonight, put it under his pillow."

At first, Cross seemed sure it was merely more snake oil for the hopeless.

"Many people have been blessed with cures, people in as bad or worse shape than Joey." Cross started to lose his skepticism, desperate to hang on to anything.

"Guaranteed cures?"

"There are no guarantees, Michael." She didn't have to tell him that. His skepticism returned, hitting him firmly in the gut.

"I didn't think so."

"You've got nothing to lose," Veronica said, trying to reassure the dejected Cross.

"Only my son," he answered softly.

Veronica knew what it was like to lose a son. She lost hers in a hunting accident. She also knew there was nothing she could say to ease his pain.

Cross thanked her for her kindness and went to the office. Work would keep him from total despair, if only for a little while. Focusing on the impostor pope, as crazy as it sounded, would keep him sane.

He decided to go to the research department before checking in with Sol. Teri was there waiting for him. She had a file of photos and background data on Pope Paul VI. Myopically, Teri read over Cross' shoulder as he went through the file. A Pepto pink bubble inflated and deflated next to Cross' ear. He didn't seem to notice Teri popping the bubbles with her large front teeth. Instead, he was totally absorbed in some photos of the pope. Teri popped an enormous bubble when she saw two photos side by side.

"Wow! There really are two popes. Look at the differences in their noses."

"Ya think?" Cross could not believe what he saw. Now he felt he had to listen to Veronica's messages. This was the bit of concrete evidence he needed. He also started to put hope in that rose petal.

"Don't you see the differences," piped Teri. She measured the distance of the nose from the bottom of the impostor's ear. They looked at each other in total amazement.

"Can you get voice tapes of these guys and have them analyzed?" Cross was on a crusade now.

"Sure. Hey, before you go, look at this list from the Trilateral roster."

He took the list, but seemed unimpressed.

"Yeah, so?"

"Check out this name."

"That mother fu...sorry, Teri. I love ya, kid."

Cross pecked her on the cheek and ran out of the room. Teri ran her fingers over her cheek and smiled.

By the time Cross headed for home, he was beyond tired. Not knowing what to expect when he opened the front door, put his nerves on hyper-drive. He pulled into his drive and sat for a moment gathering what thoughts he could catch. Cross had to be at his best, not only for Joey, but also for Annie.

When he got out of his car, he noticed a blonde middle-aged woman in a car parked in front of the house. She was doing a crossword puzzle. Relieved that a goon hadn't been staking out his home, he trotted up the stairs. The front door was open and he was surprised he could hear laughter, Joey's laughter, coming from the living room.

Little Joey sat in the lap of a tall, dark haired man Cross had never seen. He got defensive, but Annie diffused him before he got to the couch.

"Michael. This is Joey Lomangino. He heard about our Joey and stopped by to see him."

Lomangino stood up, and stuck out a strong right hand, holding Joey in his left arm.

"Hey, Mike. Hope it's okay. I just thought I'd drop by and meet yous all. Lomangino's face was badly scarred and Cross noticed the man's eyes were badly damaged.

Annie smiled at Cross and took his arm. "Joey has been telling stories to little Joey.

"Great," he said warily. "I'm surprised he feels up to it."

Lomangino's face grew concerned. "I don't mean no disrespect or nothin'. Veronica Lueken told me about Joey, so I though I'd drop by."

Cross was thrown by Lomangino's ability to function. The way he appeared to look at people when they spoke and the way he was able to move about the room surprised Cross.

"Geez. I can't believe your blind. You don't act like it."

"Other than not seeing, I don't feel blind neither. But that will change. I'll see again," Lomangino said confidently.

Cross looked at the damage around Lomangino's eyes and knew that was impossible. He had run out of tolerance for false hope and pie in the sky stories.

"Pardon me for saying so, but," Cross started.

"I don't have any eyes. I know. But I'll have 'em back. The Blessed Mother said so."

Cross looked at Annie who was smiling broadly. A flash of anger hit his face. Annie, on the other hand, was still holding out for a miracle for her son and Cross knew it.

"Really, Joey? Oh, if only she would help our Joey," Annie sighed.

Joey Lomangino smiled at Annie, and then kissed Joey.

"As Padre Pio used to say, God love him, pray, hope and don't worry. I gotta go. My wife's waiting in the car."

He handed Joey to Annie and headed for the door. "Mr. Lomangino, can I walk you to your car?" Cross had calmed down and he was not sure why. There was something very peaceful about this man.

"Sure. Why not? But you gotta call me Joey."

Annie put her son to bed; thankful he wasn't in much pain. The child seemed to enjoy the time he spent with Lomangino and seemed content. Annie was not at ease though, not that Lomangino had upset her, but rather she began to feel slighted.

She headed to the kitchen and started to chop carrots and onions for dinner. Cross heard Annie's aggressive chopping and headed for the kitchen. He looked around at the china cabinet and noticed that all the silver had been recently polished. Any time Annie was angry or worried, she would polish the silver. With nothing left to shine, Annie attacked the vegetables. He grabbed a carrot as she diced the onions like a Chinese chef with a vendetta.

"Anybody I know," asked Cross, kissing her neck.

"Just working through some frustrations. That man is really remarkable, isn't he?"

"Yeah. Did you believe that stuff about his getting his eyes back?"

Cross did not know what he wanted Annie's answer to be.

"Dunno."

Annie put the butcher knife down.

"Yeah. There are so many screwed up people anymore. The world is pretty far gone."

Cross helped Annie with dinner and set the table.

"Where's Joey?"

"I put him to bed." Annie looked so tired. Cross hated to see her like that.

"That reminds me. I stopped by Veronica's place today."

Hope filled Annie's eyes. "And?"

"Well, she gave me this rose petal. We're supposed to put it under Joey's pillow." Cross felt silly telling his wife about the petal.

"What for?"

Cross scratched his head. "Veronica said they were blessed by Jesus and the Virgin Mary and that many people have been cured when they had the petals. I remember doing my research on Veronica and some actress, Susan Hayes; I think…you know the one. The red head."

"Hayward?"

"That's it. She had twenty tumors and was sent a rose petal by Veronica and supposedly - zap! The woman was cured."

Annie's face flooded with joy and just for a moment, she looked much younger. Cross smiled at her.

"What are we waiting for," said Annie. The couple rushed to Joey's room and gently placed the petal under his pillow. They said a silent prayer, then kissed Joey goodnight.

Cross had to admit that the Hayward story gave Veronica and the petals more credibility, but he was reluctant to feel any hope. He didn't want Annie believing Joey might be cured. He was afraid that if Joey died, it would be too much for her. Cross knew it would be too much for him.

He couldn't sleep and spent most of the night watching Annie sleep. There were too many things colliding in his brain keeping him awake. Even the booze couldn't quiet the ruckus. Cross could not shake the feelings that he got when going over Nick Peters' files. Something was going on and he had to unravel it.

By six, he gave up on getting any rest. He got up and called Sol, and asked him to meet him at the Staten Island Ferry. The morning was cold and dark. Cross sprang for two cups of coffee, a peace offering for Sol.

He handed Abrams a cup. "Sol, what do you know about Graham Katz?"

Abrams blew into the steaming cup.

"That's why you dragged me out here to freeze my ass off? Other then his sister hates your guts, what's there to know about a guy like that? We ain't exactly in the same social circles. Why do ya wanna know?"

Cross took out his flask and poured some brandy into his coffee and handed the flask to Abrams.

"His name came up on the Trilateral roster," said Cross, studying Abrams for a reaction.

"Where's the crime," Abrams barked.

Cross knew that by itself was not significant, but there was a trail that led to some dank holes.

"I've been going over Nick Peters' files on those people. Something ain't right. They meet in secret."

"So do cheating wives and their lovers."

Cross started to get perturbed. "They never want the press to know about 'em and some of Nick's sources say those bastards are controlling the stock market, world banks, nukes, you name it."

Abrams slurped his coffee. Cross knew he was mulling things over in his cluttered mind. "You got a problem with that Mike?"

"Wouldn't you?"

"Maybe. Can you prove it?"

"Not yet," answered Cross.

"Until you can, try not to step on Katz's balls. If what you say is true, he could do shit loads more than fire our asses."

Chapter Eight

Michael Cross came in the front door and saw Annie crying on the couch. He could hear pots boiling over in the kitchen. Looking around, he didn't see Joey and his heart stopped.

"Honey, what's wrong? Is it Joey?"

"He just seems so run down today. I thought the rose petal was supposed to work. Nothing happened. In fact, I think he's getting worse."

"Don't go anywhere. I'm gonna turn off the stove." Cross ran into the kitchen. He was angry and scared, feeling like a small boy in a big crowd just after losing sight of his mother. He turned off the burners and ran back to Annie.

"Maybe it doesn't work like that. Maybe the cure is progressive."

Realizing there was not much time left, Cross sat on the couch. He put his arm around Annie and they sat in silence a moment. Then the phone rang, startling them.

"Yeah, hello.'

Cross slammed down the phone.

"Who was it?"

"Dunno."

Flustered, Annie said, "We've had hang up calls all day long."

"Why don't we take Joey to the shrine? Maybe that will help. You go get him and I'll get the car."

They were willing to try anything to avoid the helpless feeling that had become an irritable overseer. They didn't know what else they could do. If this proved to be another dead end, Cross had no idea where to turn.

The drive to the shrine was made in silence, except for a few soothing words for Joey. Cross found a place to park reasonably close and carried Joey up to the seats for the infirmed.

Annie seemed to sense something. She thought the air felt charged and she wondered why Cross had not brought them sooner. Joey seemed lethargic in his father's arms. Cross gently cradled him as Annie bundled the boy in his yellow blanket.

Veronica Lueken arrived and went to greet the people who patiently awaited the start of the prayer vigil. When she got to Joey, she stopped and made the sign of the cross on the boy's forehead and kissed his cool cheek. Annie smiled at Veronica, who took her hand and patted her on the shoulder. Veronica started the service. A chill went through Annie like red wine through a white tablecloth as the breeze increased. She started to have second thoughts.

"Maybe we shouldn't have come here."

"It'll be okay," Cross answered. He pulled the blanket up around Joey's chin.

"The rose petal didn't work. How do we know this will do any good," she asked. Cross always counted on her second thoughts. They kept him in line many times, but this was not the time to bring them to the surface.

The crowd joined Veronica in a Hail Mary. Annie numbly recited the prayer, keeping her eyes on Veronica. The visionary's attention was drawn upward as the crowd continued to pray. A broad smile filled her face. As Annie watched, she felt her heart beat faster.

"Our Lady is going to speak. She's saying, 'We are permitting at this time, manifestations and evidences of miracles, more abundant than ever in the past history of your world. This is a means we will use to fight the armies of Satan.'"

Cross looked at Annie. Tears trickled down her face. Joey stirred and Cross kissed him and held him closer.

Still focusing on the heavenly visitor, Veronica said, "Blessed Mother, many here have petitions for you. Could these be granted?"

Annie took Cross' hand, squeezing it. It was clammy like hers.

"Our Lady said, 'Many will be granted their supplications, but many will have to bear their crosses of illness in order to purify their souls to enter the Kingdom. You will soon have a well. With this well, the waters will cure. The waters will be given to the ill."

Annie's hope sank, but Cross fought with the sinking feeling. Joey distracted them when he struggled. Cross helped the boy to sit up and rewrapped the blanket around him.

"Come to Me all mothers who weep for their children; come to me and I will solace you."

Annie slid out of her chair and fell to her knees. She made the sign of the cross, closed her eyes and prayed silently.

"I have used the petals of the roses as instruments, significant of the graces that I will bestow on you."

Suddenly, Joey sat straight up and squealed, not from pain as his parents' first thought, but from something else.

"Daddy, look at the pretty lady! She's smiling at me!"

Annie looked at Joey not knowing what to think.

Joey stood on his father's lap. "Look! She's right there!"

Cross looked up. There stood the Blessed Mother. A white veil covered her long, blonde hair. Tears flowed from Cross' eyes and an incredible happiness filled him. He fell to his knees and held Joey over his head. Annie finally turned her eyes from her son and looked up to see the Blessed Virgin. Many people in the crowd could see her as well. People gasped, then they fell silent.

"Oh my God," Cross cried. He looked up in awe at the beautiful woman, as she smiled and looked at everyone in the crowd, and then slowly disappeared.

The euphoria hadn't worn off by the next morning. The Cross' watched Joey run through Dr. Jarvis' examining room while the doctor spoke to them about the child's x-rays.

"I'll be damned," Jarvis said. "I can't see any sign of the tumors. And this happened last night, you said?"

"Yeah. All of a sudden he could see. So you think it's true? It's not just a fluke," asked Cross.

"It's strange all right. I can't see anything wrong with him. We'll have to watch him, of course. He could have a relapse."

"No, he won't," Cross said, surer of that than anything.

"Sometimes tumors come back," the doctor warned.

"Not in Joey's case," said Annie.

Cardinal Martinelli's Villa Outside Rome

The cardinal was furious. He walked around his study slapping his leg with the morning newspaper. George Hawthorne and Mikhail Makarov watched him, attempting to put up with the prelate's tirade.

"Absolutely idiotic. Look at this," the cardinal shouted, throwing down the paper on his desk. The headline read: *Pope Paul VI Dead.* Hawthorne coldly picked up the paper.

"Relax, your eminence. This is what we were after in the first place," Hawthorne said.

"Not that, you imbecile. It's the interview below the fold. Cardinal Niri practically exposed us and our plans."

Makarov rubbed his throat and jumped into the mix. "Now old man is dead, who will care? You will be elected pope this afternoon. The martyr will be buried tomorrow and our plan continues. A red flag will hang over Rome within few years."

Hawthorne got a shiver about that inevitability. Although he was one of the one-world crowd, there was just something about that red flag business that bothered him. Not that Hawthorne was dyed in red, white and blue, but if there had to be a world order, he had hoped it would have been under different colors.

"Niri betrayed me and he must pay. Half of the Italian cardinals want him as pope. Now that he gave me up to that American reporter, what's his name," demanded Martinelli.

"Michael Cross," Hawthorne offered. "Unfortunately, he does good work."

Martinelli was livid. "Cross and Niri will both regret this."

Hawthorne raised a bushy eyebrow and walked out to the terrace. Things were getting too complicated for his tastes. He decided to head back to the United States on the first available flight. Listening to the men in the study made his skin crawl. Well aware of his future, Hawthorne took a deep breath and held it briefly, before exhaling his doubts about his associates.

In Rome, Michael Cross waited for his overseas call to go through while he drank some espresso. He acquired a liking for it after giving up booze. Cross looked out his window to watch the mourners waiting to view the body of Paul VI. Light rain started to fall, but it didn't diminish the throng. Cross somehow felt responsible for the pontiff's death. He wrestled with the things he should have done until the phone pinned him.

"Yeah."

The operator's voice blasted through the phone. "Your overseas call is connected, sir."

"Thanks. Sol, ya there?"

"Hey, Mikey. What's happening?"

Cross was not sure where to begin and he was not convinced Sol would want to hear the litany.

"A lot is going down, Solly. Listen, I got the pictures of the pope's body. It's the real one and not the impostor."

"Ya sure?" Abrams was afraid that would be the case. He also thought the impostor was chopped up and dumped in the sea.

"Yeah. I'm sure, Sol."

"So, where does that put things?"

Cross was not sure. He hadn't been keeping score long enough to anticipate the next move, but he knew there would be one. He ran a theory by Abrams.

"I guess it depends on who gets elected pope. But that's not all. Guess who is staying with Cardinal Martinelli?"

"I'm a Jewish boy from Brooklyn. Waddya think I know from cardinals?"

"Mikhail Makarov and George Hawthorne."

"A commie and a CIA rat? What the hell's the deal?" Sol didn't have a clue, but he wanted to know exactly what the two had to do with Martinelli.

"If I knew what the hell was up, it would be plastered on the freaking front page, Sol."

Abrams could see it in his mind. A story like that might make his tenure more secure.

"Stay on it, Mikey."

"Count on it." Cross wasted no time. He knew Martinelli would be enclosed on the conclave soon, so he headed for the cardinal's villa. He scarcely noticed the drive, even though the sun chased away the rain. Cross was uncertain about what he would do when he got there. He knew something would come to him once he arrived.

He pulled his rental car into the circular driveway outside Martinelli's villa and parked the car. Straightening his tie, he looked in the mirror, and then headed for the front door. Cross knocked several times before the cardinal's valet answered the door.

"Si?"

"I'm Michael Cross to see Cardinal Martinelli."

The valet squinted at him and frowned.

"He has left for the conclave."

"Do you know when he'll be back?" Cross tried to look past the valet to see if he could spot Makarov or Hawthorne.

"He won't return until there is a new pope." The valet thought it was a stupid question and started to close the door on Cross.

"Well, thanks anyway." Cross headed back to his car. He looked over the estate before getting into the driver's seat. It seemed quiet. There was no activity on the grounds and he figured the cardinal's guests took off. He drove away, but stopped about a half mile from the villa near a grove of trees. Cross cut through the vineyard and the extensive garden, ending up on the terrace outside the cardinal's study. He peered through the glass and didn't see anyone. Cross tried the doors, but they were locked. An open window just to the left of the terrace invited him into the well-furnished estate. Certain he was alone; he made it to the study. He went directly to the cardinal's desk and searched through the papers left on top. Not finding anything interesting, he tried to open the desk. It was locked. He grabbed the 24 Karat gold letter opener and stuck it into the drawer on his right. It took a little work, but he managed to pop it open. Nothing of great importance was found in the first two drawers. The bottom drawer was a gold mine. Cross bent over looking through the contents of the drawer. Suddenly, he was struck on the back of the head. He fell to the floor unconscious.

Area 51

A military helicopter flew over a sign on the outskirts of the secret base that read: *Trespassers Will Be Shot*. The sign was caught in an eddy of dust as the low flying chopper headed for the compound several miles away.

George Hawthorne and his driver awaited the helicopter. As the chopper drew closer to the helo pad, the sound of the blades bounced off the surrounding buildings and irritated Hawthorne's ears almost as much as the flying dust kicked up in the wash. For a moment, Hawthorne felt like he was back in Washington.

Captain Wolfe emerged from the helicopter and greeted Hawthorne. The men got in the waiting car and drove to a remote hangar. The car entered the cavernous hangar and the large doors solidly shut behind it blocking out the world.

Hawthorne and Wolfe got out of the car and went through a set of double doors that were heavily guarded. They walked down a gray corridor of locked security doors. At the end of the sterile hallway, they entered an unmarked office.

It was starkly furnished. There was a large set of windows at the far end of the room. Hawthorne escorted Wolfe to the windows and pushed a button. On the other side of the glass, lights came on, revealing a craft so far advanced that it looked like a Hollywood prop.

"How would you like to fly that," Hawthorne asked.

"Blow me."

"Excuse me, Major?"

Wolfe was brought back to the moment.

"Major?"

"As of today, it's official."

"Thank you, sir. Mind if I ask where this baby comes from?"

There was just something about Wolfe that Hawthorne did not like. He wasn't sure if it was his enthusiastic personality that reminded him of his wife or not.

"It's a loaner."

"So can you trust the owners?"

Yes, Wolfe was too much like his wife.

"It was tough in the beginning, way back in the Roswell days. But that was before they offered to share some of their technology."

"Where do they come from," Wolfe had to know.

"Easy now, Major," said Hawthorne. Just like his wife, Wolfe had far too much curiosity to be given any particulars.

"Let's just say these guys claim to have been here thousands of years ago."

Wolfe couldn't entirely grasp what he saw and heard.

"Sounds unreal and so... I dunno. Hard to believe, sir."

Hawthorne nodded. "If I hadn't been to one of those briefings, I might not have believed them either."

"So what changed your mind?" Wolfe searched Hawthorne's eyes, and then quickly turned away. He wasn't sure if Hawthorne was completely honest, if anyone ever was totally honest. Wolfe understood that Hawthorne couldn't or wouldn't tell him everything.

"For one thing, they showed us holograms about our history. Get this. They even showed us the crucifixion of Christ."

"Jesus."

"That's the one. Since then, we've been doing business together. These little guys are going to show us how to stop the invasion of earth by some nasty pricks from the far side of the galaxy."

"You mean the giants, sir?"

"Wolfe, don't bring up that shit." Hawthorne was impressed that the man at least had some alien information in his head. He hated to start at ground zero with people, especially on the existence of aliens. He didn't have the patience and there was no sense educating anyone who might not last until the fourth quarter.

Chapter Nine

Doctor Vento stood at the foot of Michael Cross' hospital bed and read his medical chart. Vento was a small man with extraordinarily large hands. He hummed as he dragged his finger over the nurse's notes. Satisfied, he went to check the bandage on Cross' head. The heart monitor beeped steadily, providing a metronome for the doctor. The bandages were fine, although there seemed to be a little drainage, but nothing that concerned the doctor.

He checked the IV drip and tried to focus with his trifocals. Raising his head up and down until he found the perfect spot, he watched the saline drip, and then increased the flow. Cross seemed to struggle to the surface of consciousness. He began moving his lips. Doctor Vento stopped humming to listen, but Cross did not get out a sound. Vento watched him for a moment, and then scribbled some notes in the chart.

Cross opened his mouth and licked his parched lips, and then slowly opened his eyes. Vento looked over his glasses at him. His patient started moving about in the bed. The doctor immediately popped off the top of a syringe and jammed the needle into the IV line just as Cross tried to sit up.

"Just relax, Mr. Cross." Vento easily pushed his patient back down on the bed.

Cross tried to focus on the doctor. He wanted to ask something, but he couldn't think clearly. Then his eyes rolled back in his head as the sedative coursed through his veins, driving Cross into oblivion. Vento took his patient's pulse and then readjusted the IV. A gorgeous nurse burst into the room, startling the doctor.

"Doctor, Cardinal Martinelli is on the phone."

Vento left the room in a hurry, leaving the nurse with Cross.

Martinelli's Villa

The cardinal hung up the phone and smiled at his guests, Cardinal Truman and the World Teacher. Truman studied the mysterious Teacher's face trying to guess his age. He settled for somewhere in the middle thirties. The World Teacher's long black hair was tied back, accentuating the man's enormous dark eyes. The Armani suit he wore fit his 160 pounds perfectly.

"Well, your eminence, how is our little mole doing," asked Truman.

Martinelli blew his nose. "As unaware as our new pontiff."

"Excellent," said the World Teacher. "I must say, your eminence, my plan to have you step aside and throw your votes behind John Paul was a stroke of genius. No one will suspect you when the time comes."

"Yes, it is magnificent, isn't it? Tonight we will toast, if you'll excuse the saying, the Holy Father, and tomorrow we will have a new pope, one more sensitive to our needs."

Martinelli raised his glass, as did his friends. The grandfather clock chimed in the midnight hour and suddenly stopped.

Washington, D.C.

As the sun set on the Potomac, George Hawthorne and Graham Katz pulled up in front of the White House, stopping for a minute or two. Hawthorne rolled down his window to get a better view.

"Graham, I want you to start hinting in your paper that I am gonna make a run for the White House. Even though the president is one of us, I just don't think he's advancing our cause."

Katz was delighted Hawthorne spoke up. "I'm sure glad you said that, George. That's why the vote was unanimous to dump him. You should have an easy time in the primaries, if Mr. Hollywood doesn't run."

Hawthorne looked annoyed. "Oh, he's running all right. No doubt in my mind."

Katz wasn't surprised.

"How are the plans going with the United Nations?"

Hawthorne smiled. "Just fine. Within the next twenty years we'll have them strategically placed across the whole freaking country."

Things looked more promising than Katz had anticipated.

"And that's when we contrive a major calamity of sorts."

Hawthorne was pleased Katz grasped the concept easily.

"Let's allow the World Teacher to handle that, shall we?"

Hawthorne dropped Katz off at his hotel and went directly home. He was feeling a little needy and went straight to the bedroom, hoping to catch his wife still awake. He was disappointed to find that she was already asleep with a magazine on the bed beside her. Hawthorne turned out the light and took his neediness elsewhere.

Three days later in Rome, Michael Cross ripped out his IV and threw the bottle across the room, taking out two vases of flowers. He knocked everything off the bed table and climbed out of bed. The cacophony brought a nurse to the room. When Cross saw her, he picked up the bedpan and threatened her with it.

"Just stay the hell away."

The nurse backed up. "Mr. Cross, please calm down. You have had a serious head injury."

"Oh, yeah? Well, I'm fine now and I'm leaving. Where the hell are my clothes?"

She wasn't about to tell him. "You can't leave without Doctor Vento releasing you."

"Watch me."

Cross hurled the bedpan at her, but it missed and hit Doctor Vento as he entered the room. At first, Vento was shocked, but it quickly gave way to anger.

"Restrain yourself, Mr. Cross," he yelled. Doctor Vento had no impact on Michael Cross.

"I'm leaving and you can't stop me."

Vento knew he would reap the consequences if Cross escaped. Not being very physical, he tried a different approach and hoped the cardinal would understand.

"Very well. Nurse, please get Mr. Cross' things. Still, you should be careful. You had a nasty head injury in that car accident."

"Car accident? I was hit on the head," volleyed Cross. Contempt built up until it matched the intensity of his headache. He knew he could smash the poor doctor's head. Five years ago he might have tried it.

"It is true you hurt your head, but you were drunk behind the wheel of your auto. It is very lucky for you that you did not kill yourself or someone else."

"Drunk?" Even with his headache, he knew he had the doctor.

Vento folded his arms in front of him.

"That is what the police said." If Cross had any doubts that he had been set up, they evaporated like his paycheck.

"I haven't had a drop of booze since my son was cured."

Doctor Vento knew the cardinal's plan was dead on arrival and hoped that Cross would not kill him. He shoved the quivering doctor, dropping him instantly. Cross grabbed his clothes from the nurse and ran out of the room, not caring that his posterior was totally exposed.

Once on the street, Cross headed for a pay phone. He needed to call his wife. Nervous, he kept looking over his shoulder to make sure no one had followed him. A black Jaguar pulled up. Cross was ready to run, if it was necessary. The driver's window rolled down, revealing the World Teacher.

Not knowing the man, Cross tried to concentrate on his phone call.

"Mike, I've been so worried even though the doctor said you'd be okay in a couple of weeks and discouraged me from making the trip."

Cross looked back at the Jaguar. The World Teacher casually lit a cigarette and continued to stare at Cross.

"No problem, baby. Cross glanced at the car again trying to get a better look at the driver.

"When are you coming home," asked Annie. Cross knew she was anxious.

"Soon. I want to check out a few things out."

The World Teacher pulled away and tossed his cigarette out of the window. Cross watched him and saw the car absorbed into thin air. He stared hard at the last spot he saw the car. There was nowhere else the car could have gone. The traffic was thick.

"Mike, did you hear the pope's dead?"

Cross plugged his right ear to hear Annie better, but couldn't get his mind off the Jaguar.

"I know he's dead. It's not the impostor, but really Paul VI."

Annie was worried now. "No, honey. Pope John Paul, his successor dropped dead."

That was it. Cross felt he had entered another reality.

"What?"

He struggled through his altered state, his heart racing with his headache.

"The pope had a heart attack, I guess."

Cross tried to poke his nose back into reality. He was starting to feel like plastic wrap was laid over his face and he felt on the verge of suffocation.

"Have they elected a new pope?"

"John Paul II," answered Annie, sure she should fly to Rome immediately.

Cross was able to poke a couple of air holes in his new dimension and sucked in a breath of the here and now.

"Is it Martinelli?"

"No, he's Polish."

Now he wasn't sure if he hadn't gone down the hole after Alice. "How in the hell did that happen?"

Makarov's Office In The Kremlin

Mikhail Makarov answered the phone and immediately pounded the desk with his fist. The caller delivered some unfortunate news. Makarov felt hindered because he couldn't reach through the phone and strangle the inept caller.

"You had all votes tied up. How could you let Polish pig ascend to papacy? I tell you this, you guinea idiot, we will take care of this one. And when you meet again to elect pope, do not fail."

Makarov slammed down the phone cursing the cloak and dagger antics at the Vatican. Had he been in charge, the Vatican would be his and so would all of its money.

Manhattan-Two Weeks Later

Declan Cavanaugh's gray eyes peered over his reading glasses at Michael Cross. Always a good judge of character, Father Cavanaugh had the gift of reading hearts. He sized up Cross.

"Well, Michael, how are you feeling after your ordeal?"

"I'm fine, Father. Thanks. But I'm a little crazy with what's happening in Rome. I've been working two separate stories and now it looks as though they're both connected."

Cavanaugh took off his reading glasses, inspected them and decided to clean them with his handkerchief.

"I know what you mean. That was one of the reasons why I resigned my position at the Vatican after Pope John XXIII died."

"Weren't you the pope's right hand man?" Cross had only read the priest's brief bio, but he had to know more.

"Yes. I was the intelligence officer."

Cavanaugh grew slightly distant remembering those Vatican years. It was a job with so much promise, but an extraordinary amount of danger went with it.

"So, you had the inside story about everything going on there and around the world."

"I did," Cavanaugh answered humbly.

"Some sources said you were friends with Cardinal Martinelli." Cross watched the priest closely.

"Hardly, Michael. We knew each other, but we both have a great deal of distaste for one another." Cross was pleasantly surprised by Cavanaugh's answer.

"What does Martinelli want?"

Father Cavanaugh took off his glasses and his eyes narrowed slightly.

"He not only wants the papacy, but the entire world."
Cross was surprised again.

"I get the papacy, but the world? How could he hope
for that?"

Cross studied the priest's face. It was a nice face. It
gave Cross a sense he could be trusted.

"You have to think globally, Michael," smiled
Cavanaugh. Cross was not ready to do that.

"You mean One World Order kinda sh…stuff?"

"That shit, as you started to say, is where Martinelli and
his friends are headed." Cross was not ready for the One
World reality. He didn't want to consider it as inevitability.
It seemed too out there for him to bother with it.

"Father, you can't believe the world will let one person
rule the entire planet?" Cross set his jaw and started to
grind his teeth.

"I do, God help us. That is where we are headed."
Cavanaugh was convinced. Cross could see that.

"But how does that involve the Vatican?" A tension
headache was gaining ground with Cross.

Cavanaugh sat back in his chair and crossed his legs.

"Would you like some aspirin, Michael?"

"No, thanks."

"First, you must understand that not everyone in the
Vatican is corrupt. There are still many good priests who
do not ally themselves with Satan. Their allegiance is to
God and His vicar, the pope." Cross was stuck on Satan. He
wasn't sure of his existence, but he trusted Cavanaugh not
to mislead him even though the concept of the devil was
something that eluded him even in parochial school.

Father Cavanaugh took a sip of tea. "However,
Michael, you have to see that ever since Vatican II, the
Church has gone through tremendous changes, regrettable
changes. Those changes are not for the betterment of the
Church. Not only that, but look at the Church as the big

business it has become. There is a lot of power and money there. Have you read the Book of the Apocalypse?" Cross was not ready for that particular turn.

"I didn't understand it." He didn't want to understand. The apocalypse was something that would occur during someone else's lifetime, if then.

"Your answer is completely understandable, but it is not as difficult as you may have been led to believe. It's a guidebook, a reference for us. Unfortunately, it is also a reference for people like Martinelli."

"What do you mean, Father?" Cross was intrigued.

"If, I am right, and I pray to God that I'm not, he's sold his soul to the devil." Michael Cross wasn't sure he wanted to hear about this, especially from a notable exorcist like Declan Cavanaugh.

"Martinelli, along with Satan, whom I believe is the incarnate in the man they call the World Teacher, are using the events in the Apocalypse to set up the world for a takeover."

"Can you be more specific?"

Cavanaugh leaned forward slightly.

"You're aware of the Third Secret of Fatima, aren't you?"

"Sure. That's the one that's never been released," said Cross. At least he thought that's what Sister Agnes had said in grade school.

"It's criminal it hasn't been released. Well, Martinelli was part of a group who tried to steal the secret. Sister Lucy, she was one of the children at Fatima…"

"Right."

"Sister Lucy wrote down the Third Secret in a letter. I was there the day Pope John XXIII opened it." Even if Cross did not want to hear about Satan and possession, he definitely wanted to hear this.

"Then you know what the secret is?"

"There were three of us in the room that day. The Holy Father, Cardinal Billot and myself."

Cross snapped to attention.

"Billot? The Blessed Mother mentioned him to Veronica Lueken, along with Martinelli and Cardinal Cantore."

"I hadn't heard that, but I'm not surprised." Father Cavanaugh stood and stretched.

"Spell it out for me, Father."

"Now, I swore not to reveal the actual secret, Michael. But let's look at an ancillary aspect to the Third Secret."

"Okay."

"Let's say you know certain catastrophes would take place if man did not change. As you can see just by New York City, we're going down the tube as a society, prostitution, crime, and every kind of degeneration imaginable. Now, then, if you wanted to fabricate a calamity and then have a fake rendition of the Second Coming, a person or persons could quite conceivably hold the world hostage."

Cross' brain started to hurt even more. The conversation was leading someplace he didn't want to go.

"What kind of a calamity?"

Father Cavanaugh said matter of fact, "Take the warning for instance." Cross knew this was new territory for him. Declan Cavanaugh understood Cross' nature and seemed confident of him.

"At Garabandal, the Blessed Mother mentions that God is going to send a warning to every human being. A mini-judgment that will let us know where we stand with God." Perhaps Cross would have felt better if he was hearing something from a government source. His religious side was still underdeveloped, although receptive.

"That must have been mentioned to Veronica. I remember something about that."

"That's right. Well, this judgment will be a cataclysmic event in which science will not be able to explain what happened."

Joey immediately came to Cross' mind. His life was just getting back to normal.

"So what will it be like," asked Cross, hopeful that this event would only be spiritual. Cavanaugh anticipated his reaction and wasted no time.

"It will appear as though two bodies, perhaps comets, will collide over the earth. A huge explosion will take place and the sky will look rolled back. Imagine, Michael, a torn sky above the whole earth." Cross did not want to imagine anything.

"Then what?"

"We will each see our sins the way God does. No excuses." Cavanaugh looked into Cross' eyes then turned to go to the window. The day was bright and beautiful.

"Sounds painful, Father."

"It can be, but we won't hurt physically. Although we will all feel intense heat at that time, depending on the state of our soul."

"But no one will be hurt, right?" The thought of anything happening to his family made him weak and somewhat angry.

"Well, some people will die of heart attacks because of the awesome event coupled with the condition of their souls. By and large, it will have no physical effect. Time will seem to stand still and for many, the length of their personal mini-judgment will seem interminable."

"Is that it," Cross asked hopefully.

"No, there's more. You mustn't go outside. Those outside will perish. There will be poisonous dust in the air when the comet strikes. No one will be permitted to see the wrath of God."

"Comet? I thought this was going to be something spiritual?"

Cavanaugh knew that it would be something a great deal more. While some of his colleagues only subscribed to the spiritual side of the warning, Cavanaugh knew the other aspects of it detailed in the third secret of Fatima.

"It is spiritual, Michael. But God wants all of our senses awakened. The devastation will be horrible. One quarter of the population will die."

"My God. No one's ready for this," he said. Cross knew he was not even close to being ready.

"Exactly. Then when it finally calms down, we go back to our lives, which will never be the same." Cavanaugh grew distant as he talked about it, trying to envision the new world, the new reality.

"Some people will change. Those caught up in sin probably won't change and if they do, it won't last. But that warning will put us on notice for a great chastisement, if we fail to transform."

Nicotine withdrawal ran over Cross like a freight train.

"What you are saying then is that the wrong people could use these events to come to power."

"Particularly the antichrist and his colleagues. With dwindling food supplies and chaos everywhere, it's a no-brainer. He'll take the credit for the warning."

Cross was not ready to accept this. It seemed so over the top like some Hollywood extravaganza with a cast of thousands, impressive maybe, but make-believe. He prayed the warning was just a scary hypothesis made up by clerics to influence and frighten parishioners.

"Forgive me, Father. It seems like a fairy tale - a biblical fairy tale."

"Make no mistake about it, Michael. The world is in store for some terrible events." Cavanaugh looked at Cross again. There was no doubt in Cross' mind that Cavanaugh was sincere and the priest had the background to back-up what he said.

"How bad will it be," asked Cross, feeling somewhat fortified from his cigarette.

Cavanaugh looked out over the city and let out a small sigh. "For starters, the total annihilation of New York City."

Cross thought about seriously going off the wagon, but pushed the thought away. There was nothing more to say, so he left Cavanaugh to his work and took a long walk to let it all settle in his mind.

Election Day - 1980

Reporters gathered around a small television in Sol Abrams' office watching the election returns. Even though the coverage just started, it was obvious that Mark Raymond and his running mate, George Hawthorne, were delivering a severe blow to the democratic incumbent. Everyone was ready to collect on side bets.

Sol Abrams had a tight grip on his money and would have sooner pulled a tooth than to pay up. As he counted it out, he pulled the bills slowly from the wad and painfully let go, smacking the money into Cross' waiting hand.

"Ten, twenty, twenty-five, thirty. You schmuck. Who'd thought old glamour boy would win."

"Don't you read your own paper? The Ayatollah Cockamamie had better cover his ass."

One young reporter, who didn't know Abrams well, thought he could push him into a corner.

"Hey, Solly. It's early. Wanna go for double or nuttin'?"

"Wanna be outta work, wise ass? Get away from me. Hey, Mike. How does it feel to know Hawthorne has even more power?"

Cross didn't answer Abrams. He knew it was a good question, but he wasn't sure how he felt about it. Somehow it felt like he was coming down with the flu. Bored with the coverage, Cross changed channels.

Hawthorne had just changed channels as well; taking the night in like a pedophile inviting a child into his home. The phone rang. David Feller was on the other end.

"Yeah, Dave. It's great news except for one thing."

Feller and his trilateral chums wouldn't be pleased if something were wrong.

"What's that, Mr. Vice President?" Feller had high hopes for Hawthorne.

"Raymond wants me to quit the commission."

"You gotta be kidding me."

"Wish I were," replied Hawthorne.

Feller thought for a moment or two as Hawthorne listened to the tally of votes.

"So you quit. That doesn't mean you won't be one of us. Something could happen to the old man."

Hawthorne smiled. "I'm working on that."

Chapter Ten

Major Wolfe found his kicks in the cockpit of an F-16 fighter jet. He felt in control of his life for a change as he put the plane through various maneuvers. It was a peculiar ballet, somewhat like sex or so Wolfe thought. The pursuit of the target and the evasion by the opponent until it was locked-on and then ultimately destroyed, was sex at its finest to Wolfe. His basic needs were met, with little or no complaints and absolutely no guilt. Once the target was destroyed, he could free his mind for other things.

Wolfe deftly chased his practice enemy, a buddy of sorts. There was no disputing his friend's finesse behind the controls, but he was no match for Wolfe who slipped in behind the mock MIG, locked-on and artificially blew him up.

"You're history again, you mother," Wolfe laughed.

"What kind of beer do you want," his buddy asked.

"I guess that depends on the broad who brings it. See ya downstairs."

Wolfe peeled out and headed for Area 51. He landed on the numbers and taxied for a distant hangar. As he climbed out of the cockpit, a ground crewman met him.

"Major Wolfe, you've got a call from Washington back in Building 7. You can take the jeep, sir."

"Thanks, airman." The beer and the broad would have to wait. He jumped into the Jeep and headed to the phone.

His legs and body were getting used to solid ground and he decided to jog up to the front guard desk at Building 7.

"Major Wolfe."

Vice President Hawthorne had been waiting on the other end. He could have called back, but he was more interested in staying on the line. Certain the president would be calling with some mindless job for him to do, Hawthorne did his best to avoid him.

"How do you like those F-16's Major?"

"Just fine, sir. You'll have to take one for a spin."

Hawthorne would sell his first born for a chance, but then he often offered to sell his son.

"Far cry from the Hell Cat days. Listen, the reason I called is, uh, we're going to loosen up our policy on sightings," Hawthorne said, rocking in his office chair.

"Yes, sir." Wolfe was somewhat happy about the decision. "In other words, you want people to get used to seeing those babies in the skies."

"You got it. Call me when you get back to Cheyenne Mountain."

Hawthorne hung up and turned to look at an old photo on the credenza behind him. There he was a lifetime ago in the cockpit of a Hell Cat. Hawthorne hardly recognized himself. He still felt the same as he did then, eighteen and cocky, even though the mirror betrayed him every morning.

A few miles out in the Atlantic, a Soviet sub kept its sonar on a United States Coast Guard cutter patrolling just inside the coastal boundaries near Long Island.

As it headed out of range, the captain of the sub, Ivan Kosinski, watched the cutter through the periscope. The pinging of the sonar diminished. The crew remained silent. After checking his watch, Captain Kosinski did a 360 with the periscope. The horizon was completely clear.

Kosinski picked up the microphone. "Bring our guests forward." Four Middle Eastern men appeared, dressed in black. Sweat poured off of their faces. They weren't cut out for the cramped quarters. Kosinski nodded at them. He made another search of the horizon.

Satisfied they were alone, he turned to his first officer.

"Take her up, Vulgarin."

"Yes, Captain. Taking her up," the small man responded.

The massive sub broke water and found calm seas as the hatch was quickly opened. Kosinski and two crewmembers escorted the men up top. A raft was hastily inflated and the four men jumped into it and paddled to shore.

"Ready to dive, Mr. Vulgarin."

Kosinski and his men hurried down the ladder as the submarine submerged into the darkness.

Queens, New York

Veronica Lueken looked for Michael Cross in the crowd at the shrine. He arrived late with his son Joey.

"Joseph, come here and let me look at you. Such a handsome young man." Joey studied his shoes. "You must be so proud, Michael."

"I am. Joey, say hello," Cross said, lightly jabbing his son in the ribs.

"Hi, Mrs. Lueken." Joey had matured a great deal since she last saw him. Veronica ran her fingers through the top of his blonde hair. Joey stiffened slightly.

"Listen, the reason I called you, Michael, was I have a favor to ask," she said.

"Sure, Veronica."

"Don't agree until you know what it is. I had started for the grounds earlier, but I was instructed by Our Lady to take down a letter to the Holy Father. I know this is a lot to ask, but could you take it to him in Rome? It's urgent."

Cross was not even fazed by her request. He looked at his son and was thankful he was alive. Veronica could have asked him to go to Mars and he would have done it.

"Of course I could. I've got some unfinished business in Rome. Well, Joe. Waddya say? Wanna go with your old man?"

Joey rather liked the idea. "Sure, Pop."

Veronica thanked them and went to start the vigil. Cross and Joey found seats in the third row, not far from the visionary. Tonight there was a different tone to the vigil. Protestors gathered across the street. Police managed to barricade the protesters bodies, but couldn't harness their mouths. Cross kept an eye on them, concerned that violence might erupt.

Veronica quickly went into ecstasy and spoke about what she saw. "Oh! I see a commotion."

Cross was not sure if Veronica meant the protestors. Two weeks later, Veronica's vision replayed in his head.

He and his family joined thousands of people in St. Peter's Square to see Pope John Paul II. People held flowers and waved white handkerchiefs as the pope headed towards the crowd in an open car. Cross and his family were in the front row and could easily see the pope as the car got closer. Cheers and applause filled the air.

In a moment of déjà vu, Cross remembered what Veronica had said during her vision. "I hear stomping of feet and I hear people screaming!"

Then everything slowed down. Cross could not believe what he saw. Veronica's words played in his mind as the noise seemed to swell in Cross' ears.

"And I hear the rata-tatata tat...like something, I don't know, it's like pellet or..."

"Gun fire," Cross finished the sentence.

Shots rang out and the Holy Father doubled over in pain. The pope was helped to his seat as the car sped away. Cross and his family stared in astonishment. He looked down at the envelope containing Veronica's letter to the pope and froze for an instant. Then he grabbed his wife and son and got them out of the panicked crowd.

In Moscow, the new president of the Soviet Union, Mikhail Makarov delighted over the news he heard from Cardinal Martinelli.

"Your first executive order went well, maestro. Bravo," said Martinelli.

"Then pig is dead?"

"No, not yet. I do not see how he will survive. It is still too early.

Makarov stood and pounded his fist into his desk. "Martinelli, it is later than you think."

Outside the pope's hospital, Annie and Joey waited for Cross. The street surrounding the hospital was mobbed with well wishers. Annie called to her husband as he exited the hospital. He ran over to see her and kissed her.

"Hey, Dad! How's the pope?" Cross hugged his son.

"He's gonna be okay."

"God willing," added Annie.

"Can you make it back to the hotel okay?" Cross took out their room key and placed it in Annie's hand.

"Sure," said Joey.

Annie immediately started to worry. "Where are you going?"

He smiled at her, kissed her again and said, "I've got to see someone about a cardinal sin."

Annie knew that look in his eye all too well. There wasn't anything she could say that would stop him.

He managed to keep out of trouble in his digging and returned to the hotel very late. Annie was relieved when he woke her up. Cross was not ready for twenty questions and she did not push. He got into bed and ran his fingers through her hair until she fell asleep.

Even her rhythmic breathing and his fatigue couldn't seduce him to sleep. He thought about what he was going to tell Sol Abrams in the morning.

Annie awoke early and heard Cross in a heated conversation. He paced with the phone. Then he started to yell.

"Sol, I'm telling you there's more to this thing and it all ties into Hawthorne, even the assassination attempt on the pope."

Annie didn't like the sound of that. She got up and slipped on her robe. Deciding to stay in the bedroom, she brushed her hair and wondered what he might do.

Sol was in no mood for Cross.

"Are you completely nuts? You've had your head up your ass for so long working these frigging stories that you see conspiracies in your intestines."

The veins in Cross' neck could have stopped traffic.

"Cut me some slack. This is going somewhere, probably to another Pulitzer." Cross was not that concerned about winning the prize, but he knew Sol might go for it.

"I don't give a rat's ass where it leads. Get off the story or you're fired." Even Annie heard Sol that time.

"What?" Cross threw his coffee cup across the room. Joey heard the crash and stumbled out of bed.

"If you don't drop it, your shit canned."

"I can't drop it, Sol. So, I guess this is quits."

Cross slammed down the phone. Annie attacked her hair with the brush; afraid she couldn't keep her mouth shut.

Abrams slammed down the phone. Graham Katz calmly watched him, knowing that Cross had been fired for the last time.

"I hope you're happy, Mr. Katz. You just lost the best reporter any publisher could dream up."

Katz straightened his tie. "I know that was difficult for you, but your raise should make it easier to live with."

Money was just about as comforting to Abrams as food.

"Yeah. And I suppose you aren't gonna lose any sleep over this."

"Not in the least," Katz said, as he stood to leave.

"The man has family, ya know." Sol felt the least he could do was to make Katz feel guiltier than he did.

"Yes, I know." Katz smiled at Abrams defeat.

After two days of stewing and some heated conversations with Annie, Michael Cross decided to take his family for a drive in the Alps. He thought getting away from his investigation for a while would be healthy. Taking in the sights was just what he needed. Headed for a picnic, everyone was in a joyous mood. Annie had put the last few days in the back of her mind, making it easier for Cross to enjoy himself.

The breathtaking scenery took their minds off the darker reality that had been part of the lives for the last few weeks. There was a brilliant spot of light that broke through the gloom for Annie. She had discovered she was pregnant, almost an impossibility after years of failed attempts. Cross was pleased and Joey took a special delight in the news. It was the perfect day to begin again.

Their rental car struggled with the incline as they made their way to the top of a mountain. The slow progress didn't arrest their spirits. Out of nowhere, a black Mercedes Benz appeared behind their yellow Fiat. Cross did not think anything of it until the sedan hit their back bumper. The jolt pushed Annie into the dashboard.

Cross sped up and looked in the rear view mirror. He pushed the car as fast as it could go. He knew it wasn't an accident.

The Mercedes pulled out trying to pass the Fiat, but veered back behind Cross as a fuel truck raced towards it in the oncoming lane. Once the truck passed, the Mercedes pulled out on the precarious road and banged into Cross' undersized car.

Cross fought to keep control on the winding road. Quickly he glanced at the sedan, but couldn't see through the dark tinted windows. He wasn't sure what he could do with a sub-compact piece of junk, especially with his family on board.

Again, an oncoming car forced the Mercedes back behind Cross. Joey whipped his head around to see if the sedan would back off. The driver of the sedan downshifted and Joey could hear the increase of RPM's. The driver in the Mercedes shifted again and plowed into the back of the Fiat popping the transmission seals, then suddenly pulled out to pass.

Cross tried to speed up, hoping to avoid being pushed off the side of the mountain. A truck in front of Cross slowed down, forcing him to slam on his brakes. As the cars approached a narrow curve, the Mercedes pulled out, came along side of the Cross' car, and sharply turned into it, forcing the Fiat over the cliff.

The car bounced off the side of the mountain twice before plummeting further into a ravine. The Mercedes stopped briefly on the road. The driver lowered the passenger window to watch the Fiat as it burst into flames. Satisfied, the driver punched the accelerator and sped away.

Cross awoke amidst the inferno. He looked at Annie in horror. The fired had consumed her clothes. Frantically, he tried to put the flames out. It was too late. Cross could see that her skull was crushed. Her beautiful face was unrecognizable.

"Dad," screamed Joey. Cross did not seem to hear him at first.

"Help me, Dad!"

Joey's screams cut through Cross' shock. Joey's badly broken leg was trapped. The flames grew and both Joey and Cross thought the car would explode any second.

"God help me," Cross pleaded as he tried to pull Joey out of the car. Joey started to panic, but didn't say anything. He held his breath and tried to help his dad. The pain was so intense that Joey eventually fainted. Cross finally freed his son's leg and yanked him out of the car. The Fiat exploded along with Cross' life.

Joey regained consciousness and sat with his father staring at the dreadful pyre. Cross put his arm around his son. A siren burst his thoughts about Annie and the baby. He knew he still had Joey and he focused all of his attention on his son.

For the next ten years, Cross was there for Joey. Through the surgeries on Joey's leg, through rehab and driving lessons, Cross was there. Joey seemed to motivate Cross like no other person could. He still pursued his investigation and never relented. Cross never gave up the search for the people responsible for hurting his family.

Each day Cross and Joey got closer, just as Cross was getting closer to unraveling the biggest conspiracy the world had known. He knew Joey would be all right, as he listened to the cardinal one Sunday afternoon in April.

St. Patrick's Cathedral was jammed. Normally, large crowds made Cross uncomfortable, but not that day. Cross remembered the last time he was in the magnificent cathedral. He had prayed for his son's life. As he watched his son, Cross was amazed at how fast time was consumed. He glanced at the other young men who knelt alongside Joey. There were five in all, two tall young men, one short man in his early forties with hair that couldn't be tamed, and a slight man about thirty. Joey was in the middle. His hair was still quite blonde, but cut very short. He had broad shoulders and towered over the other men.

"I bless you in the name of the Father, the Son and the Holy Spirit," said the cardinal.

Cross told himself he was not going to cry, but that had little effect on the tears that welled up in his eyes.

The young men stood and the cardinal had the men turn towards the congregation. The cardinal then introduced the newly ordained priests. Cross thought his chest would split with pride as the cardinal put his hand on Joey's shoulder.

"Father Michael Joseph Cross."

Joey smiled broadly at his dad. The organist began the recessional and the cardinal walked slowly to the back of the church accompanied by the new priests.

Cross hurried to the back of the church where Joey was waiting for him.

"Thanks for everything, Dad."

"I'm so proud of you, son. I wish your mom could have been here." Cross hugged Joey a little harder, then stepped back to look at him.

"Hey, Dad. Look who's here."

"Mike, good to see yous," said Sol Abrams. He stuck his hand out, shook Joey's hand and then Cross'.

"Congratulations, Joe. Too bad Annie, well, you know what I mean." Abrams blew his nose.

"Thanks, Sol," answered Cross.

"Nice service, although the cardinal ain't got nuttin' on my cantor."

Joey laughed and then excused himself. Cross was miffed at Abrams for butting into the day, but he did not let it show.

"So, waddya doing now, Mikey?"

"Working at The Wire," Cross said quietly.

"Yeah, I thought I heard that. I also heard you never let go of that conspiracy sh…," Abrams stopped, aware of his surroundings.

"You know that crap with Hawthorne," he finished in a whisper.

Cross did not flinch. "Now that he's president, I'm going after him with all I got. With Joey on his way, there's no reason not to go for it. Looks like his own people are gonna dump him anyway."

"Think so? I dunno. I think you were wrong about the Soviet Union too, pal."

Cross could not believe he was listening to Abrams and the old line.

"Oh yeah? Don't fall for it, Sol."

"Fall for what, Mikey? The cold was is over."

"Not by a long shot."

Chapter Eleven

Halifax, Nova Scotia
A northern express battered the Park Place Ramada Hotel with torrents of frigid air and snow. Halifax was locked in with a terrible storm. Inside the hotel, a different storm brewed.

David Feller and Graham Katz led an interesting discussion.

"Trust me on this. Hawthorne is out," Feller told the attendees. "I don't care if we have to manipulate every vote, and tamper with every voting machine in the country. He's out."

Applause filled the room. "David's right," Katz broke into the applause. "Hawthorne had his chance with the Gulf War. The U.N. was ready to go. All he had to do was deliver the crisis."

Most of the participants concurred.

"That ball-less wonder pushed our plans back by at least ten years."

The World Teacher rose and immediately a hush fell over the meeting.

"What makes you so sure that your new man will have any better shot at implementing the European Union's desires and putting the United States under United Nations control?"

"Because the kid has agreed to make that his first order of business. He signed a contract agreeing to sign the executive order the day he takes his oath of office."

Unimpressed, the World Teacher walked to the front of the room like a cat stalking prey.

"What about Congress? They will not go along with such a cavalier gesture," he said.

"That's why our guy is going to sign an executive order which bypasses Congress. No one will know about it until after he has put it into effect," said Katz. He took a drink of water and cleared his throat.

Katz stepped up to the front of the room, but the World Teacher stopped him with a look. Feeling a little chastised, Katz decided to speak from where he was.

"To further guarantee results, five million dollars will be placed in his wife's Swiss bank account the moment he signs the executive order."

The World Teacher turned his attention to the group and sighed.

"My friends, you must look beyond your human failings and strive to act in a loftier fashion. Money is the root of all evil. It corrupts. A worker does need to be paid his wage, but beyond that, nothing more should be offered. These are trying times and we must aspire to achieve good. The talk of war and killing is not the direction we need to go.

"If our unification process is to be accepted, it must not come at the point of a gun, but through peace and diplomacy. Surely you must have learned that from your history. Those who oppose your plans, those who do not accept me now, must be taught, calmly and lovingly. In the end, those who deny me will suffer the consequences, but this is the time to love one another, as I have loved you. Do what you must, but instruct this new candidate well in his duties to me."

The man mesmerized the entire group. They seemed to breathe in unison. Their thoughts were cleared as the World Teacher united them telepathically. Love seemed to grow in their hearts for this unlikely leader and fervor for his cause became pronounced in each person. Instantly, they were all seeing the same pictures before them. The World Teacher appeared with a gold crown on his head and in his slim hand he held a scepter. All of the people in the room were suddenly thrust down to their knees. The World Teacher then showed each person their future and what they would accomplish, the power they would obtain if they followed him. Without saying a word, the World Teacher spoke to their hearts and minds. His voice got inside their heads, but none of them saw his lips move. His eyes became the group's sole focal point. Within seconds, the crowd was transformed forever.

From that point on, when anyone mentioned his name, the man's face appeared before them, his eyes looked into their souls. The people in that hotel meeting room would now do whatever it took to please their leader, their master. They were convinced he was the consummate leader.

Queens, New York

Veronica Lueken was weak and shaky when Michael Cross went to see her. He poured a cup of coffee for her, and then went to sit by her on the couch. As she sipped her coffee, Cross studied her face. He had often seen her ill, but not like this. It bothered him.

"Maybe you shouldn't go to the shrine tonight. You're not feeling well. You just had surgery a few weeks ago."

Carefully, Veronica put down her coffee cup. She thought about how heavy it felt. Everything felt heavier now.

"The Blessed Mother asked me to be there and I want to go. Time is short, Michael. You know I am sorry I missed Joey's ordination."

Cross smiled at her.

"He'll make a wonderful priest," she sighed.

"That's okay. He knew you were there in spirit."

"Where will he be assigned?"

"Rome," he answered. Cross was not sure he wanted his son in the Eternal City.

"Such a troubled time in Rome now days. Troubled times everywhere, Michael. I'm really worried."

Veronica's brow wrinkled and her voice started to tremble.

"Are you worried about your health?"

She waved her hand at him and smiled.

"Oh, no. The messages from Jesus and Our Lady have gotten so serious. They talk about terrorism in the United States, plagues and famines. Who would suspect that in such a rich country as ours?"

Cross did not want to believe it would happen, not in America.

"Years ago I may have doubted that, but not now. Kinda scary, but I guess it's to be expected. Maybe the warning will change things. You know, I never asked you about the Jacinta photo. What do you make of it?"

Veronica took a deep breath and let it out slowly. "Now you know the warning has to come first, followed by the Miracle and then the Great Chastisement. The date is imbedded in that photo. But even before the warning, many things have to happen. Terrorism in the United States is just the start. Things will get very bad."

"What are you talking about? How bad?"

"Michael, we'll be attacked and eventually, Russia and China will invade the United States. It will be horrible."

"Jesus." Cross thought about his dad who fought in the Pacific during World War II. God knows what he would have thought about America being invaded.

"What about the Ball of Redemption," he asked, thinking a comet plowing into the earth was preferable to an all out invasion.

"There are two comets, Michael. One comes with the warning and the second one with the chastisement."

"Two comets? And they're going to hit the earth?"

"Yes." She seemed very matter of fact about it all, but he knew she didn't take it lightly. Veronica looked at her watch.

Cross knew they had to leave for the shrine, but he did not want to go without more information.

"Where will they hit? Do you know?"

"Only God knows for sure. But some visionaries have been told the first one would hit in the Atlantic. One visionary saw England destroyed by it and a giant tidal wave will hit the eastern seaboard."

Veronica patted his hand. "We better go before I am too tired to move."

Cross drove Veronica to the shrine. She seemed more than drained. Throngs of people were waiting for her. She slowly got out of the car. Veronica seemed to be in pain, but she smiled through it. Cross ran around the car and took her arm. He could feel her lean into him and he tightened his hold on her.

They made their way through the crowd and walked to the statue of Our Lady. Veronica walked to her chair and she sat down with effort, obviously winded. Perspiration formed on her face and her lips appeared bluish.

A worker brought the microphone to Veronica. She was already in prayer and fixated on something.

Veronica spoke softly. "Our Lady is here. She wants me to tell you what she is saying. My child, and My children, I come to you with a Mother's sad heart. And I brought you forth, Veronica, to make it known to the world that there are dire events headed towards your country and the world."

Michael Cross took the microphone and tugged on the cord. He looked around the crowd and was surprised to see Sol Abrams.

Veronica seemed stronger as she repeated what she was told. "You must pray much for the leaders of your country and the leaders of the nations of the world, because if you do not, this will bring a most disastrous war to mankind. Man does not seem to learn from his past. He still goes on making mistakes to his own destruction.

"I assure you, My children, there is no freedom in Russia. It is all a delusion. They seek the monies of the world from the nations of the world. And why do you not learn a lesson? It happened in the time of Lenin, it happened in the time of Stalin. And there you are ready to give billions of monies that should be given to your nation and the free nations of the world.

"Do not be deceived, My children. Russia is not free. It is a cosmetic act to delude you. Lenin, Stalin and Makarov have a father who is the father of all liars. So what does that make them?"

Cross looked back at Sol Abrams who seemed enthralled.

Veronica's voice grew stronger and she became excited.

"Now Our Lady is pointing to her right. Oh! Oh, there. Jesus is now coming through the sky!"

Cross whipped his head around to see if he could see anything.

"He is moving very fast across the sky over to Our Lady."

Several people knelt and gasps of anticipation filled the night air.

"Now He's reached her side and is whispering something to her that I can't hear."

Veronica described Jesus. "He has on a magnificent cape with a beige gown underneath. His feet are bare except for two strips of a beige colored sandal. Jesus' hair is quite long and is caught up in the wind. His gray blue eyes are glistening. He smiled and touched His finger to his lips. I'm supposed to repeat what He says."

Cross adjusted the microphone and looked back at Abrams again, who was more caught up in what was going on than Cross expected.

"I told you that Satan and his legions of demons are loosed upon the earth. If you go up to the stratosphere right now, there is hardly an inch that is not covered by demons.

"Do not look on other planets for life, for there is none. Only those who delude you tell you this. We have allowed many to see what mankind calls flying saucers. They are transports from hell.

"All of you who now plan in conspiracy to bring about a new world religion, a religion that is not of the God you know, but a religion that is coming from the depths of hell.

"Look up there, My child. You have to look closely and repeat what you see."

Veronica's face instantly blanched. "Well, I see two men. I don't know if they're Muslims. They have a different colored skin, but they are not black. Now they're walking through a building and they're carrying with them bags, but the bags are extra large."

She paused for a moment and then moved her eyes to the right. "Jesus is saying, 'in those bags, they are carrying all the implements of destruction.'"

Veronica became agitated. "Oh, I can see now, they're pointing across the street and I recognize the ..."

Several months later, Michael Cross sat in front of his television. He was in shock. CNN ran story after story about the bombing of the World Trade Center. Cross was not sure prior knowledge made the reality any easier. The phone rang. Cross ignored it at first, and then finally answered it.

"Yeah. Cross."

It was Sol Abrams. His voice sounded shrill.

"Can you believe it? Can you freaking believe it?"

Cross did not know what to say. Sol sounded like a man who'd been crushed by a giant piece of the puzzle he didn't want to admit existed.

"Mike? Ya there?"

"I'm here Sol. It is pretty amazing. Pretty damn horrible too."

"So what happens now," asked Sol.

Chapter Twelve

Rome

Cardinal Martinelli seemed to be living in perpetual angst. He knew hell had to be easier to endure.

"I cannot believe it. The pope will not sign his resignation papers."

Cardinal Truman was amused at the prelate's discomfort.

"You sound surprised, my friend."

"Does he think he will live forever in his condition?"

"I doubt it. Perhaps God is keeping him alive," Truman teased.

"Do not be silly."

"Still, the old man is stubborn. It's his Polish roots."

Martinelli poured two glasses of brandy and handed one to Truman. Martinelli drank the entire glass. Cardinal Truman watched him under a raised eyebrow. The hard look did not go unnoticed by Martinelli. However, that didn't stop Truman.

"This will delay Makarov's exile by at least two years."

"Maybe longer," pushed Truman. Martinelli slammed the snifter down. He pulled on the sleeves of his cassock and walked with purpose to the bottle of brandy and poured another drink.

Two years later, the president squinted into the sun as he delivered a speech in the Rose Garden. Mikhail Makarov stood on the dais with him. The small audience listened politely to the speech, but they watched Makarov and he watched them.

"Now that the cold war is over and the wall has come down, we extend a warm welcome to Mikhail Makarov," said President Macon.

A light applause started.

"Although he survived a serious coup in his homeland, I'm sure we can make him feel right at home." The applause gathered enthusiasm on cue, as the players furthered their plan.

While watching the speech from a Manhattan high rise, David Feller passed out Cuban cigars to his colleagues. Graham Katz helped himself to a cigar, as did George Hawthorne, who put the stogie in his breast pocket.

"Gentlemen, our group was successful in buying some land for our friend, Makarov," said Feller.

"Yes, and that eco-thing that he's involved with is very hot right now," added Hawthorne.

Feller thought that was an excellent point.

"Everybody is busy cleaning up the globe. It's a delightful front," Katz confirmed.

His friends agreed. Things were shaping up nicely.

"And when the time is right, he'll usher in the one world religion," added Feller.

Hawthorne must have experienced anoxia from all the cigar smoke. He started to sing. "Age of Aquarius. Age of Aquar..." Hawthorne stopped himself. "Sorry, boys."

A few of the men looked at one another as though they shared a common thought. They were glad Will Macon replaced Hawthorne. Had they not gotten Hawthorne out of the White House, their plans would have been halted like a husband having sex with his mistress when his wife walked in. If Hawthorne had been in charge, everything would have fizzled.

Feller broke up the collective consciousness.

"The European Union will have their currency in place before 2002. Now that they've assured us they won't handle U.S. dollars, the United States will eventually capitulate or see no trade money."

Katz thought there was an obstacle to a smooth transition. "You'll have to get the pope to go along with Makarov on that one world religion."

"He won't be able to resist," Hawthorne spoke up, hoping for redemption from his colleagues.

Feller nodded, then took the conversation in another direction.

"I was speaking to the Director of Resources for the United States Army. Our new president has ordered the establishment of detention centers all across the United States."

A shiver went up Graham Katz's spine.

"The sound of concentration camps gives me the creeps."

"I can understand that," Hawthorne said, smacking Katz on the back. "But we need to have a warehouse for people who don't go along with the program. Besides, they won't be in there long before they're exterminated."

Hawthorne thought he had made Katz feel better. Katz, however, could only think about his parents who died in Auschwitz.

"You don't still believe in God, do you Katz," Feller's lip snarled as he popped the telltale question.

"After the Holocaust, I didn't think God was alive," Katz said softly.

Feller walked over to him, straightened Katz's tie, and then pushed up on the knot.

"It's a good thing to put an end to the nonsensical practice of worshipping something that isn't there. We'll never change things praying for divine help that's never going to come," Feller derided.

Katz got the message. He could almost smell the burning flesh of the ovens. To him, God was dead.

Rome

The pope prayed to his ever-alive God to spare him from Martinelli's visit. Cardinals Truman and Cantore joined him. They had nothing but contempt for the old man who stood defiantly before them.

"Sign the paper," ordered Martinelli. The Polish resistance met him.

"I have no intention of signing this."

Cardinal Truman decided to take another approach. He knew the pope was isolated. His friends had either died or retired. Truman tried to soothe him with compassion, however feigned. He may as well have poured alcohol on a diaper rash.

"Your holiness, we only have two things we are concerned about: the church and your health. In all candor, you are not doing all that well," oozed Truman.

The pope looked at Truman with dismay and then with sternness only a father could level. A knock at the door didn't break the pontiff's stare.

"Come," he said with new strength. Monsignor Joseph Cross entered the papal apartment. He walked over to the Holy Father and kissed his ring. The pope was relieved his aide had arrived.

"Ah, Joseph. Have you met the three wise men? Monsignor Joseph Cross meet Cardinals Martinelli, Cantore and *Tru*-man." The pope had a sparkle in his eyes.

"Your eminences," Joseph responded. He knew what the men were doing and he had come to run interference.

"Joseph, these three want me to sign this one of a kind document that goes against the statutes. You know that a pope holds office until he dies. Retirement only comes with death, dear cardinals."

The pope handed the document to Joseph.

"Your holiness, I don't thing that the young monsignor would be interested in…" Truman started.

"Nonsense."

Martinelli jerked the document from Joseph's hands and stormed out of the apartment. Truman and Cantore barely tossed an amenity at the pope before leaving the apartment.

The pope smiled at his young monsignor. "Good timing, Joseph."

The pope tried to get out of his chair, but couldn't. Joseph helped him to his feet and steadied him until he got his balance.

"Surely you aren't going to sign that paper and resign."

"God willing, no."

"Your holiness, I've always wanted to ask you why you just don't excommunicate the cardinals who practice heresy and consort with the devil."

"They would claim I am crazy if I got rid of vast numbers and then they would get rid of me anyway. I still hope and pray that some will change. Their souls are at stake. We have to do all that we can do, but we also have to realize that scripture must be fulfilled." The pope slowly walked to his bedroom.

"I told one of my colleagues from Poland something the day I was elected. If I succeed, you will not see me again. If I fail, you will not see me again. Besides, Joseph, the longer I can hang on, the longer the reign of the antichrist will be put off."

Joseph helped the pope into bed and stayed with him for a while. He had grown very close to the pontiff and was saddened at the prospect of losing him. Joseph had caught the attention of the pope early in his priesthood, exemplifying the finest qualities in a priest. His promotion to monsignor came quickly. When the Holy Father had requested him to work as his chief assistant, Joseph didn't hesitate at the chance. Still, he realized that the pope would suffer a horrible death. At least that was what many prophets had said. Even the pope had intimated some of the details.

Normally, he had no cause to doubt those prophecies. They had been tested and passed. That night, however, had him praying they were wrong, that the prophecies were meant for another time, even though he knew in his heart they weren't.

Michael Cross followed his former boss to Jackson Hole, Wyoming on a hunch. When he arrived, he found Graham Katz, George Hawthorne, David Feller and President Macon on the links. Cross thought to himself about the strangeness of the foursome.

Although he could not get close because of the Secret Service, Cross got out his electronic surveillance gear to listen in on their conversation. He searched for the best position, trying to look unobtrusive. He went through the back yards that bordered the lush course, looking for a protected spot. He thought an agent saw him. Cross picked up a hose and started to water the lawn. As he sprayed the grass, he casually made his way to an impressive willow tree and took up his position.

He aimed his electronic ear at the group as they walked up the eighteenth fairway.

"That was a stroke of genius donating that land in Utah to the U.N., Mr. President," Feller said.

The president had always been high maintenance and appreciated Feller's stroke.

"They've had their eyes set on that rich coal out there. It's the largest coal reserve in the world next to the one in Indonesia."

Katz took a toothpick out of his mouth and advised the president. "Better not mention Asia, Mr. President. You're in enough hot water."

The president laughed. "Isn't that the truth? But it won't matter."

A cellular phone rang on the hip of a Secret Service agent. He answered it and then drove his golf cart up to the president.

"Mr. President, you have an urgent call."

"Here I am trying to beat par and some joker's gotta piss me off."

"Thank you, Agent Brown. This is the president." He stopped walking and then turned his back to his entourage. Cross turned up the volume and then checked to see if his tape recorder was running.

President Macon's face got red. "Take 'em out. Don't let them get into Washington with those documents."

The person on the other end must have had trouble hearing him.

"I said take them out. Shoot the bastards down," Macon nearly shouted. He shut off the cell phone and put the antenna down and tossed the phone back to Agent Brown. The foursome continued towards the green in silence.

The other agents dispersed giving the men some space for conversation. All of them were intrigued about what just happened. Hawthorne took advantage of the space. He took out his nine iron, sized up his shot and the president.

"Are you on schedule for putting the Untied States under U.N. control?"

"Yes, George. Sure hope the people don't hate me for it." He almost sounded genuine.

Katz watched Hawthorne's ball miss the green and hit a sand trap. "Even if they do hate you, so what," he said.

Hawthorne headed for the trap, but stopped briefly. "You know what I told McFadden, that reporter, and I wish I hadn't. If the American people had known what I'd done…"

The other men answered in unison. "They'd have lynched you in the streets."

Hawthorne almost looked hurt.

Cross checked his tape recorder and then spotted an agent looking in his direction. Carefully, he backed out from under the willow and cut through a yard to get away.

That evening, Cross went to the airport. He got there in time to see the president make his way through the lobby. Air Force One was ready to go, but the president had to press more flesh. An agent stopped Macon right in front of Cross.

"Mr. President, is that a go on the C-130," the agent whispered.

Macon nodded. He left the terminal and ran up the stairs to his plane. Cross stood up to watch the plane take off. Air Force One barreled down the runway and lifted off. He watched it disappear into the night.

A reflection in the window caught his attention. Two secret service agents buzzed about something. Cross could not make out what they were saying, but the hair on the back of his neck stood up. Nonchalantly, he watched as the men went out to the tarmac. One of the agents boarded a C-130. Cross dismissed his gut feeling and headed for the payphone.

He dug into his pocket for his calling card and punched in Sol's number.

"Hey, Solly. I got to talk to you about something."

The C-130 started its takeoff roll and bathed the terminal in noise and vibrations.

"Mikey, Art Lueken has been trying to get you."

"What?"

Sol screamed into the phone. "Veronica's husband has been trying to get you."

Once the C-130 lifted off the noise level returned to normal.

"Why? What's up?"

"She's really bad. It doesn't look so good, kid."

A large explosion rocked the night and a plume of orange fire consumed the darkness. The windows of the terminal rattled and people started to scream. Cross dropped the receiver and bolted for the door.

Chapter Thirteen

The next day, Michael Cross was in Queens speeding down Veronica Lueken's street. He double-parked in front of her house. He got out of his car and was nearly hit by a truck trying to get around him. The driver honked the horn. Cross resisted the urge to flip him off. Running up Veronica's stairs, he nearly coughed up a lung and swore he would think about giving up cigarettes.

Cross pushed the doorbell three or four times and got no answer. He ran back to his car and drove away. The car radio blasted out some awful tune and he quickly changed the channel until he found the news. He lit a cigarette and ignored his cough.

"No official confirmation about the crash of the C-130 carrying some of the president's Secret Service detail. As for the president..." the newscaster said, before Cross turned off the radio.

"What in the hell is he up to?" He took a left and headed to St. Mary's Hospital.

San Francisco, California

At the Presidio, Secret Service Suburbans were parked all around Mikhail Makarov's headquarters. Fog consumed the agents who were on duty. Occasionally a ship's horn broke the stillness.

Inside, Makarov was playing chess with the president. The World Teacher sat in a high backed chair contemplating his own moves. The president struggled with what he would do next.

"Mr. President, I want to assure you that our kilo class submarines are now in position," said Makarov.

"About like your queen who's gonna knock the balls off my king."

"Really, Mr. President. You should try to refrain from such colorful terminology," the World Teacher said.

"Yes, sir. Forgive me. I forgot myself."

"Have you decided which American city we will target," Makarov asked.

"It should be large enough to cripple the country so that you, as president, can turn to the U.N. for help. New York City would be an appropriate place. It's evil and therefore any move against it is completely justified. You would be doing the world a favor. If the markets went down, that would certainly help our efforts," said the World Teacher.

"I can't believe we're talking about hitting a United States city. Man, that's crazy."

"As I said, evil must be destroyed if your world is to have lasting peace. The Masters approved of the annihilation of whole countries that rose against Israel."

"I thought you were a man of peace and love."

"I am. I am also just."

The World Teacher loved a good debate, but he knew Macon was vacillating and he didn't want to lose him.

"Just do it and you will be a great hero. You will be immortalized as the great man that you are. There is an important position that you will fill once this plan has been set into motion. Have courage and just do it."

Makarov listened carefully to the two of them. He knew the World Teacher could convince anyone.

"Then it will be alright?" Macon sounded like a little boy before taking a vaccination shot.

"Why would I lie," asked the World Teacher.

Macon looked into his eyes and felt suspended. His mind cleared of all his anxiety. A calm came over him and his sense of importance grew.

St. Mary's Hospital, New York

Every tube imaginable was attached to Veronica Lueken. Wearily, she looked up at all the paraphernalia. She had been hospitalized quite often in the last few years, but she knew this stay would be different. Veronica seemed to accept it.

Michael Cross knocked on her door. He was shocked by her appearance. He couldn't hide it from her, but it didn't seem to bother her.

"When I heard you were worse, I got worried." He kissed her on the cheek.

"There's nothing to worry about, Michael. I'm glad you're here. There's something I want you to do for me."

"Anything."

"You don't know what I'm going to ask. You must learn not to jump in headfirst until you know how deep the water is. Now then, people need to know that those concentration camps I've been talking about really exist. I want you to prove it to the country. Promise me you'll prove they exist. Michael, America has no idea."

"You know I'll do all that I can," he said.

Veronica took a labored breath and seemed to relax.

"Don't put it off, Michael. Please. And keep working on your investigations." She strained to reach a bag on her bed table.

"Take these tapes and listen to them right away. You've missed hearing them. I want you to get caught up to speed."

Cross took the bag and smiled. "I promise."

Veronica tired. Her hand with the IV was badly bruised and her skin had lost its elasticity. Cross could not get over the change. He felt compelled to stay with her until she fell asleep. It wasn't long before Veronica drifted off. The thoughts about her collided in his brain, jamming his concentration. She had made him realize so much, but he had a long way to go. He wasn't sure how to get there without her help. His need for nicotine overwhelmed him. He left and hurried to the parking lot.

He got into his car, lit a cigarette and then popped a tape in the cassette player.

Veronica's voice boomed through the speakers. "This Ball of Redemption will be sent upon mankind. My child, I took you from your bed of pain and illness to bring you here to tell the world to prepare now. It is almost too late.

"We have asked also, urgently, and have had great cooperation from the Earth's masses of people, to Rome to tell them, look up and see what lies beyond your windows; a ball that is fast hurtling towards Earth. Even scientists have failed to recognize the speed of this ball."

Veronica apparently saw the ball and her reactions were caught on tape. "It's frightening! It's bouncing around like it has no control," said Veronica.

"Our Lady said, 'this one will not be destroyed, for mankind has listened but not followed a schedule of prayers and repentance. This has not been done to the satisfaction of the Eternal Father. All must get down on their knees and beg for the repentance of mankind."

Cross lit another cigarette and started his car. He was about to pull away, but stopped. The words on the tape captivated him.

"Jesus says, 'I see murder ahead now, My child, in your city of New York. Many shall be mowed down. It is an attack by a communist nation.

"One last thing, since Lucy has been silenced, it is necessary that the world knows the truth.

"I will also send this message out through one more seer in the world, and if it is not abided by, I have nothing to do but to allow the Chastisement to fall upon mankind."

Cross felt hollowness clear to his soul. It was something he had never felt before, not even when he lost Annie. He drove around for hours listening to the tape and trying to drive off the horrible feeling. He almost headed for a bar to drown it, but forced himself to drive home. Finally, sleep overtook him and he escaped for a few hours.

In the morning, Cross began to keep his promise to Veronica. He booked a flight to Omaha. Hurriedly he grabbed The Times before boarding and started to read before the plane rolled down the runway.

The 737 was half filled. Cross was assigned a seat in the middle of the plane. He grumbled as he read through the news, somewhat amazed by how differently The Times covered the news since he left.

He turned to the center of the front section hoping to find something of interest. A full-page ad jumped out at him: *The Christ Has Returned!*

The ad revealed to the world that the World Teacher was ready to make his presence known, claiming he was the true Messiah. Cross wadded up the paper and headed for a phone at the back of the cabin. He dialed a number, oblivious to the stewardess who tried to pick him up.

"Have you totally lost it," Cross asked Sol Abrams.

"My wife doesn't think so. Why?"

"Why did you run that ad about the World Teacher?"

"You saw that, huh? Well, it's about revenue, Mikey."

"So you sold out to the idiot tabloids?"

"I woulda figured you knew all about him. He's in Rome all the time. Lately, he's been seen with Martinelli."

"Martinelli? But that means he's in on trying to get rid of the pope."

Cross felt like he was having another bad dream.

"He can't be a bad guy, Mikey. He's performing miracles right and left. He's trying to resolve the Middle East situation along with the U.N." Abrams sounded convinced.

"Swell," answered Cross.

"So where are you headed?"

"I'm headed to Nebraska. Talk to you later."

Cross hung up and ran his credit card through the phone. He dialed another number. The blonde stewardess brushed up against him and this time he noticed her, but his son answered the phone stealing his attention.

"Joe?"

"How are you, Dad?"

"I'm fine. Listen…"

"How's Sol?"

"Sol's okay too. Joe, you gotta get out of the Vatican. Get a transfer or something. You've got to stay the hell away from the World Teacher or whatever the hell he goes by this week. He's evil, Joe. He's gonna try something with Martinelli against the pope."

Pushing his worry aside, he focused on the concentration camps.

Michael Cross went to several states looking for the camps. He found several. Most of the centers were empty, but many of them had guards on duty, but what they were guarding was still a mystery. He couldn't engage any of the guards to discuss what they were doing or the people they were to guard.

He had gotten a tip about a monstrous camp east of Anchorage. It was at the end of a rail line. There was only one way into the area.

Near Anchorage, Alaska

Cross traversed rough ground and a dense forest by horseback. There were no known roads that led to the prison. He brought a guide with him who knew the area well. Jack Carey knew Alaska better than he knew his wife. He understood the risks of getting caught. Cross was quite clear about that. With the tree cover, satellites were not a problem, but there had been reports that soldiers had been seen in the area.

After a full day of riding, the men decided to camp near a spring. Jack unloaded the packhorse and Cross did his best to help. It had been twenty years since he had been on a horse and his backside reminded him they had another day's ride just to get to the prison's perimeter.

Cross felt older than Jack who had just turned seventy. Jack's gnarled hands were still strong and Cross hoped he would be half as strong by the time he reached seventy.

Something crashed through the trees. Cross reached for his Remington. A deep blowing sound told the men they were not alone. Cross cocked his rifle and aimed in the direction of the sound. Jack slowly pushed the barrel to the ground.

"Relax, Mike. That's just a big buck telling us we're in his neighborhood."

"Ok." Cross' heart started to beat again.

"Don't hunt much, eh?"

"Nope, just stories."

"Why don't you build us a fire and I'll see if I can shoot us a turkey. You can build a fire, right?"

Cross smiled. "Guess I deserved that."

"Start some coffee too. It's goin' to get chilly tonight." Jack adjusted his well-worn Stetson. The old man headed off into the trees. Cross unpacked the coffee pot and walked to the spring to get some water.

He wished he had lived a hundred years ago, when the West wasn't so populated. So much weighed on his mind. The outdoors took him away. There wasn't a phone or power line for miles. Cross doubted there were other people in the area. That was fine with him. He hoped he wouldn't find a prison camp at the end of the trail. The reality of it had no place in his mind.

Firewood was plentiful. Cross had no trouble gathering enough kindling and even managed to start a nice size fire. The wood was good and dry and he knew it wouldn't smoke much, keeping their presence hidden. His senses came alive. Smells were stronger and sweeter than anything he remembered. Cross lit a cigarette and the taste was wonderful. It was like his first drag in the morning, only more delightful. He could get used to this kind of life.

As he watched the fire, his mind wandered everywhere and then nowhere in particular. He took a stick and stoked the fire. Realizing the coffee pot was too close to the flames, Cross moved the pot gingerly with his fingers. He quickly licked his index finger and examined it. It had already formed a blister. He got up and went back to the spring and submerged his hand in the icy water. He saw a man's reflection in the water and he turned around sharply. Expecting to see Jack, Cross grew alarmed when he found out it was someone else. He thought he recognized the man, but he wasn't sure.

The stranger was tall and dark, about thirty or thirty-five. He had large black eyes, larger than Cross had ever seen.

"Hi," said the man in a soft voice.

Cross stood and wiped his wet hand on his pants.

"Can I help you?" Cross felt uncomfortable.

"Perhaps I can help you."

Cross noticed the man did not seem to be dressed for the climate. He had on an expensive jacket. "Armani," Cross thought to himself. There was something weird about the guy and he was sure he had seen him somewhere.

"How about some coffee," the man asked.

Cross looked him in the eyes and became very uneasy. The man's eyes seemed devoid of light.

"Hope you take it black," said Cross. A gunshot ripped through the canyon, startling him. Cross dropped the cup of coffee into the fire. The hot coffee sizzled as it hit the flames. Cross laughed aloud. His jitters got the better of him.

"It's been one of those days." Cross poured another cup of coffee and went to hand it to the man, but the man was gone. He wasn't anywhere to be found.

Jack came into the camp lugging a large turkey.

'We'll eat good tonight.'

"Jack, did you see anybody on your way back to camp?"

"Nope."

"Are you sure?"

"Yep. I'm old, but I ain't blind. Something get into you, boy?"

"There was a guy here and when I looked up, he was gone."

"Well, where did his tracks lead?"

"Tracks? I dunno." Cross searched the ground. Jack helped a bit, not sure about Cross.

"Boy, I only see your tracks and mine. Sure you weren't napping and dreamed it?"

Jack cocked an eyebrow and rubbed the whiskers on his chin.

'Well, if we're gonna eat, you better get to plucking them feathers."

It took Cross a while to dress the bird. The more feathers he plucked the more he thought about the stranger. He gutted the bird with Jack's supervision. Jack was far too hungry to let a greenhorn spoil his dinner. Spotting some pinfeathers, Jack took out his lighter and singed them. He was not sure what to make about Cross' visitor.

"Drink much, do you," asked Jack.

"Used to. Gave it up."

"Been awhile?"

"Years." Cross shot down Jack's theory.

The men ate in silence and bedded down for the night. Jack was asleep as soon as his head hit the bedroll. Cross had to work at it. He added more wood to the fire. By 3 a.m., he'd given up on the stranger. Cross had worked it to death. He focused on the morning and fell asleep. The smell of bacon frying in the pan yanked Cross from his dreams.

"Hungry, Mike?"

"Starved."

"Well, grab a plate and let's tackle breakfast and get on with the ride."

Cross could have eaten the enamel steel plate. He scarfed down his breakfast.

"Got the horses ready. Let's get the dishes done and head out."

Cross was anxious to leave. They traveled most of the day. By late afternoon, Jack stopped to give the horses a rest. He got down and took out his binoculars from the saddlebag.

"Why don't you mosey up that hill and I'll bet you'll see whatcher looking for."

He handed Cross the binoculars.

"Coming, Jack?"

"You go on. I've got to get some circulation into my ass."

Cross knew how he felt. His butt had been numb for the last five miles. Now he ached all over, but he dragged himself to the top of the hill. He looked out over the ridge. About three miles away, he could see a structure. Focusing the binoculars, he made out the prison camp. It was huge. His sources told him the camp was designed to hold nearly a half million people. Now he believed it.

Scanning the area, he noticed the razor wire on top of the fences was rolled in as if to keep someone in rather than to deter someone from breaking into the facility. As he looked around the camp, he saw armed personnel on duty, but no sign of any prisoners.

He made his way down the hill to grab his camera.

"Satisfied," asked Jack.

"Jesus, Jack. It's the biggest damned thing I've ever seen. I'm gonna get some pictures.

"Best be careful, boy. Don't take too long. We gotta high tail it out of here. Daylight's being chewed up like a grizzly on an ol' Coho."

Half way up the hill he started to wheeze and he swore at himself under the breath he had left. By the time he got to the crest, he felt dizzy. He hugged the ground a moment or two and then laid flat. Cross pulled off the lens cap and got the camp in the viewfinder.

"Quite a sight, isn't it?"

For a second, he thought Jack had changed his mind about the climb, but then he realized he was in trouble. Although Cross was grateful it wasn't the stranger from the night before, he wasn't happy to see this man.

"Jesus, where did you come from?"

"I didn't mean to alarm you."

"Who the hell are you?" Cross got a better look at the tall young man. His blonde hair caught the sun. The man looked like he was glowing.

"My name is Rafe. Do you have enough of a lens for the shot?"

"Yeah, one of the best. Are you going to arrest me or what?"

"What makes you think that?"

The young man smiled at Cross.

"Well, I figured I'm trespassing and you're in camouflage. You look like you belong down there."

Cross hurried and took the pictures; afraid the burly guy really was going to arrest him.

"There is more to the picture than just the camp, Michael."

"How do you know my name?"

Cross thought he had lost it completely.

"That's part of my job."

"Are you a fed?"

"No. You don't have to worry about me."

Cross was not so sure. He bagged his camera and got ready to run. He had his camera confiscated before and he was hoping to make a run for it.

"Before you go," Rafe said. "I think you should investigate those missing suitcase bombs. You know, the ones the Russians can't find. They've been strategically placed throughout the United States and you need to make it your business to find out about them before it's too late."

"Waddya mean too late?"

"It's time to go. There's a patrol coming up the trail. Hurry."

Cross did not wait to find out if the man was right. He ran down the hill, and got on his horse. Jack and he galloped for a good two miles, finally fading into the thickness of the forest. It had been a bizarre trip and the men he met stayed on his mind.

Washington, D.C.

Armed with data and photos of several concentration camps, Cross attended a presidential press conference. He knew he wasn't popular with President Macon and stood the risk of being ignored. As soon as the president finished his opening statement, Cross did everything he could to get the president to call on him.

The president called on everyone around Cross. In the remaining minutes of the conference, the president finally called on Cross, thinking the worst questions had already been asked.

"Mr. Cross."

"Thank you, Mr. President. Sir, why is the United States government building internment camps in this country?"

"We haven't had camps utilized in this country since World War II, Mr. Cross."

The president tried to call on someone else, but Cross pushed his follow-up question.

"I have pictures right here, sir, which clearly show these camps are in operation today."

Cross held up a large photo. The press corps went nuts. The room buzzed and cameras whirred. The entire corps focused on the picture, except for Macon.

"I have sources, sir, which indicate these prisons were built and manned by federal authorization."

"I don't have any idea what you're talking about."

"Helen, do you have a question," the president asked, hoping the seasoned reporter would come to his rescue.

Before the reporter could open her mouth, Cross ran up to the podium and smacked down the photo in front of the chief executive.

The Secret Service went for Cross and got him around both arms and pulled him out of the room.

"Who are these detention centers meant to hold, Mr. President?"

The room was in an uproar and cameras zoomed in on the president's magenta face. Macon turned and left the room and headed for the Oval Office.

That night, the news lead with Cross' demonstration, but he did not get to see any of the coverage. He had been jailed. Even being estranged from his freedom and his cigarettes didn't bring him to regretting his actions. Cross knew he was right. It took him until the next morning to get a hold of some help.

Cross finally got Sol Abrams on the phone.

"Sol, you gotta help me, man."

"I've been trying to get in touch with you."

"I'm being held in the DC jail on some trumped up charge. I need you to spring me."

"I'll see what I can do. Listen, Mike. There's no easy way to say this. Veronica Lueken died late yesterday."

Cross did not know what to say.

"Mikey?"

He heard Sol, but couldn't bring himself to answer him. Cross hung up the phone and fought back tears. On an emotional level, Veronica's death touched him more than he thought possible. Without her, Joe would have died. She was family to him, but she was also a valued source. He didn't know if he could ever find anyone to take her place.

Chapter Fourteen

Sol Abrams drove up to the curb at La Guardia Airport. Michael Cross spotted him as he exited the terminal. The traffic was awful. Cross got into Abrams' Olds. He was happy to see him.

"Thanks for the lift, Sol."

"I'm gonna put it on your tab."

A man in a dark suit and sunglasses made a note of Sol's license plate and got into a waiting car. He tailed the Olds hanging back slightly.

"It's good to see you, Mikey. Sorry I couldn't get yous out until after Veronica's funeral."

"Thanks for sending flowers for me."

"That's also on your tab. How's about telling me what got you so riled that you made the national news?"

Cross did not hear Sol. He was distracted by thousands of birds acting strangely. It was as if they all heard a cue and responded in unison.

"For the love…will you look at that," Cross exclaimed.

"What? A broad?" Abrams nearly drove into the oncoming lane.

"No. Thousands of birds are flying out over the ocean. Look at 'em go."

Sol swerved again. "Never seen anything like it. A little early, isn't it?"

"Hey, Sol. Pull over here at this parking lot. I wanna grab my car. There's something I have to do."

Sol pulled over as quickly as he could, considering the traffic. The men in the car behind them pulled over and parked just beyond the copper Olds.

Cross got out of the car. He looked up at the sky again, and then walked to his car. A shiver ran down his spine. Perhaps he sensed the man walking behind him. He was more focused though on where he was headed. Cross had to see Declan Cavanaugh.

The man behind Cross watched him get into his car and drive off. He ran back to his vehicle and easily caught up to Cross in the heavy traffic.

Cross pulled into a parking ramp and was tailed to the fourth floor. He parked his Chevy and took the stairs down. One of the men behind him took the elevator and the other followed Cross into the stairwell.

It was a short walk to Father Cavanaugh's apartment building. The doorman recognized Cross and let him into the lobby. Once the two men saw where Cross entered, they waited outside the building.

Cross knocked on Cavanaugh's door. His housekeeper opened the door and led Cross into the living room where Cavanaugh was seated.

"Michael. Great to see you. Where've you been?"

"Jail."

"Jail? You must be right about something."

"How d'ya figure?"

Cavanaugh showed Cross to a chair. "If I ever have a question about whether I'm doing the right thing, I can always be sure by how much I'm hassled by the devil."

"In your line of work, exorcisms and all, you must run into him a lot."

Cavanaugh smiled. "More than I'd care to, which is not at all. I could tell you stories that would... well, that isn't why you're here."

"You're right, Father."

Cross took out a cigarette and tapped it on the back of his hand.

"I've got a few questions. You've mentioned the World Teacher before. What do you know about him?"

Father Cavanaugh had no discernable reaction, but Cross wasn't aware the priest didn't want him to see it.

"What do you mean?"

"A group claims to know who he is and when he's going to declare himself."

Father Cavanaugh crossed his legs and ran his hand through his white hair.

"Yes. Yes. The Times had a big spread. If you are asking me if he is *the* Messiah, we know he isn't. If you're asking me if he's *the* antichrist, I can't answer that right now."

He had read Cross' mind, Cross smiled to himself.

"We'll have to see if this fellow comes up with some fantastic plans to save us from financial collapse and there's a food crisis in our future as well. Of course, the antichrist will be instrumental in the Mid-East peace plan."

Cross thought Father Cavanaugh had a great deal of information, but was holding back.

"What I do know for sure, Michael, is you don't want to read about him or look at his picture. He will get inside your mind. It's as though you open a door and invite him in. He never refuses an invitation. When he officially arrives on the world scene, throw away your television and computer."

Cross was taken aback by what he said. Cavanaugh remained very calm, but he could see Cross was unsettled with his answer.

"Aren't you overreacting?"

"Trust me, Michael. His powers will be great. No one has seen anything like him ever. He will spin a web with all sorts of allure."

Cross got up and walked around the living room with his thoughts.

"Father, you're the only one I can ask who won't think I'm crazy. At least, I hope not."

"I'm listening, Michael."

"I had a strange encounter last week, two actually. I was investigating concentration camps and went to Alaska because I heard they had a facility out there."

"I'll bet you found it."

Cross held back the drapes and looked out nervously.

"Yes, I found a camp or what I think is a camp."

"And your encounter?" Father Cavanaugh had infinite patience, but he knew Cross was afraid of verbalizing his question.

"Well, that's just it. I'm not sure I really had an encounter." Cross kept his back to the priest.

"Was it at the camp?"

"No. It was on the way there. You see I was making coffee while my guide was off hunting dinner. All of a sudden this guy was standing right there with me."

"How did he get there?"

"I dunno. I never heard him walk or ride into the area. He spoke to me and I was gonna give him some coffee, but Jack was on his way back to camp and the guy split."

"Where did he go?"

Cross stuffed his hands into his pockets and decided to blurt out what happened.

"He disappeared into thin air."

"I see."

"Father, I'm not crazy am I?"

Cavanaugh stood up and walked over to his desk.

"I know you're not crazy, Michael. Did you recognize him?"

"That's just it. I wasn't sure."

"Would you recognize him again if you were to see him?

Cross could not figure out why Father Cavanaugh did not challenge him about how the man disappeared. He asked the priest, even though he wasn't sure he wanted to know.

"Father, is it possible that this guy was not human?"

"You mean was he a demon?"

"I don't know what I mean."

"He could be one or the other or both."

"Well, how could a human being just disappear?"

The palms of Cross' hands got clammy.

"It may have been some sort of illusion, Michael."

Cross knew it would come back to his sanity. He walked over to Father Cavanaugh's bookshelves and glanced at the titles. A part of him wanted to crawl inside one of the books to hide.

Father Cavanaugh returned to his recliner. He saw his housekeeper peeking around the corner at them.

"Is there something you need, Kiri?"

"Would you like some coffee, Father," she asked, startled at being discovered.

"Yes, thank you. Now then, Michael, where were we?"

"I'm crazy."

"Sorry, don't think so. These things have happened to any number of people. It's happened to me. And I'll admit it makes you question your senses."

Cross relaxed a bit and went over to the sofa and sat.

"Tell me, Michael. Did he say anything to you?"

"Just hello and he asked for some coffee and then poof."

Father Cavanaugh nodded. "Well, he might return to see you."

"Great." His stomach tightened.

"Do you wear a St. Benedict medal and crucifix?"

"I just wear a St. Michael's medal."

"That's a start. I have some in my desk drawer." Cavanaugh sprang up and went back to his desk. He opened the top drawer.

"Here is your coffee, Father," Kiri interrupted. "Would you like me to pour," she asked.

"I'll let Michael do the honors."

Kiri left the two and returned to her listening post.

"Here you go, Michael. Wear them in good health."

"Thanks." Cross decided to end it there. He didn't want to bring up the second man he saw, unsure about who it was and what problems may accompany him. With Veronica gone, he had other issues, other questions that stuck in his mind.

"Father, on a different subject, do you see the warning happening anytime soon?"

Cavanaugh stirred his coffee and took a healthy bite from a pecan cookie.

"Well, that depends. The way the world is going, it could be soon. But certain conditions have to be met. Sit down and we can go over some points and enjoy more of these cookies. I believe we will see great calamities before the warning, such as wars, and attacks on our country."

"Then the warning?"

"Things will be very bad. When things seem to be at their worst, that's when the warning will occur."

"Where does the antichrist figure into all of this," asked Cross.

"He should declare himself shortly after the warning. People will have a last ditch effort to get right with God."

"So does the warning just happen or will there be an indication it's on the way? You said things would be bad, but is there any one thing that points to the warning?"

Father Cavanaugh got up and poured more coffee. He filled Cross' cup and thought about how much to say.

"Seven days before the warning, a white cross will appear in the sky. It will be seen by everyone for twenty-four hours."

"Anything else?"

"Yes, small animals and birds will disappear. They will be able to sense something is about to happen, much like an earthquake. People will also feel a spiritual event is about to take place. I've got some books you should read concerning the visions at Garabandal. There are other books that discuss the warning, the miracle and of course, the Great Chastisement with the three days of darkness."

Cavanaugh carefully picked the books from his library.

"What comes after the warning," asked Cross.

"The miracle, with a few things in between," Cavanaugh smiled wistfully.

"Isn't that when Joey Lomangino gets his eyes?"

"That's what we've been told. Here you go, Michael. These will get you started."

Cross took the books and walked towards the door.

"After the miracle, Father, then what?"

Cavanaugh sighed and said, "After that we'll reap the whirlwind."

"I was afraid of that. Well, thanks for your time."

"Not at all."

Father Cavanaugh shut the door and returned to the living room. A shadowy figure was waiting for him. The priest wasn't in the mood for another battle, but he wasn't surprised by the demon's appearance. It could have been the hideous odor, that telltale scent. He didn't know what kind of battle it would be. It didn't really matter to the weary priest. He knew there wasn't any choice but to go through the trial. The demon gathered more of an appearance. Kiri couldn't see the demon, but she felt his presence. She became very ill at her listening post, went to her room and then locked the door.

The demon's face was distorted and long. The mouth was too small to harbor such massively deformed teeth. Suddenly the demon leapt at the priest and tackled him. Father Cavanaugh felt his collarbone break, but he was in too much pain to scream.

The demon pounded him for several minutes. Cavanaugh's prayers were answered. Momentarily satisfied, it left. He was unconscious and badly beaten. Kiri stayed in her room for the next two hours, scared to come out.

Cross made it home with the armload of books, and decided to read them right away. He got two packs of cigarettes from the refrigerator and tossed them on the dining room table. The sliced turkey in the fridge reminded him he hadn't eaten all day.

He sniffed the turkey to make sure it hadn't gone bad and then made three sandwiches. Grabbing a soda to go with them, Cross settled in for some heavy reading. Losing track of time as he poured over the books, he figured he had been at it for at least a pack and half. There was so much information to cover that he couldn't walk away from it. Cross was so completely entranced by the material that he failed to notice he was not alone.

A man entered the dining room. Cross got up and was met with an iron fist that dropped him. Five men ransacked the house. They emptied closets and bookshelves. Dishes in the cupboards were thrown to the floor. Furniture was overturned and pictures were taken off the walls, some of them destroyed. The men became furious when they couldn't find what they wanted and stormed out of the house.

Cross woke up to Sol Abrams' fat face looking down at him.

"Shoulda ducked, Mikey."

Abrams removed a washcloth from Cross' head.

"Tell me about it. Did they take anything?"

"I couldn't tell you."

Cross sat up slowly and looked around the house.

"Jesus, Mary and Joseph. Guess I'll have to stay with you tonight, Solly."

"Are you kidding? I came over here to hide out. Katz fired me today and I didn't want to go home to face my wife."

Cross got to his feet, not sure he heard Abrams correctly. He staggered over to the fireplace and went to the third brick below the mantle, just to the left of center.

"Maybe they hit you harder than I thought. What in the hell are you doing? Lie down until the cops and the paramedics get here."

"I'm looking for something."

Cross pulled out a brick and dug out an envelope and some cassette tapes. He made sure everything was there and then returned it all to the compartment.

Sol didn't ask. He knew Cross would not tell him about that stuff. Abrams also knew that another hiding place would soon be found. Even if he thought about seeing what all the stuff contained, he knew Cross would kick the hell of him.

Sol helped Cross to the couch as the police and paramedics rolled up outside.

He was taken to a midtown hospital and had a terrible time enduring the never-ending wait in the emergency room. Sol stayed with him until hunger hijacked him. A nurse came into the cubicle to take Cross' vital signs.

"Hey, Mikey. Now that the nurse is here, I have a piece of pie calling my name."

"Yeah, I'll bet you do. It's hollering 'Hey fatty, what's another five pounds?'"

"Your mother," Sol answered on his way out the door.

"How's your head feeling, Mr. Cross?"

"Pounding away." He tried to read her nametag, but couldn't focus well enough.

"Young."

"Hardly," laughed Cross.

"That's my name. You were trying to read my ID."

He squinted again at her nametag.

"Let me guess. The 'L' is for Loretta."

"I go by Lori. Now just put this thermometer under your tongue. My mother was a big Loretta Young fan."

"M-m."

The doctor will be in to stitch that cut in a little while. We've had a busy night."

Cross nodded. He absorbed her face and her body. She was beautiful, but she didn't flaunt it. Lori took her looks as second nature and often forgot she could cause palpitations in most men. Obviously, Cross was one of them.

"Still a little upset with that beating," she asked, removing the thermometer.

"Huh?"

"Your pulse is a little fast."

"Oh. No, I'm fine. But I think you're to blame for the pulse rate."

"I'll bet you say that to all the nurses. How much do you smoke?"

He fought his headache. Cross was not sure if he should answer her. He didn't feel up to a lecture.

"Two packs give or take."

"A week?"

"A day."

Lori just cocked an eyebrow and then hung her stethoscope around her long neck.

"I'll be back."

Cross watched her leave. He dozed off for a few minutes until he heard the curtain pulled back. Cross sat up and smiled, hoping it was Lori. A gruff resident with a suture kit met him.

"Let's see your head, Mr. Cross." The resident roughly examined the cut just above Cross' left eyebrow. He popped off the cap of a syringe of xylocaine.

"This might hurt a bit."

The resident was right. Cross nearly came off the table. He thought about hollering, but Lori came back into the exam room to help the doctor. Cross quickly stifled the scream, but then the resident stuck the needle into the center of the three-inch gash.

"Jesus, man. I'm not some lousy anatomy dummy."

"Just one more stick and then we'll be set, Mr. Cross." The resident was unmoved by his pain.

Lori took hold of Cross' wrist and squeezed as hard as she could as the last injection went into the wound.

"That's it, Mr. Cross. You can relax now," said Lori. Her soothing voice calmed him. Cross focused on her as the doctor went to work. Lori's pager went off.

"Excuse me, Rob. I've got to get this. Do you need me for anything?"

Cross thought the doctor would be nuts not to need her.

"Nope," the resident replied.

She met Sol on the way out.

"Excuse me, lady," said Sol as he watched her walk away.

"Hey, Mike. You'll never guess who's here."

"I give up."

"Declan Cavanaugh."

"Visiting somebody? Ouch! Will you watch it, Doc?"

"No. He's a patient. I saw him in the elevator. He didn't look too good."

"How much longer, Doc," Cross asked impatiently. "Ow!"

The resident tied the last knot.

"I'm done. I would have been done sooner, but you squirmed more than a three year old."

"Yeah? You're using a dull needle. You tried to numb it up and I still felt it. Can I go now?"

"Sure. Just take it easy for a few days. Come back in about ten days and get the stitches taken out. If you have any blurred vision or sudden headache, come back to the ER right away."

The resident feigned a smile and left. Cross tried to jump down from the gurney, but felt woozy.

"Easy now, Mike. What's the rush?"

"I wanna go see Father Cavanaugh. Sol, while I get dressed, can you find out what room he's in?"

"812. I thought yous'd wanna know."

Cross made it to Father Cavanaugh's room with Sol's help. He peeked in the room and saw that Cavanaugh was sleeping soundly. From the hall, he could see the priest's arm was in a cast.

"Excuse me, sir," a nurse stopped Cross.

"Visiting hours are over. You'll have to come back tomorrow."

"Can you tell me what happened to Father Cavanaugh? I'm a friend of his."

"His collar bone was broken and his shoulder was dislocated."

"Do you know how it happened?"

"Probably a fall. The father is getting up there. You'll have to go now. Our patients need their rest."

The next day was dark and rainy, but that did not deter Cross from visiting his friend. He was surprised to see him sitting up in bed, attempting to eat his breakfast.

"Tell me, Michael, you didn't happen to bring Jack to see me?"

"Jack?" Cross thought perhaps Cavanaugh had hit his head.

"Mr. Daniels. Did you bring some with you?"

"Sorry, Father."

"Ah, it's just as well, I suppose. Still, it would have gone well with my orange juice."

"So, was Jack responsible for your fall?"

"Fall? Nonsense. I got into a fight."

Cross did not know what to make of the elderly priest.

"A fight at your age, Father?"

"At my age? What does age have to do with it? Sit, Michael. You're making me nervous."

Cross dragged a chair next to the priest's bed and sat.

"Who beat you up?"

"One of the devil's own."

"Did you call the police?"

"And tell them what?" Cavanaugh cautiously drank some tea.

"Tell 'em who did this to you."

"Ah, me boy, they'd think I was daft."

"Why? Just turn the guy in, Father."

"I told you, Michael, unless you've gone deaf, that one of those damn stinking demons did it."

"What? During an exorcism?"

"No. He just showed up and asked if I cared to dance."

Cross did not know if Cavanaugh had a stroke or not. He seemed okay.

"Blasted hospital food."

"Father, are you telling me that a demon knocked on your door and picked a fight with you," Cross whispered.

Cavanaugh leaned into Cross and whispered, "Not exactly."

"I thought not."

"He just showed up in the living room and there we were, engaged in combat. Now don't be looking at me through the black eye on your face. I haven't lost my bobber. So, are you hurt?"

"I'm okay. I'm more interested in finding out how the hell you got here."

Cavanaugh wadded up his napkin one-handed and pushed the tray aside.

"I told you. Michael, if you're going to be snooping further in to the truth, you may as well know right here and now that there are battles being fought on several levels, seen and unseen. They're going to be more prevalent too. So, get used to them."

"But Father, you should be more careful."

"I do my best. Each new day, I'm older but I'm also one step closer to eternity. We all are. Get used to the fact that the unexplained will become commonplace. The veil between this world and the next is getting thinner every second. Soon, we'll all be able to see demons and have to fight them, one on one."

Cross thought his concussion must have been worse than the doctors told him. This wasn't making any sense to him.

"What in the hell do the demons look like?"

"They're ugly bastards, Michael. But they all vary, same as human beings. Some may look almost like you and me, while others have a more reptilian appearance. Trust me, they're as ugly as sin."

"Has this sort of thing happened to you before, Father?"

"On occasion. This was a bad go-round. I don't know what's worse-the demons or the people who took a contract out on my life."

"You mean someone ordered a hit on you?"

"Yes. That's why I'm always careful about where I go. I've got friends with the State Patrol and the police who act as my bodyguards. But in the end, when your number is up, it's up."

"Is there anything I can get you?"

"Mr. Daniels, if it won't be too much trouble."

Cross smiled as he got up. He shook the priest's hand and left with too much on his mind. The more he learned about the global conspiracy, the less he really understood. He popped two Advil and stopped at the drinking fountain to chase them with some water.

"I thought you would be home resting," said Lori Young.

Cross looked up and saw her. He wiped the water off of his chin, feeling like a five year old. Lori was more beautiful than he remembered.

"I had to see a friend."

"Did you find her?"

"Him, actually."

Lori smiled and started to walk away. "Get some rest," she said.

"I will." Cross thought about asking her to have coffee, but he could not get his lack of courage under control. He felt a little dizzy, but attributed that to her cologne and not to his head. Cross left the hospital feeling old, too old for Lori and too old for his own good.

Sol drove him home. Later, Sol cleaned up the house while Cross rested on the couch. Abrams hated to clean, but it beat going home. Whatever motivated him was fine with Cross. His splitting headache changed his mind about doing anything. He couldn't think and he couldn't sleep. Instead, he merely existed; content to live from one cigarette to another.

Chapter Fifteen

It took Sol several weeks to face his wife. When he finally arrived home, she met him with two suitcases filled with his clothes. Cross allowed him to stay for a while longer until Mitzi Abrams calmed down.

Normally, Cross would have been driven crazy by Sol, but he had opened a new door in his investigation that led straight to Washington, D.C., leaving Sol the run of the house.

As Cross tried to put the pieces together, he had trouble understanding why certain factions within the Vatican had contacts with a segment of the CIA. He couldn't uncover what they had in common.

Late one spring evening, Cross was contacted by his source in Virginia. He took a red-eye flight to Reagan International where Hugh Klebbans met him. Cross had known him for five years. Klebbans sought him out when he had inside information about George Hawthorne. He and Hawthorne went way back and had mutual friends. Klebbans was known for his reliable information and Cross did not hesitate to meet with him.

The men drove through the rainy District until Klebbans found an obscure hole in the wall. He parked down the street and the men walked back to the Redskin

Bar. A downpour ensued, soaking Cross' cigarette. He hated to lose one of his allotted smokes.

They found an empty table in the back of the bar. Cross quickly lit another cigarette.

"What'll you have, Mike?"

"Ginger ale in a short glass."

"Oh, that's right. You gave up the booze. Hey, man, if this will bother you, I'll…"

"It's fine, Hugh. I can handle it."

A waitress came over and took their order.

"Scotch, rocks. Make that a double and a short ginger ale," Klebbans said.

Cross watched the big screen television. A report was on about the Yankees and spring training.

"Mike, got something you need to know."

The waitress returned with the drinks. Klebbans smacked a twenty on her tray and looked over his shoulder at the other customers. He bummed a smoke from Cross and downed half of his drink.

"Mike, you're going to see an airliner go down."

Cross forgot about the Yankees.

"Waddya talking about, Hugh?"

"I'm telling you, a U.S. airliner is going to be shot down. This is some serious shit, Mike."

"Who is your source on this, Hugh?" Cross knew Klebbans' track record. His heart started to beat a little faster.

"It's a guy in the FBI. I had it confirmed with an agency guy I know. You can trust the information."

"When's it gonna happen?"

Klebbans finished his drink and snapped his fingers for the waitress.

"My guy's saying summer."

"Jesus, Hugh. Why? Who's gonna do it?"

"That's a good question."

"Want a refill," asked the waitress.

"Please. Mike?"

"I'm fine."

"Thanks, honey," said Klebbans.

"Check into this. A guy told me that some surface-to-air missiles were taken off an army base in Maryland."

"Missiles?"

"Yeah. My hunch is you'll find the men behind the airliner deal if you can track those mothers down."

"Doesn't give me much time."

"I'll get you all the intel I can, but they're on to me, Mike. I gotta get out of town."

"How are you fixed for cash?"

"I'm okay for now. Listen, Mike. Watch your ass. The people behind this one are connected, man."

They finished their drinks in silence and left the bar. Klebbans dropped Cross at the airport where he rented a car. Tentative about what he would do next, Cross got a hotel room and made some calls. Not one of his contacts was home.

He took out the phone book and tried to see what Army bases were listed. Cross found a few, but was uncertain how to find out about the supposed theft of the missiles.

At 3 a.m., he finally got through to one of his contacts. Cross asked about any missing missiles and was given the name of a woman who could help him.

He checked out of the hotel early and headed for Maryland. All he had was a phone number. When he was a few miles from Ft. Detrick, he called the source on his cell phone.

"This is Michael Cross. I got your number from a mutual friend. We need to talk."

He briefly explained what it was about and the woman on the other end gave him directions to a meeting place. She said she would need an hour. Cross stopped at a coffee shop near Fort Detrick. He bought a copy of the paper, had three quick cups of coffee and a piece of toast. He left promptly at 7:45 a.m. and drove to the meeting spot.

A young woman parked her Cavalier next to his rental. She checked her hair in the mirror and glanced at Cross who was reading the sports pages.

She rolled down the passenger window.

"Excuse me, sir. Are you Michael Cross?" He matched the description Cross gave of himself.

"That's me."

"Let's go, okay?"

Cross threw the paper in the back seat and grabbed his cigarettes off the dash and the keys. He got into the black Chevy and they drove quickly out of the area.

"I only got your first name, Shari."

"That's all you're going to get."

"Okay. I need to ask if you know anything about some missing missiles from Ft. Detrick."

"What's it to you?"

"If you do know something about those missing missiles, then you sure as hell know that it isn't a good situation."

"Like I don't know that," she huffed and stomped the accelerator.

"Take it easy, kid. Pull in that supermarket lot over there."

She found a place to park in the crowded lot.

"Now then, how do you know the missiles were stolen from the base?"

My boyfriend was on guard duty that night. He got his butt reamed because the brass and the FBI thought he might have been in on it." Shari was nervous and picked at her blue fingernails.

"Was he?"

"Absolutely not."

"Did he see anything suspicious?" Cross took a liking to the girl. Her brown eyes were honest as well as beautiful.

"The only thing he saw was an Army truck leaving the base. He told me he thought it was an inside job."

"Can I talk with him about it? I promise I won't give him up."

"You can't."

"Look, kid. I really promise. I won't give him up."

"He's dead, Mr. Cross."

"How did it happen?"

"They said it was suicide. But it couldn't have been."

Tears easily formed in her eyes and trailed down her reddened cheeks. Cross put his hand on her shoulder. "Why not?"

"How many guys do you know kill themselves the day before they pick up a new sports car?"

"None, I guess. How did he die?"

"A bullet to the head."

She blew her nose hard and then wiped her eyes.

"God, I'm sorry, Shari."

"So am I. They claimed he shot himself while out on patrol. They told me they found the gun in his left hand. One shell was missing. That was so strange."

"Strange how?"

"Eric was right handed."

Cross made sure Shari would be all right before getting out of the car. He didn't want her to drive him back to his car in case someone would see her.

He went to a pay phone and called his boss at The Wire. Cross decided not to inform him about the missiles. There was more legwork that needed to be done.

Over the next few weeks, Cross worked diligently trying to come up with the names of the major players involved. He managed to get a small story by his boss

about the stolen missiles. He was surprised nothing came of
the piece. Even the major networks glossed over it.

Cross thought that was odd. He tried to work on the
story in between his other assignments, but the trail had
gone cold. Leads dried up and Hugh Klebbans had no
further information. By May, the FBI, on some nebulous
charge had detained Klebbans. Cross had reached a dead-
end.

In June, Sol and Mitzi Abrams reconciled, much to
Cross' relief. Abrams' appetite and his bad habits were
hard to endure. Cross was happy for Sol. Especially since a
national magazine had hired his former boss for more
money than The Times shelled out. Mitzi was ecstatic.

She threw a party in mid-July and Cross was invited.
He was thankful that the guests were old friends and
family, even better, none of them were in the media.

The evening was warm and everyone sat around the
pool. There was a fabulous view of Long Island Sound. The
water was calm and tranquil as the remaining light tickled
the waves.

Sol had outdone himself on the steaks. Everyone was
well fed, too well fed in Cross' case. He asked Sol to walk
with him along the shoreline. A gentle breeze blew the
lingering strands of hair on Sol's round head. Abrams
continually brushed them down with his hand.

"Why don't you just shave those three hairs and be
done with it," Cross laughed.

"Listen, you jerk. You think you're so damned
gorgeous with all that hair of yours? Lemme tell ya, pal.
Girls really dig bald men."

"Whatever you say, Solly. Hey, I'm glad things are
working out for you and Mitzi."

"Yeah, me too. Thanks."

They walked further up the beach. A blonde man
approached them. Cross thought he knew him, but he was

not positive. When he got closer, Cross knew it was the mysterious man from Alaska.

"Hello, Michael."

"What are you doing here?"

"Working." The man walked calmly by Sol and Cross.

"Who was that big guy, Mikey?"

Cross stopped to light a cigarette.

"Hey, Mike. Look! Fire works."

Cross looked up and saw a hot yellow streak climbing in the night sky. Then suddenly, a massive explosion ripped through the blackness.

"Jesus Christ," Sol yelled. "What in the hell was that?"

Cross did not want to believe what his gut was telling him. He looked for the blonde guy and wondered if he had any connection to the explosion. Cross saw him and ran up to him.

"What is going on, Rafe?"

"I told you, Michael. I have to work to do and so do you."

"Mike, wait up," wheezed Sol. His fat legs rubbed together while he ran like two giant logs of sausage.

Cross turned to look at Abrams and then looked back. Rafe was gone.

"You got your cell phone? I wanna call a guy at Kennedy to see if they got that explosion on radar."

"I left it at home," Abrams gasped.

"Forget it. I'll meet you back at the house." Cross ran back to Abrams' house. The other guests asked him if he saw what had happened. He ran past them into the kitchen and grabbed the phone. His mind raced in place. Frustrated, he slammed the phone down. He ran to his car and drove to the harbor.

He hitched a ride on a boat headed out to sea. The captain had seen the explosion while gassing up his fishing boat. Wasting no time, they headed out at full throttle. The

ocean was ablaze. Rings of fire could be seen for miles.
Cross took photos as they got closer to the burning debris.
He prayed it wasn't what he thought it was, but his soul
knew that it was an airliner.

Cross tried to settle his thoughts. Rationalizing that it
may have been a mid-air collision, he focused on looking
for survivors. He borrowed the captain's cell phone and
called The Wire to report the story.

By dawn, no survivors had been spotted. Cross could
not imagine how anyone could have survived. He went
back to shore with more questions than answers.
Immediately he went back to his investigation.

The early news reports included eyewitnesses who
claimed to have seen a yellow streak in the sky before the
explosion, confirming what Cross had seen. Then the
reports suddenly stopped. It appeared the media had taken
another direction and not entirely by choice.

Cross went back to Sol's and picked up his cell phone.
Sol and Mitzi were huddled around the television. They had
plenty of questions for Cross, but he told them he had to go.
He said he would call them. Sol saw a familiar look in
Cross' eyes and got up to leave with him, but Cross did not
go for it.

Once outside, he punched in Hugh Klebbans' number
and jumped in his car. The phone rang about ten times
before Klebbans picked up.

"Yeah."

"Hugh, this is Cross."

"Didn't I tell you, Mike, just like I said? That baby was
shot out of the sky."

"There's no real proof yet, although from what I saw,
you may be right."

Cross headed for Manhattan and he knew the traffic
would be hideous.

"Did you see Peter Harbison agreed it was a freakin' missile," said Klebbans.

"No kidding. So what exactly was gained by shooting the airliner down, assuming you're right?"

"Just another piece to a God-awful puzzle. You know this will ruin the airline industry."

"Yeah, if people are shooting down planes, the impact will hit more than just the airlines."

"That's why you're never going to hear them say a missile was to blame. They know better. But, eventually the news will get out."

Cross had more questions, but the did not know where to start.

"Hugh, are you hearing anything else from your guys?"

"Yeah. Nothing I can give you now. I'll be in touch. Keep working the story and you'll see I was right on this one."

Klebbans was right. After the wreckage was pulled from the Atlantic and reassembled, residual chemical traces consistent with a missile strike were found on parts of the plane. The media mentioned it with earnest, but then settled on the more acceptable explanation about a gas tank malfunction, allowing Americans to drift back into complacency and resume uninformed lives.

Cross continued with his research. He got even closer to Declan Cavanaugh in the months following the downing of the plane. The priest served as an encyclopedia for Cross. His vast knowledge about many inner dealings in the Vatican and around the world helped Cross to tie together the bulk of his work.

Cavanaugh was always happy to help, especially when it came to prophecy and New York City. He always told Cross that people needed to keep their eyes on the sky, but Cross didn't know if that was because of the recent crash or other things.

It didn't take him long to discover that Father Cavanaugh was referring to many things. One October night, Cross heard Cavanaugh on the radio discussing a myriad of apocalyptic events. Aliens and UFO's came up, as they normally did. Again, Father Cavanaugh urged the radio audience to keep watching the skies. He also intimated that the United States was headed for trouble.

The following afternoon, Cross visited Cavanaugh at his apartment. He needed to get more information. For years, he had seen sinister forces in the Vatican connected to UFO studies. The Vatican built an observatory in Arizona to keep tabs on UFO activity and to track the prophesied comets.

Father Cavanaugh opened the door before Cross knocked.

"Hi, Father. How'd you know someone was out here?"

"I not only knew someone was out here, but I also knew it was you. Come in, Michael."

"Thanks."

"I thought you knew that I'm psychic."

"No, you never mentioned it."

"Well, it can unnerve people, especially when they know I know what they're thinking."

"I'll bet you're great at parties," Cross smiled.

"Now you wouldn't have me abuse my gift now would you? Sit down."

"Well, doesn't your gift help out in tight situations?"

"It can. You've got something on your mind. What is it?"

"I do. But first I want to know how you're doing?"

"Here, Michael. Try one of these cigars. I'm doing well, thanks. I've got to go in for an x-ray on my shoulder next week, but I think I've healed. Not bad for an old man."

"How 'bout I drive you to your appointment?"

"Fine. Now spill it, Michael."

Cross lit the cigar and collected his thoughts. The rich tobacco had a calming effect on him. He thought about switching his cigarettes for some stogies.

"I heard you on the radio last night. It sounded as if you believe we're going to see a real UFO invasion. Is that what you meant by watching the skies?"

"Yes, partly. I think we're going to see all sorts of amazing things and the UFO's are part of that."

He crossed his legs and noticed his shoe was untied. He bent to tie it.

"Is that why the Vatican built an observatory in the desert?"

"Ah, yes. You know about that. But they're also watching for comets and asteroids."

"But the UFO thing, you think it's real?"

"That depends on the meaning of real. They're a deception designed by the devil which will make us rethink the creation of Man. Don't be surprised to hear that God is merely a by-product of man's imagination."

Cross thought for a moment. He took a good look at Father Cavanaugh who was immaculately dressed even though his arm was in a cast. His white hair had become a little sparser, but the man looked well.

"So all of these sightings are real?"

"Some, but most are illusions."

"Does the government know that?"

"I suspect not."

"If you're psychic, wouldn't you know for sure?"

Declan Cavanaugh smiled. He liked the give and take with Cross. Normally, he made Cross work for the answers. It made him grow.

"Some believe what they want or need to believe. I think that this great deception will be done with the blessings of the government."

"We're just going to allow them to invade?"

Cross was having trouble accepting aliens as inevitability.

"Invade is such a curious term. You see, I believe they're already here. Aside from a few manifestations, I believe they are here, but invisible to most people. They're in a different realm. Soon the veil to that realm will get thinner and thinner. You'll have wall to wall demons."

"Demons?"

"Demons, not cute little grays from space as they claim."

Cross nearly choked on the cigar smoke.

"Want some water, Michael?"

"No, thank you. I'm fine." He coughed again. His eyes watered.

"What are the demons doing here?"

"Fighting the battle for souls."

"Excuse me, that just seems so…"

"Incredible? It is but it is also quite real. Can you imagine people seeing those demons everywhere? Why, the whole world will be at risk of insanity."

"Yeah." Cross grew quiet and Cavanaugh let things sift down. He knew he said enough. They agreed on a time for Cross to take him to the hospital and then Cross left.

He punched the button for the elevator and waited for a minute or two before the elevator finally arrived. Cross walked into the empty car and pushed the lobby button.

"Going down I see," said a man directly behind Cross.

"You startled me. I didn't see anyone when I got in."

The hair on the back of his neck stood straight up and he felt an unusual chill. The man walked to the other side of the elevator where he could better see Cross. Suddenly, all the floor buttons lit and the elevator came to an abrupt stop between floors.

Cross had a real need for a cigarette and he did not know if his slight claustrophobia or the man brought it on.

It really didn't matter. He pushed the lobby button
repeatedly.

"In a hurry," asked the man.

"Kinda."

Cross finally got a good look at the guy and realized he
had seen him someplace. He turned quickly and pushed the
emergency button. The bell sounded and Cross felt like it
was the start of the first round of something. At first, he
wasn't sure if his imagination was toying with him. He
didn't know why the dark haired man had made it all the
way from Alaska. To Cross, the world did not seem that
small.

"How have you been," the man asked.

Cross did not want to answer.

"I said, how are you?"

"Fine. Do I know you?"

Cross was hoping he was wrong about meeting him.

"We've met."

"I don't know your name." The elevator lurched a bit
and then stopped again. The emergency bell was getting on
Cross' nerves, but not as much as the man standing next to
him.

"William."

"Huh?"

"My name is William."

"Got a last name?"

"Mann. William Mann."

Cross couldn't wait for the doors to open. He watched
the lights of the floors go out one by one. His stomach
churned like a Ferris wheel on a sticky summer night.
Cross felt hot and cold at the same time. His mouth began
to water.

"I'd like to talk with you," Mann said.

"I'm very busy." Cross did not know why he said that.

"You're not busy now."

Mann put his hand on Cross' shoulder, as the elevator door opened. Cross immediately hurled all over the floor. The doorman ran up to Cross.

"You alright, Mr. Cross?"

"Yeah, sorry about the floor. Did you see that guy get off the elevator just now?"

"No, sir. You were the only one who popped out. Sorry about the car getting hung up like that. That's the first time that's happened since I've been here and that's twenty years.

All the way home, Cross thought about the having a strong drink. He fought the urge until it left him shortly before he went to bed. It had been a long day. Cross climbed into bed and grabbed the television remote. Sick of the news, he found some football highlights and settled in for the night. He couldn't get comfortable, however. There was a funny feeling in his stomach. Cross was not sure if he was hungry or not. The elevator ride hovered in his memory and in his stomach like a harrier.

Flipping through the channels, food on the TV enticed him. He headed to the kitchen to make a sandwich. As he left the bedroom, and walked through the hallway, Cross noticed a chill, a chill that ran deeply into his bones. He retrieved a sweatshirt from the couch and put it on as he went to the kitchen. He seemed a little warmer. Cross thought he might be coming down with something. He just felt off.

The phone rang and he debated about answering it. His stomach growled. All he wanted to do was eat. There was some fresh corned beef in the fridge. He took it out along with some hot mustard and cheese, and then answered the phone. There was no one there.

Cross thought how bad the sandwich would be for him, as he piled on four slices of cheese and a mound of corned beef on some rye bread. The phone rang again.

"Yeah." He tucked the phone into his shoulder and spread a glob of mustard on his sandwich, waiting for the person on the other end to say something.

"Hello?" No one answered. He checked the caller ID. The call registered as out-of-area. After putting the mustard in the refrigerator, he snagged a Coke. Cross stuck a good portion of the sandwich in his mouth and headed back to the bedroom.

He got back into bed, but decided he needed some chips. Going back to the kitchen, he found some Doritos. The phone rang again.

"These people are starting to piss me off." He let the phone ring. It rang three times and then stopped. Cross pulled open the bag of Doritos and shoved two into his mouth. The point of one chip nailed the roof of his mouth.

"Damn it." He laughed at his inability to chew and got back into bed, content he was set for the night.

A sandwich and a half bag of chips later, Cross finally felt full. He changed the channel to the catch the news and went to brush his teeth. The Channel 2 News had just started. As he squeezed out toothpaste on his toothbrush, the lights went out. They quickly came back on and the news blared in the bedroom. Cross flossed his teeth and went to bed. He was glad the news was boring for a change, so boring that Cross turned off the TV and the lamp by his bed.

After peeling off his sweatshirt and tossing it on the floor, he punched his feather pillow a couple of times then tried to sleep. A chill came over him again. Cross got up to make sure the window was closed. It was. He retrieved his sweatshirt from the floor and put it back on. On his way back to bed, his little toe caught the caster on the bed frame and bent back sharply.

"Dammit. Dammit. Dammit," He yelled all the way back to bed.

He punched his pillow again and then closed his eyes. Mann's face appeared before him. Cross flung open his eyes. The room was dark except for the red numerals on his alarm clock. He hunkered down under the covers and closed his eyes. Sleep gently began to creep up on him. Cross sunk into the softness of the bed and drifted off to sleep.

Suddenly, there was a terrific weight on his legs. He tried to kick at it through his twilight sleep, but the weight remained. Cross felt trapped. He awakened, tried to throw the covers off and found a cold, black shape sitting squarely on his legs.

His heart raced and he reached for the light. He flipped the switch, but nothing happened. He fumbled in the dark to get his gun from the bed table.

"That really won't be necessary, Michael," a deep voice sounded. He watched the black object slowly take shape. A beam of light from behind Cross' head shone on the figure. It was William Mann.

"Jesus Christ," screamed Cross. He had never known fear like this.

"Jesus," he screamed again.

Mann disappeared. Cross tried to turn on the lamp. This time it worked. He jumped out of bed and searched the entire house, turning lights on in every room as he went. His heartbeat began to slow, but his nerves were shot. Again, the urge for a stiff drink hit him. He searched the cupboards for any liquor and couldn't find any. Cross lit a cigarette and tried to calm down.

He thought about calling Declan Cavanaugh, but then tried to dismiss what had happened as a nightmare. Sleep didn't interest him the rest of the night. Cross did not care.

The next day he made it a point to investigate William Mann. There wasn't much to go on at first. There were a few William Mann's in the phone book. Cross checked every one. They bore no resemblance to his late night visitor.

He then checked the public library and discovered some newspaper articles about him. Apparently, Mann was a philanthropist involved in a few projects with the United Nations. For the most part, though, Mann led a solitary life. He had no wife and no children and there was little evidence of a girl friend.

Cross made photocopies of the articles and stuck them in his wallet. He did his best to find out more about the wealthy Mann.

The following week, he picked up Declan Cavanaugh to take him to the doctor. Cross used the opportunity to ask the priest if he knew anything about him. Traffic was heavy and Cross knew Cavanaugh would be up for conversation.

"Say, Father. Have you ever heard of William Mann?"

They were stuck at a red light. Cross looked at the priest to see his reaction. His eyes widened slightly.

"Yes."

Cross did not know if he should tell him about seeing him in the elevator in Cavanaugh's apartment building or about the bedroom meeting.

"And you want to know what interest he has in you," Cavanaugh smiled.

"I forgot you were psychic," laughed Cross. "Then do you know…"

"That he paid you a visit? Yes. Were you frightened?"

"He scared the sh…the crap right out of me."

"No doubt."

"Who is he?"

"Now that's an perplexing question." Cavanaugh didn't want to unduly frighten Cross.

The light turned green and traffic crept forward.

"Perplexing how?"

"William Mann is somewhat of an enigma." Cavanaugh rolled down his window.

"And? Is he dangerous?"

"I suppose he could be. I've heard reports about him. It seems he possesses certain abilities."

"Such as," Cross pushed.

"Let's just say transportation isn't a problem for him."

"You can say that again. What is he like?"

"I haven't had the dubious pleasure."

Cross glanced over at him. "But I saw him at your apartment building. He was in the elevator.

"Look out, Michael!"

Cross nearly hit the bumper of the cab in front of him.

"That is a tad bit distressing that he was in the building."

"So, is he dangerous?" Cross felt Cavanaugh was evading the question.

"Depends on the person you ask. He's supposedly very spiritual, fasts a lot, that sort of thing."

"And what's your take?"

"If you see him, run like hell."

"If that's an option," Cross muttered. He easily recalled Mann sitting on his legs and his heart started to beat faster.

"What is his interest with me, Father?"

"I don't know for sure. Off hand, I think he's interested in sidetracking you from your work."

"My work?"

"Yes. Well, more specifically the work you will be doing in the future."

"And what's that, Father?"

"That's for you to figure out, me boy."

"Thanks," Cross grumbled.

"By the way, Michael, you might want to lessen your cigarette intake. Your heart would greatly appreciate it. Every thing in moderation."

Cross was afraid he was right. His heart seemed to be putting up some resistance lately.

"There's the hospital, Father. I'll drop you off and park the car. Will you be alright?"

"I can manage. I'll be on the ninth floor after my x-ray."

"See ya in a few."

Cross drove to three parking ramps before he found a place to park. He stopped at a small convenience store and bought three packs of cigarettes. On the walk to the hospital, he thought about the things Declan Cavanaugh had mentioned. He wondered about the work he would do. Cross was getting weary of conspiracies and thought he needed a respite, some sort of diversion that would recharge him.

The hospital was busy as Cross made his way to the main entrance.

"Hey, stranger," a voice shouted from behind him. Cross didn't pay any attention and went into the hospital through the revolving door.

"Hey, you!"

He felt a tap on his shoulder and turned his head.

"Hi, Lori," he said.

"You don't look like you're been beaten up, lately. Why are you here?"

"Brought a friend in for an appointment."

"Nothing serious, I hope."

"Nope."

"Do you have a couple of minutes?"

Lori Young searched his eyes. Cross seemed to avoid eye contact.

"A couple, why?"

"How about a cup of coffee? My shift doesn't start for forty-five minutes and I could sure use the caffeine."

"Where do you want to go?"

"The cafeteria is fine. Okay with you?"

"Sure."

Lori made small talk with Cross as they took the elevator down to the basement. He felt awkward and wasn't sure if it was her beauty or his personality that made him feel like a sixteen year old with acne. His feet stumbled over everything in his path. Her dark eyes noticed everything about him. She attributed the three-day stubble to his desire to be sexy. He was thinking he should have shaved because he looked like a bum.

Cross bought two cups of coffee and two pieces of chocolate cake.

"I hope you're hungry. I don't eat desserts."

"You're kidding," he said, embarrassed. "Well, you know I just haven't been able to give up sweets since..."

He shut up. He wasn't sure he wanted her to know about his alcohol problem.

"Since?"

"Since I found out I couldn't live without chocolate."

They drank their coffee in silence. Lori wanted to talk, but she was waiting for him to say something.

"You still work here, huh." If Cross could have kicked himself without her knowing it, he would have. He couldn't believe he would say something so lame. Lori seemed so eager that he felt uneasy. Cross thought she had staked her claim and he did not know how he felt about it.

"How about you? What are you doing now?"

"I'm working at The Wire."

"The night club?"

"The Wire news service. I'm a reporter." He wasn't sure if she was pulling his leg or not.

"Sounds interesting."

He smiled. She had a ready smile that reached to the freckles on her cheeks. He noticed her well-manicured nails and the expensive watch she wore. Lori couldn't take her eyes off of him. To her, Michael Cross was perfect. They stumbled around a couple more awkward silences. Cross finished one piece of cake and decided to pass on the second. He checked his watch and she checked hers.

"Okay, I'd better run."

"Me too."

"Thanks for the coffee," she said.

"No problem."

He knew she wanted more, perhaps even dinner. Lori hoped he would ask her out, but he was tongue-tied and slightly disinterested. She thought about asking him. They got in the elevator. Lori pushed one and Cross hit nine. The crowded elevator kept them from talking. Lori squeezed her way out of the elevator on the first floor.

"See ya."

"Yeah, Lori." Cross wanted to say more. At least he thought he did, but let it go. He got out on the ninth floor. Declan Cavanaugh was waiting for him.

"How'd it go, Father?"

"I'm fine. I'm ready to leave."

"Hope you weren't waiting long," Cross said.

"Was she pretty?"

Cross grinned. "Yes. Very."

They caught the next elevator down and got out on the first floor. The exit was just past the emergency room. Cross failed to see Lori as they headed for the door. Lori didn't miss them. She watched them as they walked out of the hospital.

The hair on the back of Cavanaugh's neck stood up. He made a quick sign of the cross and walked out the door. The sky had gown dark. It rained on the men as they walked to the car.

"Didn't know it was gonna rain or I would have brought an umbrella."

"You're thinking if I'm psychic, why didn't I see this coming," said Cavanaugh.

"You know that's unfair. Okay. Why didn't you bring an umbrella then?"

"Weather generally isn't all that important. Besides, I like the feel of rain."

The elderly priest still had a spring in his step and kept up with Cross. They made good time to the parking garage. Cross paid the fee and waited for the attendant to drive his beloved Impala down the ramp. Normally Cross never allowed someone else to drive it, but he didn't want to look like a jerk in front of Father Cavanaugh.

Cross took out a cigarette and lit it, then remembered what Cavanaugh had said about his heart. He promptly dropped it, but it was difficult to see the smoke go to waste.

"I'll take one if you don't mind, Michael."

"I didn't know you smoked cigarettes. Here you go."

Cavanaugh took a large drag and slowly exhaled. "All things in moderation, Michael."

"Yeah. I should scale back for sure. Hey, I've been meaning to ask you something. You keep making connections with things that are going to happen like the UFO invasion and terrible things that will happen to New York City and the world. You've tied it to the third secret of Fatima. You said Sister Lucy was alive, right?"

"Yes. She'll live to see the secret come to fruition."

"How old is she?"

"Close to ninety or so."

"But that means…"

"Things are getting close."

"Do you think I'd be able to interview her?"

"That would take special permission from the Vatican and her bishop."

"Maybe Joe would help me."

The men heard the screeching of brakes and the occasional roar of an engine. Cross' heart sank to his feet. He looked at Cavanaugh and saw a twinkle in his eyes. Suddenly, the red Impala appeared at the top of the ramp. The attendant stomped on the gas and then slammed on the brakes when the car reached the street. The Chevy came to a stop just before hitting the sidewalk. Cross' face was redder than his car.

"Patience, Michael," laughed Cavanaugh as he got into the car.

Cross thought about chewing out the kid, but contained himself. He got in and readjusted the seat and rear view mirror. It just didn't feel like his baby. Cross slowly pulled out on the street and headed for Cavanaugh's apartment. The rain increased as they negotiated the traffic.

Chapter Sixteen

Even with Joseph Cross' help, the Vatican approval for an interview with Sister Lucy took several months. While waiting for the approval letter, Michael Cross kept busy. He began to tug on loose threads that were sewn into the U.N.'s plans for global domination. The assorted threads all seemed to lead to the same place.

Cross discovered that the current global conflicts were started or controlled by certain people within the U.N. and by some presidents and prime ministers as well. He spent time in Bosnia and covered the war for The Wire. His theories about the U.N.'s goals had to be kept to himself.

Upon his return to New York, Lori Young made it a point to see Cross as often as she could. She was quite attracted to him. He wasn't sure how he felt about her. There wasn't anything he considered a drawback when it came to Lori. If anything, she was more than he expected and he suspected she was more than he needed.

It was obvious she really liked him, if not loved him in some way. He liked her company, but he dodged her attempts to sleep with him, attributing his romantic reluctance to the onset of middle age. His desire for her was overwhelmed by his desire to work, to expose a consuming conspiracy. At first, the magnitude of it all made him feel removed from people, removed from the need for a relationship. Finally, he recognized that strong friendships helped him cope with the truth he uncovered.

Lori Young was supportive of his work, but she didn't know whether to believe his research. Her life was caught up in the here and now, heartbeat to heartbeat. To her, the bad guys were the crooks in Manhattan who kept her job filled with trauma and death. It was real and palpable. She understood that the way she thought she understood Michael Cross.

When Cross received the letter from the Vatican, Lori was determined to convince him to take her with him to Portugal. Cross was not sure if he wanted her to go. He preferred to stay focused. At times, she was a distraction, no matter how pleasant. Cross knew she could not be part of the interview with Sister Lucy. He didn't want her to feel abandoned, nor did he want to entertain her as she hoped. Cross knew she had sights on marriage and a family, but he could not bring himself to let go of Annie. He never gave himself permission to date after she died. The thought of getting entangled with a woman and the possibility of children unsettled him.

Yet, the beautiful nurse was good for him. She kept him centered, not as Annie had done, but in a way that kept him from being overwhelmed by the austerity of his work.

Two weeks before Cross was ready to leave for Portugal, Lori showed up at his house. She brought over twice-cooked pork, extra rice and alcohol free beer. Lori wasn't sure how to convince him to take her along, but she had a few ideas.

"Ya know, Lori, you didn't have to go to all this trouble," said Cross.

The smell of dinner reminded him how terribly hungry he was. She grabbed some dinner plates and scooped the dinner out of the cardboard containers. Cross cracked open a fortune cookie and popped half of it in his mouth, then tossed the fortune.

"Hey, you're supposed to wait for dessert, Michael. What did your fortune say?"

"I dunno."

"Where is it?"

"I tossed it in the ashtray."

Lori put the plates down on the dining room table and retrieved the fortune from the ashtray. Her nose wrinkled as she pulled it from the ashes.

"C'mon, Lori. Let's eat."

"It says you're going to kindle a new flame." Lori put her arms around him and kissed him. He kissed her back, but his stomach growled so loudly it made them both laugh.

"You want sweet and sour sauce, right," he asked.

"You're impossible."

"Only when I'm hungry."

They both sat down and Cross wasted no time. He ate with a vengeance. Lori watched him as she picked at her food. She got up from the table and got her purse.

"Where are you going? Dinner's getting cold."

"I wanted you to see these travel brochures."

Lori placed six or seven brightly colored pamphlets in front of him and sat down.

"Are you going somewhere?"

"Well, what would you think if I went with you to Portugal? You could show me the sights and we could take a romantic tour of Europe. Maybe we could go to Italy and you could see your son."

"I'm going on business. You know that."

"You're entitled to some pleasure too, aren't you?"

"Sure, but…"

"But what?"

"I just figured I'd go alone, do the interview and come home."

He went back to his dinner hoping that was the end of it. Lori started to cry and her mascara started to run. Her lip began to tremble.

"Oh, Lori. Don't do that. If it means that much to you, of course, you can go with me. I just can't do the whole tour thing."

"That's okay. Portugal's fine, Michael."

"Do you even have a passport?"

"Yeah. I am already to go. You'll see. It will be great."

He smiled at her, not convinced it would be anything but a hassle.

Cross tried to see Declan Cavanaugh before he left. He hoped to get some advice about the interview. However, Cavanaugh was on tour promoting his latest book. Cross received a copy and was looking forward to reading it during the long flight to Portugal.

Sol Abrams drove Cross to the terminal at Kennedy International where Lori was supposed to meet him. The spring day was bright and sunny with just the hint of a chill.

All the way to the airport, Sol gave Cross a hard time because he did not put up any interference. He was in too good of a mood to allow Abrams to get under his skin. Sol thought he might be losing his touch. He pulled up to the curb and got out to pop open the trunk.

Cross pulled out his bag and shook Sol's hand.

"Thanks, Solly. You better get going or you'll get a ticket."

"Michael!"

Lori emerged from the terminal and wrapped herself around Cross.

"Now I see why you were in a hurry to get rid of me," said Sol.

"Sol, this is Lori Young."

"Pleased to meet yous. So the two of yous're going to Spain?"

"Portugal," Cross answered.

"Whatever."

"Michael, I have got to make a call to my sister. I'll meet you at the gate."

Cross smiled shyly.

"Nice to meet you, Sol."

The men watched her as she walked away. Cross felt like disappearing into the pavement because he knew what was next.

"And you brought a book to read? You schlub."

"We're just friends."

"If you wanted to go to Spain with a friend, why didn't you ask me?" Sol laughed heartily.

"Portugal."

"Huh? Oh, yeah, sure."

"I gotta go, Solly."

"I can see that. Well, have a safe flight and send me a postcard. I wanna know why you didn't let me know about her sooner, Mikey."

Cross shrugged and was glad to leave Sol. As he checked his bag and caught up to Lori, he thought about why he hadn't introduced her to his friends yet. He couldn't find an answer.

The flight was uneventful. They arrived in Lisbon a day ahead of the scheduled interview. Cross rented a car and they drove to the Shrine of Fatima, where Sister Lucy first received her visions. He was amazed at how well he and Lori had gotten along. The trip had been relaxing and the sights were phenomenal.

Cross had never been to Portugal and was in awe of the ancient Roman ruins. The history of the country fascinated him. Lori enjoyed the 12th Century architecture in the churches and manor houses. Throughout that first day, she did not give Cross a sense that her biological clock was ticking madly. He was thankful and started to appreciate her. By mid-afternoon, he started to let his guard down. If she noticed, she never mentioned it.

Lori bought a bottle of wine with lunch at a quaint café. Cross had no trouble sticking to his Perrier. By the time dessert arrived, they were holding hands and for the first time, it felt natural to Cross. There was enough time to take a tour of the shrine before driving to Coimbra. In the midst of the tour, Lori's cell phone rang and she excused herself. Cross was only slightly curious about the call. He got caught up in the history of the Fatima visions and the historical data on the three visionaries.

"Sorry about that. Did I miss anything?"

"They're just talking about Lucy as a little girl. Is there a problem," he whispered.

"No. It was just my sister. She wanted to know how we liked it so far."

Cross took some notes, while Lori snapped a few photos. He noticed that she didn't have much enthusiasm for the history of Fatima. Lori looked a little tired and he thought jet lag had struck her right between the eyes. He also thought the wine might have been to blame.

By the time they made it to Coimbra, they were both exhausted. They found their hotel and checked into separate rooms. Lori was so tired; the accommodations did not seem to bother her. After a late dinner, they said goodnight. Cross went over his questions for the interview and enjoyed one last cigarette before turning out the light.

He thought about Lori down the hall. Fatigue set in before he could wonder why he wasn't in her bed. Lori took a shower and made another phone call. She was looking forward to the morning.

The next morning, Cross was slow to wake up. He thought he had plenty of time before he had to go to Sister

Lucy's convent. When he checked his watch, he was shocked to see he had to meet her in twenty minutes. He called Lori's room and told her that he had to miss breakfast. She said she understood.

Cross hurried into the bathroom to take a shower, bypassing his morning cigarette. The hot water hit his face blasting his sleepiness away. He poured a dollop of shampoo into his hand and then rubbed it into his hair. Quickly he rinsed it out, but a little shampoo ran into his eyes, burning them.

He didn't hear Lori come into the bathroom. It wasn't until he grabbed a towel and wiped his eyes that he noticed her.

"Got room for me," she asked as she pulled the shower curtain back.

"There's room, but I gotta go." He was upset Lori wanted to play games.

"I'll see you after the interview." Cross rushed to finish his shower. Lori didn't pay any attention to what he said. She climbed into the shower with him. Her long arms went around him and she kissed him. Cross got lost in the kiss, so lost he did not want anyone to find him. He forgot about the interview for a moment. Lori saw to that. Then, he abruptly pushed her away and got out of the shower.

"I told you I gotta go. You shouldn't have come in here."

He looked at his watch. The interview was in ten minutes. Barely drying himself off, Cross got dressed. He ignored Lori's attempts at distraction, while he ran his electric razor over his whiskers. She didn't let his temper deter her. Lori was all over him until he blew up. Cross took her by the arms and forcibly put her in a chair.

"This isn't fair, Lori. You know I don't have time for this."

"Why don't you take the time? You can reschedule the

interview."

"No, I can't. Even if I could, I don't want to." Cross grabbed the room key, his briefcase and his jacket.

"Let yourself out."

He slammed the door behind him. Thankful the convent was not far, he pulled into the parking lot at nine o'clock sharp. Cross ran up to the door and rang the bell. He straightened his hair and pushed Lori out of his mind. Lori was not going to ruin this once in a lifetime interview, no matter how enticing she was.

A middle-aged nun answered the door. Cross was surprised to see she was wearing a full habit. He hadn't seen many nuns who wore the full habit anymore. It reminded him of grade school.

"Good morning, Sister. I'm Michael Cross. I have an interview with Sister Lucy."

"You may come in Mister Cross." The sister's English was fairly good. He followed the sister into the convent and was taken to a parlor.

"Please wait here. I will bring Sister Lucy to you."

"Thank you, sister. Is it alright to smoke?" He caught himself thinking about his posture.

"Well, we don't usually allow it."

"That's okay, Sister." He smiled at her. Cross took out his pen and pad along with his tape recorder. He ran his fingers through his damp hair and tired to focus on the interview. It took fifteen minutes before Sister Lucy appeared in the parlor.

"Good morning, Sister. I'm Michael Cross."

Sister Lucy didn't wait to have Sister Angelina translate for her.

"Hello," she answered, smiling at him. Sister Angelina asked Cross to be seated and then she helped Sister Lucy to a chair. The ninety-year-old religious slowly sat down.

Cross was amazed that the nun looked rather well. Her dark eyes still had a great deal of brightness in them.

Cross was not sure if they could speak freely. Sister Angelina seemed to have a great deal of influence over her. He did his best in asking questions of the sister. She was very straightforward with her answers, but Cross could not help but feel that she really could not open up in front of the other nun. However, a lot of ground was covered. She patiently explained all she could about the visions of Fatima.

There was something so holy about her that made Cross feel in awe of the demure woman. Although she did not give too many specifics of the third secret, she did tell Cross that they were living it and that the answers could be found in the Book of Revelation. She cited two chapters for him to read.

After an hour, Sister Lucy seemed to tire. Sister Angelina helped her up and ended the interview.

"Sister must rest now."

Sister Lucy smiled at him and reached for his hand. She gave Cross a piece of paper and was careful not to let Sister Angelina see it. When she withdrew her hand, Cross put his hand and the note in his pocket.

Cross was feeling somewhat off balance after the things she told him. He tried to sort through his thoughts on the way to the car. Lori was sitting in the car waiting for him.

"How did the interview go?" He didn't know whether to be angry with her or not. Cross did know that he didn't feel like company, not even hers.

"It was fine. Why are you here?" He tossed his briefcase in the back and got into the car.

"I thought we could have lunch. You missed a hell of a breakfast and I thought you'd be hungry."

"Not really, but if you're still hungry I can drop you off somewhere."

He lit a cigarette and slowly inhaled.

"Of course, we could go back to the room and finish where we left off."

He started the car and took another drag. Exhaling through his nose, Lori thought he looked like an angry dragon.

"Look, Lori. Maybe this wasn't fair to bring you along. You expected a vacation and I want to work."

"I just wanted us to get to know each other better."

"I realize that. It's just...well I dunno." He put the car in reverse. The engine whined and so did Lori.

"You don't like me, do you?"

Cross put the car in drive, but stepped hard on the brake.

"You know I like you. But right now work has got to come first." Cross could not believe he had to discuss this with the weighty words of Sister Lucy still fresh on his mind.

"I don't want to hurt you, Lori. Honest. Listen, there's something I have to do and I can't take you with me. I'll drive you to the airport and put you on a plane for home."

He stepped on the gas and her heart. They headed back to the hotel. Lori had started a slow burn.

"I want to go with you. I don't have to get back to work for ten more days."

"Lori, I can't do it. I've got to check out a few things."

They didn't say another word. Lori packed her things and Cross loaded the car. The trip to Lisbon passed in silence. Cross found a flight headed to New York City and stayed to make sure Lori caught it. He waited with her until the plane could be boarded.

"I'm sorry, I know you didn't have much fun."

"It's okay. I understand, I guess. Where are you going," she asked.

"I'm not sure yet."

"Alright, you don't have to tell me. Do you still want to see me when you get back?"

"Sure," he said tentatively, anything to get her to leave.

She stormed onto the plane. Cross felt relieved. He made sure Lori's plane took off before buying a ticket to Rome. He checked his luggage and went to the assigned gate. There was still an hour before his flight. He decided to check his phone messages. All the pay phones were busy and his cell phone battery died. Cross left the gate area and walked through the crowded concourse looking for another phone. He finally found one. Cross got out his phone card and dialed home. Declan Cavanaugh had left a message that intrigued Cross. He placed a call to Cavanaugh.

"Father, Mike Cross. I got your message. What's up?"

"Ah, Michael. Did you hear about the lights over Phoenix last night?"

"Lights?"

"It seems there was a monstrous UFO sighting. Several craft were supposedly spotted."

"This is on the level?"

"Straight and level."

"Jesus."

"This is just the beginning. Anyway, how was Sister Lucy?"

"Fine. It was quite an interview."

"Well, I won't keep you, Michael. I just thought you would like to know."

"Absolutely. I'll call you when I get home."

Cross hung up. He went back to the ticket counter and traded his ticket to Rome for a flight to Phoenix. Cross could not find a direct route and it took him a day and a half to make it to Arizona.

The delay gave him a chance to read about the strange sightings and to line up eyewitnesses for interviews. His boss seemed to go along with his detour even though he was late to the party. He had a friend at Luke Air Force Base that agreed to talk to him, if Cross would assure his anonymity. The brass was all over its fighter pilots who scrambled the night the lights were first spotted.

Phoenix, Arizona

Cross touched down in Phoenix about noon. He rented a car and called Pete Luft to see where they could meet. Luft had a couple of days leave and waited for Cross at a local golf course.

The two men met in the parking lot of the El Caro Golf Club.

"Sure has been awhile, Mike."

"It's good seeing you, Pete. How's your mom?"

"She's doing okay."

"Great. Did she ever remarry?"

"Nah. When dad was killed in Nam, it just seemed to do her in."

"I can understand that. I really need to call her. It's been too long."

"I'm sure she'd appreciate it. Hey, I brought a buddy's set of clubs and thought we might as well play a round while we talk."

"Oh, man. It's been a long time."

"Good. Then you won't want to keep score."

Cross changed in the locker room while Luft paid the green fees and rented a cart. The midday sun felt good to Cross.

"I can't believe it's March. The sun is great," said Cross.

"Yup. It's spoiled me."

They each took out a driver and got in the cart and drove along side the first tee.

"White or blue tees, Mike?"

"How 'bout red?"

"I'm not letting you tee off from the ladies tees. White okay?"

"Fine." Cross knew the ladies tees would have been better for his game and his ego. He took a few practice swings and looked around the course. There were only a few players and they must have called in sick to work. Cross watched Luft tee up the ball and then hit a monster drive down the center of the fairway.

"We're not playing for dough, right?"

"Not this round, Mike. I'll go easy on you."

Luft got in the cart and lit a cigar. He was amazed at how good Cross' swing was. It was relaxed and fluid. Cross took two practice swings and then addressed the ball.

"Don't laugh, Pete."

"Just hit it."

Cross looked down the fairway and then back at the ball. He pulled the club back and hit a great shot, landing about twenty yards shy of Luft's ball.

"Not bad for an old man," said Luft. Cross laughed and got in the cart. He looked around again.

"So, are you going to tell me what the hell was in the sky the other night?"

Luft looked over his shoulder. He felt comfortable no one was around to hear them.

"It was strange. First, I got to tell you they told us not to talk to the press. So my ass will really be in a sling if the old man finds out about this."

"I won't use your name. I promise." Cross lit a cigarette. "The papers said the National Guard was dropping flares or something a couple of nights ago. Is that what this sighting is all about?"

"Nope."

"I didn't think so. The pictures I saw weren't consistent with flares, no telltale smoke and the lights I saw just didn't look like flares."

Luft stopped the cart near Cross' ball. He got out and looked at the lie. Tossing his cigarette on the grass, Cross pulled a seven iron out of the bag and lined up the ball.

"You won't reach the green. You'd better use a five iron."

"Did you fly up the meet the ship, Pete?"

Cross hit the ball and it landed thirty yards from the green.

"Okay. Next time, I'll use the damned five iron. So, were you up there?"

Cross picked up his cigarette and got back in the cart.

"Yup. I was there." Luft drove the short distance to his ball. He got out, chose his club and took a practice swing. Cross thought he looked uncomfortable. Luft was tall, about six feet five. He stooped a bit over the ball, but Cross thought something else was making him tense.

Luft topped the ball. It dribbled a few feet ahead of him.

"Dammit." He walked up to the ball and tried it again. This time the ball landed hole high. Cross drove up to him and went to find his ball.

"What did you see?"

"You have to swear, Mike. Nobody's going to know I talked, right?"

"Right."

"Okay. There was a humungous ship. It was kinda blue-black and honking big."

"How big?"

"About a mile or so long."

"A mile?" Cross got a little pale at the thought of it.

"Maybe larger. Perhaps a mile and a half in span. I saw at least seven lights on the thing. It flew from Northwest to Southeast and looked like it was barely moving."

"What was the altitude?" Cross stopped the cart by his ball.

"Had to have been below five thousand."

"Then even people on the ground could have gotten a great look at the thing."

"They did. Lots of video was shot that night."

Cross couldn't have cared less about his next shot. He chipped the ball on the green, but was too involved with Luft to see where it landed.

"Nice shot. Some of the videos didn't do it justice, especially the lights. They'd go from white to red."

"So, is it one of ours?"

"Nope."

"Did you guys catch up to it?"

"We got close and then it shot off, straight up and then it disappeared from radar."

"Was that the end of it?"

"No. There was another ship. This one was triangular. That baby had to have been two miles long."

Cross stood still. He was dumbfounded.

"Then there was another sighting near the Estella Mountains. Some guy got it videotaped. Jesus, Mike. I thought we were under attack. There were two other ships near the base. They vertically ascended and completely disappeared before our guys could get there."

"My God! They had to have caught them on radar."

"Nope. Those mothers crossed over Prescott, Tucson and Phoenix airspace and not one controller admitted they were visible on radar. I'm telling you, this is the real freaking thing. God, I was so shaken up, they had to help me out of the cockpit. My legs wouldn't support me."

"That's nothing, Pete. I would have had a heart attack."

They finished the hole in silence, trying to pretend things were normal.

"Mike, what are you going to do now?"

"That's a good question. Have you ever seen or heard about this stuff before now?"

"Just talk. The brass clamps down on this stuff pretty fast."

"Did you hear some guy claimed to have seen beings in the windows of the ships?"

"Yup. I saw 'em too, not well, but I saw something in the windows."

"Lemme ask you a question, Pete. Did the base lose power?"

"Some of the guys said power was briefly interrupted when two of the ships flew near the base. Why?"

"Just wondering. Kinda blows our defense if they can shut us down."

They finished their round and went separate ways. Luft said he'd keep in touch before he drove off. Cross went to find a motel and something to eat. After he devoured two burgers, fries and some soda, Cross got back in his rental car and called Father Cavanaugh from a pay phone.

"Father, looks like these things are genuine articles. From my friend's description, these things sounded like the mothers of all ships."

"I was afraid of that. Things are gearing up then."

"Gearing up for what?"

"Those ships are the calling card of the antichrist. The great deception may soon be upon us and when that happens, millions of people may be vaporized. Keep in touch, Michael. I have to go."

As always, Cavanaugh left Cross with more questions. This time, he was uneasy about finding out the answers.

He spent the next five days interviewing eyewitnesses and looking at videotape. The Air Guard's explanation of flares had holes big enough for one of the super crafts to fly through and then some. After weeks of investigations, Cross firmly believed there was something to the lights in Phoenix. They were not produced by flares, but belonged to several UFO's.

The reports from eyewitnesses all seemed to concur. There were beings on board the ships and most witnesses believed they were not human. That fact forced Michael Cross to re-evaluate the crash at Roswell in 1947 and other sightings throughout the United States.

Cross spent most of his summer near Roswell talking with former military personnel and their relatives about the events surrounding the crash. His exploration drew the attention and the anger of the government. Round the clock surveillance was the reward for his hard work.

During interviews, Cross was told about the many premature deaths of people who were connected with Roswell. One woman, whose father had seen one of the alien survivors, informed Cross that her dad's death came shortly after he went public with the information.

Cross finally believed the tabloids were telling the truth. The twenty-four hour tail confirmed he was on to something big.

Chapter Seventeen

By July, Cross was ready for a break. When Pete Luft called asking Cross to meet him in Las Vegas, he could not wait. There were questions that Pete had answers to, but Cross knew it wouldn't be easy to get around the surveillance. Still, he had to try.

He took a red-eye flight to Los Angeles hoping to lose the tail on him. As expected an agent picked him up once he left the plane. Cross quickly blended into the crowd and ducked into a restroom to change clothes. Cramming his things into his overnight bag, Cross pulled out a ball cap and shades and then left the restroom. He went to a pay phone and called Luft. Cross asked him to change his plans and to meet him in San Diego. Luft agreed.

Knowing he could be quickly found if he rented a car, Cross took a cab to a local Honda dealer. He bought a used Gold Wing and headed south. It had been years since he'd been on a motorcycle, but it all came back to him. Cross loved the wind in his face and the occasional bug in his teeth. The utter freedom provided him with some peace. A short glimpse of his youth returned and his investigation was shoved to the back of his mind for the one hundred twenty mile trip.

It took Pete Luft several hours to make the drive, but by evening the two men sat down for a steak dinner.

"Anything new on those ships, Pete?"

"The brass has been going crazy trying to seal up the leaks. I'm taking a really big chance talking with you."

"I appreciate that. I've had pricks on my case for months now."

"Yup, but if you keep pushing things, they'll fly right up your ass."

"You know we can't let this go. Those little gray bastards have the capability of taking us all out."

A waitress brought them a menu. Luft ordered a beer. Cross envied him a bit. For the first time in years, alcohol tried to seduce him.

Luft leaned forward and lowered his voice. "There's something you need to check out in Denver. It's an underground base filled with those mothers."

"You're shitting me," Cross said. "Where in Denver?"

The beer arrived and the smell made Cross' mouth water. He lit a cigarette to smoke out the temptation.

"There's a new site for the airport. Right under there, you'll find more than your mind can handle."

"Like what?"

"For starters, they've got prisoners down there helping to build the base."

"Where in the hell is the army?"

"Some say they're in on it."

"For God's sake, why?"

"You tell me, Mike."

"Well, how can these gray bastards hold people hostage?"

Luft got nervous. He scanned the room and then leaned forward again.

"I got it on good authority that the guys running the show aren't just the grays, but some honking ass creatures."

Luft downed his beer and wiped his mouth with the back of his hand.

"What?"

"I swear to God, there's some funky shit going on down there and it was all related to these sightings."

Cross got quiet. He wasn't sure Luft had his head screwed on right.

"Can anybody get down there to check this out?"

"Have you lost your friggin' mind?"

"Regardless, can I get down there?"

Luft waved for the waitress.

"Bring me a double vodka."

"Maybe you could get in there. But someone would have to set you up with false ID and that's next to impossible."

Cross did not want to let it go and Luft knew it. Underneath it all, he wanted Cross to investigate the underground base.

"But it probably can be done," Luft said.

"Well, I don't want you taking any unnecessary chances, man," said Cross.

"I'm a fighter pilot, just like my old man was. I'm used to taking risks. Give me a couple of weeks."

Their dinners arrived and they ate quickly. Cross decided he would do a little cross-country touring on his Gold Wing and head to Denver. With or without Luft's help, Cross was determined to see things for himself.

Luft agreed to call Cross when he got the plans solidified. Cross left San Diego early the next morning on his way to Colorado. He decided to forget about the 50th anniversary of the Roswell crash.

The long ride to Denver was uneventful. With plenty of time for reflection, Cross soaked up the incredible scenery. Living in New York most of his life, he felt somewhat deprived. He could only fully appreciate the magnificence of the great American Southwest from pictures in some book or by flying over scenic wonders at 30,000 feet. His world was defined and confined by Manhattan.

The journey gave him distance from the harsh reality of work. Aliens and government conspiracies were a million miles away. That quickly changed after Cross arrived in Denver. He took a room at a low rent motel hoping to stay below the government radar. As soon as he got settled, he FedEx'd his address to Luft and waited for a return package.

Cross took a badly needed shower and got into some fresh clothes. His two-week beard gave him a new look, one he liked. He put away his razor and decided to check out the new airport site. The mobility of the motorcycle gave Cross more freedom. He could ride into places that a car couldn't handle. In a pursuit, he knew he had a better chance of getting away. Not seeing anything unusual around the airport perimeter, Cross parked the bike and walked around the terminal.

He couldn't get past the strange murals on the walls. They seemed to attract a lot of stares from travelers. Some people were taking pictures of the elaborate drawings. Cross stopped to look at the murals and watched the crowd. Every once in a while, he felt a thrumming coming through the floor.

At first he thought it was just the crowd of people trudging through the terminal, but after several minutes, he knew it was something more. Even when the crowd dwindled to a handful of people, there was an underlying vibration. He even noticed a painful hum in his ears.

Cross left the terminal and got on his motorcycle. He started it, popped the clutch and then stopped. Declan Cavanaugh was on his mind. He thought he should call him to let him know what he was planning to do. He took out his cell phone and then put it back in his jacket.

He put the bike in gear and rode to a nearby pay phone. Cross did not want to use his phone card. He dug deep into his jeans to find some change. After dropping three bucks in quarters into the phone, Cross dialed Cavanaugh's number. Just as the phone rang, Cross noticed a suspicious man leaving the terminal. He thought the guy looked like William Mann. Cross was sure of it. Father Cavanaugh answered the phone.

"Hello?"

Cross did not hear him. He watched Mann head for a long black limo.

"Hello?"

"Father, Michael Cross. I wanted to touch base with you. I'm at the Denver airport checking out a tip from a source. There's supposedly..." Cross paused for a moment as Mann got into the limo.

"I'm sorry, Father. I've got to call you back." Cross hurried back to his bike and followed the limo to the Brown Palace Hotel.

As the limo pulled up to the hotel, Cross hung back. He stopped about fifty yards up the street and watched William Mann get out of the car. The doorman seemed to know him and said a few words to the man, who smiled and gave the doorman a tip. Then Mann stopped and glanced in Cross' direction and smiled before he entered the hotel. A strange feeling hit Cross. It was a feeling that completely chilled him. He waited for a few minutes and then parked his bike. Cross straightened his hair and took out a fifty-dollar bill from his wallet. He pulled the bill tight with his fingers and walked up to the doorman.

"Excuse me. Could you please tell me the man's name who just came in here wearing a white suit?" Cross waved the fifty in front of the pudgy doorman.

"It isn't our policy to intrude on our guest's privacy."

Cross took out another fifty and gave it to the man.

"However, there are exceptions. His name is William Mann."

"So he was telling the truth," Cross caught himself talking aloud.

"What's he doing here?"

The doorman got tight lipped. Cross cocked an eyebrow in disgust. He took out another fifty, but this time he held on to it.

"What's he doing here?"

"He rents the penthouse. He's a regular." The doorman knew he could take his girlfriend to Durango for the weekend if he could just get Cross to come up with a little more cash.

"Do you know what he's does for a living?"

"He don't need to work, Mack. He's a billionaire." The doorman snatched the bill. Cross knew he could take it from there. Now he had to find a cash machine.

"Got an ATM around here?"

"The lobby."

"Thanks."

Cross was not surprised to see that Mann was nowhere in sight. In a way, he was quite relieved. He got five hundred bucks in cash. It wasn't until after he made the transaction that he realized the government could locate him. He sloughed it off and went to call Father Cavanaugh back.

"Sorry about earlier. I ran into William Mann again."

"Really?"

"Anyway, that's not why I called. I've got a tip about an underground base at the Denver airport. I'm here to check it out."

"Some government thing, Michael?"

"Sorta. My source says it's a joint effort with the aliens."

"Best be careful, Michael. You're involved in a dangerous game."

"I gotcha, Father."

"How long's it been since your last confession?"

Cross was taken aback.

"Uh, a while. Why?"

"It would be an excellent idea to go to confession before venturing into that mess."

"I'll see what I can do."

"I hope you mean that," said Cavanaugh.

Cross did not know if he meant it or not. He did know that Cavanaugh had a pretty good record of knowing what was coming his way. Deciding not to blow off the advice, Cross headed for Assumption Cathedral.

After confession, he went back to the motel. Lying down for an hour, he hoped to get some rest. Lori entered his mind and sleep was put on hold. He called her, but before she answered he hung up. Cross was not sure why. Not wanting to be bogged down thinking about their relationship, Cross thought about making it down to the base or whatever it was under the airport. Knowing he really couldn't prepare for something so foreign, he forgot about it.

Nine o'clock took a long time to arrive. Cross was waiting at the door when the FedEx driver pulled up. He took the envelope from the driver and went back into his room to open it. Ripping open the back, Cross sat on the bed and took out the contents of the overnight pak. There was a brief letter from Luft. There was also an ID badge.

All Cross had to do was get an ID photo taken and stick it in the badge. He was to meet a guy by the mural at the airport around four that afternoon. He was to wear black BDU's and black boots. The beard had to go. Cross quickly shaved and left for a mall to get his photo taken. There was a twenty-minute wait for the processing. He then went to a military surplus store and purchased everything he would need. By the time he got back to the photo lab, his picture was ready.

Cross returned to the motel and remained there until three in the afternoon. He left for the airport carrying serious trepidations. The sky grew cloudy and lightning could be seen flashing through the mountains. Arriving at the airport just before the storm, Cross parked his motorcycle and slowly walked to the terminal. Unsure about the person he was supposed to meet, Cross kept a watchful eye on the people around him.

The terminal was quite busy. He had no trouble blending into the crowd even in the black BDU's. He walked over to the murals and studied the wall while he waited. A middle-aged man stood next to him taking in the murals. Cross glanced at the small man and hoped he wasn't waiting for him. The man had a soft look about him, nothing like the type of guy Pete Luft had described.

After checking his watch, Cross walked about twenty feet from the murals and scanned the crowd. He began to think his contact wouldn't show.

Cross rubbed the back of his neck. A tension headache built up until it spilled over his entire body like a dump truck load of gravel. Every joint in his body ached. Waiting only made the ache worse.

A large black man in black BDU's tapped Cross on the shoulder.

"You ready to go to work," the man asked.

"Uh, sure."

"Let's go this way."

The man was huge. He easily dwarfed Cross.

"By the way, my name is Zack Williams," he said over his shoulder. "But you can forget it as soon as you leave. You got that?"

"Got it." Cross understood completely. They walked a short distance and stopped at a security door. Zack took out a plastic card and ran it through the card reader. The door unlocked and the men entered.

Zack looked down the hallway. It was empty. He leaned over the stairwell and didn't see anyone.

"Y'all listen to me now. We're going to go down these stairs. We've got five floors to go. There are card readers on each flight. If we get caught, I'm telling you right now, you're on your own."

"Got it." Cross' stomach got it too. He needed a cigarette, and cursed his dependency.

"Stay behind me."

"Ok." He thought that Zack would totally eclipse him. Cross was comforted by the man's size. As they walked down the stairs, he guessed that Zack was close to seven feet tall. He had to weigh three hundred pounds and that was all muscle. Zack was light on his feet though and had the grace of a big cat.

They made it through four floors without any trouble. Approaching the last security door, Zack stopped and turned to Cross.

"Man, you're gonna see some awful ass shit down here. You got a good heart?"

"I guess. Why?"

"You're gonna need it. Now stay to the side of the hallway."

Cross did not know what to expect. Zack slid the security card into the slot and the light on the door turned green. He took hold of the door handle and slowly turned the knob. Hot air immediately washed over them. It was unbelievably humid. Sweat beaded on Zack's shaved head like rain on newly waxed car.

The hallway was dimly lit. It was lined with doors, but Zack walked to the elevator at the end of the corridor. He pushed the down button. The elevator quickly arrived. The doors slowly opened. Cross held his breath. Nobody was in the car and Cross breathed.

"Here's the tough part."

Cross did not say anything. Zack pushed the "M" button and the elevator swiftly descended. The men's ears popped.

"Listen to me now. Don't look surprised at anything you see because these mothers will know you don't belong down here."

It was too late to turn back. Cross had the feeling the trip would be worth it, if he lived to tell about it. The elevator door opened and the men were met by bright lights that illuminated the rocky walls and the laboratory environment.

"Be cool now," advised Zack. They walked along the stony walkway. Cross could see activity below them, but his brain fought with the reality. In the midst of men in black fatigues were gray alien beings. At first Cross thought he was seeing extras in a movie. He couldn't grasp the situation. There was sense that he was having a nightmare, that this couldn't be real.

Zack stopped half way through the area. He took out a notepad and pen.

"Just pretend we're talking business here." Zack put his enormous leg up on the lower railing and leaned over the top rail.

"Act interested. You okay?"

"Yeah. I guess." Cross lied.

"Now wait a minute or two and you'll see some of the major players."

"What's going on here?"

"This is the upper part of the base."

"What's it for?"

"The government and the grays are working together on a supposed defense project promulgated by the other guys."

"Other guys?"

"Other guys. We'll get into that later."

"What are they defending?"

"Nothing that I can see. A couple of us think they're really playing offense."

Cross tried to watch the gray beings as casually as he could. Their large heads and huge black eyes drew his attention. An undersized mouth was located just above a somewhat pointed chin. Their noses were small. The group dispersed and Cross was somewhat relieved. He felt like a kid at a freak show, not knowing what was real, not wanting to look, but unable to take his eyes off of them.

"We're gonna go deeper. Now don't you think about getting caught. There are creatures around here that can read your thoughts. This next area is gonna be something."

Cross could hardly wait. Zack led him to another elevator and they went down an additional five floors. Zack handed him some earplugs and Cross gladly stuffed them in his ears. The rising drone was beginning to hurt. Abruptly, Cross felt extremely ill. He got sick to his stomach and his skin color turned pasty.

"You're feeling the EMF. It isn't gonna get better. So you're gonna have to suck up and deal."

The elevator stopped.

"Get ready."

The door slowly opened. Now the heat was oppressive.

"Why is it so damned hot in here," Cross asked.

"If we went any deeper, we'd be at hell's front door."

Great earthmovers were working in tandem clearing a tunnel. Heavy equipment was everywhere. So were the grays.

"What are they doing here?"

"They're amassing an army and making room for their ships. About five miles to the right, there's a shaft that goes straight up to the surface. They fly their ships straight the hell out of here."

"Where do they go?"

"Anywhere they freaking want."

Zack escorted Cross further into the base.

"Okay, man. There's a guy I want you to see. Watch him closely and try not to give your thoughts up."

Zack approached a man almost as tall as he was. He was dressed in black fatigues and had five stars on his collar.

"General, that report you requested is on it's way to you, sir."

"Thank you, Captain Williams.

The general looked quite normal to Cross, who was not sure if the man was an alien. He appeared the same as every other human being did. Then Cross saw something in the man's eyes. As Zack continued to talk with the general, Cross noticed something in his eyes when he blinked. It seemed as though the general's contacts were bothering him. The area was quite dirty and Cross dismissed it at first, but then one of the contact's came off the general's eyes.

Cross was horrified. The blue contact slid onto the white of the eye revealing a green iris with an elongated pupil. The man blinked and Cross thought he was going to faint. A third eyelid came over the reptilian eye.

"Excuse me, Captain Williams. This environment is really taxing on my lenses. You'll have to excuse me. I need to go find a mirror."

"Very well, sir." Cross could not believe Zack remained so calm.

"Did you see that, Zack?"

"I was hoping you'd see something like that."

"And that's an alien/human?"

"Well, the body used to belong to somebody, but what's inside is the real McCoy. Seen enough?"

"Yeah. How many of those guys are down here?" Cross asked as they headed for the elevator.

"A few hundred, but there are more up top."

"What do you mean up top?"

"You know, in the real world."

"You gotta be freakin' kidding me," Cross whispered.

"Nope. Now let's get your nosey ass out of here before we end up being dinner for one of those guys."

Cross thought he lost it. He couldn't believe what he had just seen was real. It took everything he had to stay in his boots.

"Stay with me, man. Slow down."

Unencumbered, the men safely returned to the concourse level of the airport where the world continued in ignorance to the reality below the surface. Zack took Cross to a locker room and gave him a green maintenance uniform.

"Hurry up and change. It'll be safer."

Cross numbly discarded the black fatigues and barely remembered changing into the green uniform. He concentrated on putting some order to everything.

"Is there anyway to tell what these guys are up to?"

"We're working on it. We hope you'll help. We need a guy on the outside, a reporter like you who can let the world know what the hell is going on."

"Who would believe me?" Cross was shaken. Zack opened a locker and took out a flask.

"Here. Take some of this and get away from here."

Cross opened the flask and took the first drink he'd had in years. By the fourth swallow, Cross had the courage to leave.

"Thanks, Zack."

"Take it easy. Remember, you don't know me."

"After this afternoon, I don't even know myself."

Cross left the airport and headed straight for a liquor store. He bought a fifth of scotch and went back to the motel.

Across town at the Brown Palace Hotel, William Mann was in a meeting with some of his associates. He seemed distracted. His thoughts were on Michael Cross. Mann was intrigued by Cross. He felt he knew quite a lot about him and assessed the best way to approach him.

The idle conversation of his colleagues bored him. He thought he would amuse himself with Cross. Mann had hopes of recruiting him for future work. He pictured Cross in his mind. Mann saw him riding his motorcycle through the fog. As Cross went into the motel, Mann could see and feel what he was going through. Mann excused himself and went into the bedroom of his suite.

Looking into the mirror on the dresser, Mann saw Cross drinking heavily. He sat down in a chair by the bed and closed his eyes. Cross caught a look at himself in the mirror as he poured more scotch down his throat. He didn't like what he saw, but he hated what he had just witnessed more. He kicked off his boots and plopped down on the bed. Unsure about reality, he closed his eyes and tried to forget the entire afternoon.

"Finding any relief, Michael?"

Cross' eyes flew open. Standing over the bed, William Mann stared at Cross.

"What are you doing here? How in the hell did you get in?" Cross' head spun like a roulette wheel. He thought for a moment that the visitation was alcohol induced.

"You let me in."

"What do you want?"

"I think the better question is what do you want?"

Mann's presence gave Cross a bad feeling.

"I just want to be left alone."

Mann sat on the bed. "Misery loves company. You've had quite a shock today. Perhaps you should have more to drink. May I join you?"

Cross shot a look of disbelief at Mann.

"Get out."

"I think we should have a chat."

"Whatever the hell you're selling, I ain't buying."

"Not even if it helps you with your investigation?"

"What investigation?"

Cross was unsettled, but he could not attribute any of it to the booze.

"Isn't that why you're drinking again?"

"Get out."

Mann got up and walked over to the mirror and was absorbed by it. In an instant, he was gone. Cross was so shaken; he took another drink then realized he had enough. He threw the bottle into the mirror, breaking it.

William Mann jumped back in his chair. He opened his eyes and took a deep breath. The phone rang and one of his associates knocked lightly on the bedroom door.

"Telephone, William. It's the princess."

Mann took another deep breath and then picked up the phone.

"Your highness, what may I do for you?"

Chapter Eighteen

Cross slept off the scotch. A few hours later the phone rang. He pulled himself to the surface of consciousness and answered it.

"Yeah." His tongue stuck to the roof of his mouth.

"Pete Luft. Mike, they're on to you. You have to get out of there."

"What's up?"

"Get the hell out of there. You've only got a few minutes. I'll be in touch later."

Cross hung up the phone, gathered his things and left. A few minutes later a dark sedan pulled up outside the motel. Four men got out and questioned the desk clerk about Cross. The clerk took the men to Cross' room. When they didn't find him, the leader of the group got on his cell phone and got more people involved in the search.

Cross did not know where to go. He knew whoever was after him would look for him riding the Gold Wing. Making his way to Aurora, he found a used car lot and traded off the motorcycle for an old Ford pickup. After gassing up the truck, Cross headed for Western Nebraska. By the time he got to Kimball, he figured it was time to call Luft. He couldn't get an answer. Then he tried Declan Cavanaugh.

Cross tried to tell the priest all that he had seen. Cavanaugh was not surprised with the story of the underground base or its occupants. Cavanaugh listened calmly to Cross and then urged him to head for a priest's house in Wisconsin until things cooled down. Cross thought about it and decided to drive straight through to Manhattan. He thought the more people who saw him, the better his chances would be.

Declan Cavanaugh knew he would be all right, but Cross had to hurry. They agreed to talk as soon as Cross hit the city.

The drive across the sandhills gave Cross time to think about what he would do. He knew he would have to back off on his investigation for a while. That bothered him. The truth had to come out, but he wasn't sure if this was the time to expose it. By the time he reached Interstate 80, he decided he would give the appearance of backing off and would resume the investigation using another approach. Unsure of what that would be, he let it go. In Omaha, Cross made up his mind not to drink again. William Mann had gotten to him. He thought perhaps he had been seeing things. Deep down in his stomach, he knew it was part of that new reality, something he would learn more about if he dared.

William Mann left Denver behind and flew to London. Princess Helena had scheduled a meeting with him. He was always at her disposal. When she arrived at his West London flat, Mann greeted her wearing long white robes. His face was covered with a black curly beard. Mann's long black hair hung loosely over his shoulders.

"Helena, don't you look lovely," he said. Mann kissed her hand and walked with her into his study. The room was elegantly furnished. The princess took a seat on a floral couch while Mann sat in a large wing-backed chair.

"I'm so very glad you made time to see me."

"It's always a pleasure, dear lady. With what may I help you?

The princess blushed slightly and bit her lower lip.

"You see I am very much in love…"

"And you want to know whether or not to marry Abu Zarzi."

"I'm not sure how things will go over."

"Everything will work out for the best. You mustn't worry about the Queen or your ex-husband. You have your own life. Go live it."

"Yes, I shall then. Thank you."

"I've been quite pleased with your work on the land mines. You're quite popular with that stance, but then, I told you before you married Geoffrey, that your popularity would be phenomenal."

"That's all been a little hard to take, hasn't it?"

The princess stood and took Mann's hand. She looked into his eyes. They seemed bottomless, with almost an oily quality to them, but entrancing nevertheless.

"When you get back from France, everyone will come to see you, I'm sure."

"How did you know I was going to France?"

William Mann just smiled. He escorted her to her waiting car. She got in and drove away. He watched for a moment, and then returned to his flat.

"I shall miss her," Mann said to his butler.

"Yes, sir," the old man replied.

As Mann walked back to his study, his beard disappeared from his face and his white robes changed into a charcoal suit. The butler was used to Mann's transformations and paid no attention.

Cross went to Cavanaugh's apartment. He had to get things straight in his head. His brain was covered with what he called dirty laundry, almost reaching the mildew stage. After weeks of playing tug of war, he hoped Cavanaugh would clear up a few things. Cavanaugh was getting ready to spend Labor Day at a friend's cabin in the Adirondacks, but he made time to see Cross.

William Mann preoccupied Cross' thoughts. Before he went to sleep at night, he could see Mann's eyes staring at him. Cross felt naked and uncomfortable when Mann entered his thoughts. He had to ask Father Cavanaugh if he knew anything more about him and if he could free his mind from Mann's tentacles.

"Michael, what can I tell you? It appears to me that this William Mann has extraordinary capabilities. I haven't met him personally, but other people have."

"And?"

"He does a lot of good work."

"I dunno, Father. The guy walked through the damn mirror in my motel room. It wasn't the booze. I swear it."

"I believe you, Michael. Now, even though he may do a lot of good, to me the man is, at the very least, consorting with the devil. If he can move in and out of dimensions, you're dealing with a demon. Saint's of course could bilocate, but this is on a different level."

"Bilocate?"

"Be in two places at once, but my senses are telling me this man has aligned himself with hell."

Father Cavanaugh knew more than he was willing to tell Cross. He knew Cross was not equipped to handle the facts about William Mann. Cross was easily outclassed and ill prepared right now.

"You can see into the future, Father. Who or what the hell is he?"

A scream came from the kitchen. Father Cavanaugh's housekeeper came running into the living room.

"Princess Helena is dead!"

Over the next several days, the world was glued to television in an unparalleled outpouring of grief. Princess

Helena's death affected almost everyone. Michael Cross was amazed by the enormous response evoked by her death. He didn't know if it was her beauty that touched everyone so deeply or who she was that mattered the most. She was a princess of a beleaguered and ugly world who for a brief moment brightened lives, fostered hope and brought alive a fairy tale. Her death stopped the world and shattered the myth of happily-ever-after.

Rumors surfaced about the car crash, which killed her. Some thought the paparazzi was responsible. Others felt her ex-husband had her killed. In the weeks that followed the funeral, there were even rumors that the princess survived the dreadful crash and was living in Australia, hidden by her supporters. Cross found evidence for several theories, but was not in the mood to pursue them.

The Wire had sent Cross on several hot stories in trouble spots all over the world. The grind wore him out. Globetrotting used to give Cross a high. He thought he had reached a mid-life crisis. Fatigue chased him like a crazed stalker. When he looked in the mirror, he couldn't get past his graying hair and the deep lines in his face.

Upon his return to Manhattan, Cross was ready for a break. He got a few days off. Cross awoke one morning and decided to get new clothes, some things that would beat back time. He purchased men's hair color and new cologne as he geared up for Lori.

She hadn't deserted him, in spite of being hurt by his general malaise. Her patience, and what he thought was her love, broke through his veneer warming his heart.

He was ready to take the relationship to another stage. Tonight, he planned to make passionate love to Lori. He thought it was time. The mirror concurred he was not getting any younger.

The couple went out for lasagna and returned to Cross' home in high spirits. Lori noticed Cross was more interested in her and spent the evening giving her his undivided attention. She loved it. There was no competition with his conspiracy theories. When he kissed her, she felt like she was sixteen and so did he. Sparks flew and Cross could have sworn he saw them. He kissed her again and chastised himself for not making love to her sooner.

"Let's go to the bedroom, Mike. Let's not wait anymore."

They started for the bedroom. Indigestion caught Cross in the hallway.

"You go on. I'll be right there. I've got to take some bicarb."

"I'll be waiting," she sighed. He went to the kitchen and got the bicarbonate out of the cupboard and a glass. As he ran the water, his indigestion got much worse. Hurriedly, he filled the glass and shook the powder into it. Barely waiting for it to dissolve, he downed the entire glass. Waiting for the proverbial burp, he was too uncomfortable to think about Lori. Finally, a gigantic burp forced it's way up and out. He felt better and headed for the bedroom.

Lori lit candles and got into the bed. Her clothes were strewn all over the floor.

"The candles are a nice touch," he said as he made his way to the bed, undressing as he went.

"I'll show you another nice touch." For once, Cross did not need to be persuaded. He did need to feel sixteen though. He had to recapture his youth. Guilt wasn't allowed anywhere near him. Tonight, he didn't care if he was married to Lori. He just needed to feel alive.

They wrapped themselves in a torrid frenzy. Lori felt like he really cared about her. She imagined living the rest of her life with him. He began to enjoy their relationship. Lori was someone he needed. Age was a state of mind and his body almost agreed with him until something hit him hard in the chest. Cross gasped for air and then clutched his chest.

Lori looked up in horror. "Mike? Oh, my God!"

Cross' eyes widened and he fell face down. Lori rolled him over. His eyes were open and he was unresponsive. She felt for a pulse and couldn't find one. Frantically, she crawled over him to get to the phone. She call 911, gave his address with a rushed description of his condition and then dropped the phone and started CPR.

Cross could see her and hear her, but he couldn't feel anything. Even the horrific pain was gone. Suddenly, Cross felt as if he was being sucked through a straw. He couldn't breathe and with a whoosh, he was floating above the bed. Lori worked tirelessly as he watched her. He wanted to tell her he was all right. Cross shouted to her, but she obviously could not hear him.

She prayed out loud in between compressions and breaths. He wondered how long the ambulance would take to arrive. Then his vision narrowed and the room was swallowed in darkness. He felt extremely cold and once again he felt as if he was being sucked through a straw. A bright light appeared and Cross thought he was dead.

He didn't see any of his relatives. He didn't see anything but an intense white light. Suddenly, he felt ashamed. An inexplicable horror enveloped him. His life passed before him and abruptly stopped as he made love to Lori.

Instantly, Cross was grabbed by two monstrous demons and hurled into Hell. The intense heat was unbearable. He saw friends of his who beat him with iron rods as he passed by them, burning him with searing pain.

"God forgive me," he screamed. Cross was hurled even further into the abyss. He saw world leaders tied to chairs, tormented by prostitutes. As he reached the lowest depth of hell, he was dragged before the throne of Satan.

"God forgive me. Please get me out of here!"

Everyone in the bowels of Hell screamed at hearing God's name. Satan stood over Michael Cross with such venom in his eyes that Cross wished he would go blind.

The paramedics arrived and immediately went to work on Cross. They got the paddles out and gave him a jolt. Cross jumped as he trembled before the prince of Hell.

"They can't get you back, Michael. You are mine now."

Satan put his long gnarled finger over Cross' heart, scorching him badly. Cross could not believe the pain he felt. He screamed, but the pain only intensified.

As he writhed in pain, Satan allowed Hell's residents to torture him by unimaginable devices.

"This is your eternity, Michael Cross," Satan said.

"I've been waiting for you for a very long time."

The paramedics stuck Cross with a dose of lidocaine. They still couldn't establish a heart rhythm.

Abruptly, Cross was sucked out of the bowels of Hell and landed at the feet of Jesus.

"One mortal sin is all it takes, Michael."

"Oh, God, forgive me. Please have mercy on me."

Cross was never more sincere.

"My Mercy knows no limits, Michael. In my Mercy, I wanted you to see what your actions have brought upon you."

Cross felt such extraordinary love and peace from Jesus that he didn't want to leave. He didn't dare raise his head to look at Jesus.

"Much is expected of you, Michael. You've let yourself down. You've let Me down."

"Please don't send me back to Hell. Please!"

"I want to show you the future, Michael. Earth will be tested by fire. Billions of people will die because of man's folly and man's sins. Man's penchant for war and nuclear bombs will get the best of all of you."

Cross saw the entire world engulfed in war. He saw husbands and wives killed by their children. People were insane, destroying everything in their path. Mushroom clouds formed over the planet. Much of the United States was destroyed. Cross began to experience intense pain and sorrow. He was overwhelmed with misery.

"Here is the one behind all of the bloodshed, Michael." Cross saw a man in the distance. The whole world was listening to him. Then suddenly he came face to face with William Mann.

"Behold, the Beast, the antichrist. He is preparing the world for Hell. He will be called the World Teacher."

"He's got to be stopped," Cross said.

"Are you willing to go back and help to fight the Beast?"

"Yes, Lord."

"Then amend your life or you will return to Hell without reprieve."

The paramedics worked on Cross all the way to the hospital. His heart had finally begun to beat on its own. Cross felt a pull as he knelt before Jesus. He felt exhausted and seemed to melt into a coarse liquid as he was pulled back to earth.

"You have much work ahead, Michael. But the choice is ultimately up to you."

He stayed in a coma for two days, but on the third morning, he awoke, stunned and weak. Alone in the room, Cross panicked. He had tubes running in and out of his body and electrodes attached to his chest. Cross felt like a sick marionette. Overwhelming fatigue clung to him, but he fought it trying to stay awake.

His mouth made the Mojave seem like a flood plain. Cross tried to get up and inadvertently pulled on his nasal canula. He put his head back down and tried to make sense out of things. It was hopeless.

A nurse came in to check on him and was surprised to see him awake.

"How are you feeling, Mr. Cross?"

"I've felt worse, I think."

"You had us all worried. Your son is here. After I take your vitals, I'll send him in."

"Thanks." Cross was so tired he could not keep his eyes open.

The nurse pulled back the covers and undid the bandage on his chest.

"What are you doing? What's the bandage for?"

"After your heart attack, the doctors gave you a quadruple bypass. How did you get that burn?"

As he reached a higher degree of consciousness, he began to feel squashing pain. He hurt everywhere.

"What burn? Heart attack, huh? I feel like a truck hit me."

"You can have some more morphine."

The nurse checked his IV and then put a syringe into the line and injected the painkiller.

"Now you just rest. You're really doing quite well now. I'll tell Lori you're awake."

Cross stiffened. He remembered something. His memory wasn't fully intact, just snippets of pictures flashed before him. Instantly, he saw a glimpse of Hell, but the morphine coursed through his so quickly, he drifted off to sleep.

Almost immediately, he began to dream. He saw a firing squad march into a courtyard. The men, all dressed in black with black berets on their heads, turned toward him and raised their rifles. He could hear a command to fire and Cross awoke.

"Dad?"

"Hmm?"

"Dad, how are you feeling?"

"I'm still here."

"I'm glad about that."

"Joe, what are you doing here?" Cross could not believe the weakness he felt.

"When I heard you had a heart attack, I flew back here as fast as I could." Joe didn't want to admit how scared he was. His father had always meant a great deal to him.

"It's great to see you, Joe. I need to go to confession."

Cross felt urgency for confession like he had never known. He felt a need for absolution every now and then, but this time it weighed heavily on his mind.

"I can hear your confession, Pop. You got the last rites from Father Cavanaugh you know."

"Really?" His mouth was parched and his lips were badly cracked. He licked them, but it didn't help.

Joe poured some water for his dad and lifted his head up so he could drink.

"Thanks, Joe. Don't take this wrong, but I need another priest to hear my confession."

Joe smiled and helped his father with another sip of water.

"I understand. I'll ask Father Cavanaugh."

Cross continued to struggle with fatigue, but he pushed himself. "If he isn't available, I need someone else right away."

"Just be calm, Pop. I'll get you a priest. Now rest for awhile."

Lori Young walked in on them. Joe smiled at her and leaned over to his father.

"Dad, you have company."

"Huh?" He opened his eyes and saw Lori. Immediately, he started to remember what happened to him and how it happened. "Joe, please get that priest."

Cross did not want to tell his son about the experience he had until he worked it around in his mind.

"I'm on it. Excuse me, Lori."

Lori smiled and went over to Cross, kissing him on the forehead.

"You're doing much better, Mike. How are you feeling?"

"I could use a smoke."

"You've seen the last of cigarettes. Anything else I can get you?"

"I just want to sleep." He knew he didn't want to talk even if he had felt up to it.

Lori kissed him again and stroked his hair as he drifted off to sleep.

After three weeks, Cross was able to leave the hospital. In spite of exhaustion, he felt so much better that he threw his cigarettes away when he got home. Joe stayed with him for a few more days. Cross loved his company, although he felt he was keeping Joe from his duties at the Vatican.

"Joe, who's helping the pope while you're gone?" Cross shut off the television so he could concentrate on his son.

"Monsignor Hurley."

"I feel guilty that I'm keeping you here."

"No need. I was due for a vacation and so were you. It's nice we can spend time together again."

"Yeah." Cross seemed to be miles away at times and Joe noticed it. He worried about his dad. He had seen people change emotionally after major traumas and he was uncertain how his dad was handling things.

"Hey, Dad. You know with all the stuff you've been through, sometimes it helps to talk about it."

"Hmm. I wouldn't know where to begin. Even if I did talk about it, it just seems too crazy."

"Try me," said Joe. He smiled. Inside he felt a little strange with the tables being turned. He was no longer the little boy with problems.

"Well," Cross paused. "I dunno. I think I had a near death experience."

"That shouldn't surprise you. You were well on your way."

"I made it all the way to hell, Joe. All the way." Cross could not look at his son.

"Do you want to talk about it?"

"Jesus. It was awful. I mean way beyond anything I heard from the nuns. You know?"

"Yes, but obviously God gave you a second chance."

Joe didn't need to remind Cross. He knew he had been spared and completely changed by what he saw.

"And I intend to make good." Cross meant it and Joe felt it.

"That's great. I know it isn't easy."

"That's only the half of it. I was shown the antichrist."

"Really," Joe answered. He looked down at his shoes.

"I know you probably think I'm nuts."

Cross felt a little nutty talking about it, but he hoped Joe would understand.

"You're not crazy. There are those of us at the Vatican who have been keeping tabs on him."

"Then you really believe all that business?"

"Absolutely. I believe in it as much as I believe in heaven and hell."

"So what can we do about him?"

"We can pray he won't come to power in our lifetime."

Cross wanted a more proactive answer, something akin to nuking him off the planet.

"But from what I have been shown, I don't know if it can be avoided."

"Prophecy has to be fulfilled. Sadly, we know the pope will be killed. He knows it. Yet, we keep praying because prayer can do wonders." Joe sat back in his chair and looked at his dad.

"Someone must have been praying for me or my ass would have fried."

Joe laughed and Cross laughed a bit. His chest was still sore, but he even enjoyed feeling the pain.

"What are you going to do now, Dad?"

"I'm gonna get back to work as soon as I can and try to figure out all of this."

Chapter Nineteen

Cross spent the next six weeks resting and doing research. He looked at things differently now. His view of people had changed as well. It was almost as if he had obtained another sense when it came to people. At times he could read their hearts and that proved to be a terrible burden. Cross put space between himself and many of his friends. He put the most distance between Lori and him. It was something he felt he had to do. His life had been solitary for so long that it didn't seem like a sacrifice. Sure that he had to get right with God and himself, Cross spent a great deal of time in reflection.

With Father Cavanaugh's help, he reached out to more visionaries and compiled an extraordinary library of messages, all pertaining to the last days. The similarities of the messages only confirmed to him that the world was on the ropes. He felt driven. Uncertain about how he could fight the antichrist, he decided to reveal the plans of the antichrist's main friends.

Cross drew fire from the FBI and other agencies, but kept at it. His boss at The Wire admired the work he was doing and knew Cross was on his way to another Pulitzer. Cross was completely transformed by his heart attack and his near death experience. Now, he was fit and focused. His enemies tried to do something about it.

At first, he experienced monetary problems. Checks would bounce when there was more than enough money to cover them. His phone was tapped and on occasion, disconnected. A campaign to discredit him fizzled and that's when things got really personal.

He started to have problems when he left his house. Cross would suddenly feel ill when he drove. He immediately went in for a checkup. The doctors couldn't find anything wrong with him. Then he noticed that several times per week, oncoming traffic would suddenly pull into his lane. He mentioned it in passing to Father Cavanaugh, who explained that he was under demonic attack. The priest told him to use holy water around the house and even in the car. Cavanaugh assured him that it was necessary.

For a time, Cross was religious about using the holy water, but when things returned to normal, he would forget to use it. One night when Cross was editing a significant story about the New World Order, he encountered a few problems with the dark side.

His phone went crazy, constantly ringing, but no one was on the other end. The lights in the house went off and on, until they remained off. Cross went to the window and looked out. The rest of the neighborhood had power. Not wanting to quit his work, he lit several candles and went to his old typewriter to pound out the final paragraphs. He heard a bang in the kitchen that sounded like a drawer had slammed shut. Then everything was quiet.

He got back to work and was quickly absorbed. Suddenly, he felt hot air hitting the back of his neck, as if someone was standing behind him breathing on him. He stopped typing for a moment and turned around just in time to see a butcher knife flying through the air headed directly for his chest. At the last second, he jumped out of the way, but the butcher knife caught him in the arm. He was impaled on his desk. He pulled the knife out and was stunned by the pain. The knife missed any arteries, but he was cut very deeply.

Cross struggled with reality while he wrapped his arm with his handkerchief. He could see no one in the room. Then an icy chill wafted over him. All of the candles were extinguished by a cold blast of air.

Trying to remember where he left the holy water, Cross stumbled around in the dark. He was pushed and shoved by something he couldn't see. Terrified, he tried to make it to the bedroom. That was the last place he had the holy water. As he went down the hall, he was tackled by something that felt like three hundred pounds of iron.

Something grabbed his throat and started to squeeze. For a moment, Cross thought he was finished. He pried off two monstrous hands from his throat and wrestled with a rancid smelling creature. He screamed for God's help and fought the beast. Cross struggled to his feet. His heart was way ahead of him. He reached the bedroom and fumbled for the holy water. He sprayed the room and remembered what Father Cavanaugh had told him to say.

He pointed to the floor and said, "In the name of Jesus, I command you to leave this place and go back from whence you came."

Everything got quiet except for his poor heart. Cross lit a match and went to light a candle, when the lights came on. He thought about calling Father Cavanaugh, but realized it was too late. In the light, he noticed how badly his arm was cut. He went to a twenty-four hour clinic and had it taken care of. Cross put off seeing Father Cavanaugh until morning.

When Cross arrived at Father Cavanaugh's apartment, he found the priest preparing for a visitor. Kiri was helping to move some things out of the guest bedroom.

"Let me help, Father," said Cross.

"Sounds grand, Michael. I don't seem to be as strong as I used to be."

"You're not moving, are you?" Cross picked up a heavy trunk and moved it out of the room. His arm made him wince.

"No. I've got someone who will be staying with me. It seems to be a possession problem."

"Is that wise, Father?"

"It will be alright. I don't think the case is that serious. I hope not anyway."

"Do you normally take your cases home with you?"

"This is a special circumstance." Father Cavanaugh looked over the room and thought everything was in order.

"Thank you both for your help. How about some coffee?"

"Yes, Father," Kiri said, as she ran a dust cloth over the dresser and left the room.

"How've you been feeling, Michael?"

"That's why I'm here. There's been some strange stuff happening."

The men walked to the living room. A knock at the door detoured Father Cavanaugh. He looked through the security hole in the door.

"We finished just in time."

He opened the door. A little girl stood in the doorway with her mother.

"Mrs. Hernandez, please come in. Alicia, how are you," he asked as he extended his hand to the little girl. She didn't take it. Her mother nudged her, but she glared back at her.

"Please come in. We were just about to have some coffee. How about some milk and cookies, Alicia?"

Alicia bore a hole through Cavanaugh, but remained silent.

"This is Michael Cross. He's a friend of mine. Do come in and sit."

"I should go, Father," said Cross, feeling like an intruder.

"You just arrived. Surely you can have some coffee before you go."

"No, thanks. I'd better go."

The little girl bothered Cross, but he did not know why. She was a beautiful child.

"Let me walk you to the door," said Cavanaugh. Alicia stared at the priest, as he walked Cross out of the room.

"Why don't we have lunch next week, Michael? We can have a nice chat then."

"Sure, Father. Hey, if you don't mind my asking, is the child the one with the trouble," he whispered.

"Afraid so."

"Poor kid. She's incredibly beautiful."

"And incredibly tormented."

"She's awful young."

"Unfortunately, that doesn't matter." The priest's eyes grew sad.

"If you need anything, just call, Father."

Cavanaugh smiled and patted Cross on the back. "Thank you. God bless you."

Cross was bothered the child was having problems. All the way home, he hoped she didn't go through what he'd just experienced.

He managed to get through the rest of the week without any further incidents. Cross was looking forward to having lunch with Father Cavanaugh at the Russian Tea Room. There was plenty to talk about and Cross wanted to know how to rid himself of the demonic activity.

Cross waited for Father Cavanaugh for over an hour. When he didn't arrive at the restaurant, he called the priest's apartment. Kiri answered the phone.

"Hello."

"Kiri, this is Michael Cross. May I speak to Father Cavanaugh?"

"No. Father is in the hospital. He had a stroke."

"When?"

"Last night."

"Where is he?"

"St. Luke's."

"Thanks, Kiri." Cross grabbed a cab and hurried to the hospital. He thought about how well Cavanaugh looked last week. He worried about whether his new case was too much for him or if something else had caused the stroke. Cavanaugh had been working on a revealing book about the Vatican, which had made several people very nervous about its pending release. He wondered if that had anything to do with it.

Father Cavanaugh was a man used to pressure. He had marvelous coping mechanisms grounded by his unshakeable faith. Cross envied him that. The cab ride seemed endless.

At the hospital, Cross found out that Father Cavanaugh had been placed in ICU. The waiting room was filled with the priest's friends who wasted no time in giving Cross all the details. Even though Father Cavanaugh suffered from moderate paralysis on one side of his body, the prognosis was good that he would recover. Several of his friends expressed their gratitude over the fact that Cavanaugh had suffered no mental or speech impairments. Each person in the waiting room had been deeply touched by him. Knowing they could share future conversations and debates with the priest proved to be a rallying point. Father Cavanaugh was thankful that the work on his book could continue and his work with Alicia could resume.

He made remarkable progress and returned home within a few weeks. A cane and a faltering gait didn't stop him from his work. On rare occasions, he was frustrated with the inconvenience of it all.

Michael Cross was amazed at how well Cavanaugh did and once the priest's stamina returned, he sat down with him for a talk. Cavanaugh looked frail at times and a little gaunt, but his eyes and mind were clear. He had missed Cross a great deal and looked forward to their discussion.

Father Cavanaugh sat back in his recliner. A crooked smile crossed his lips.

"It is wonderful to have you over again, Michael."

"I'm glad you're home. Are you still working with that little girl?"

"Yes. It will take longer, but she'll be freed eventually. Father Hennessy took her for the afternoon giving us some time to chat. How are things going?"

"My work is fine. I'm making progress, although it's been slow. I've had a lot of demonic junk in the house."

"Have you now?"

"It reduced to an all out brawl a few weeks ago."

Cavanaugh frowned. "I hate to hear that. Were you hurt?"

"Nothing serious. It was frightening but I got through it."

"Yes. Have you had your home blessed?"

"No, not yet."

"I'd be happy to Michael, but perhaps Father Hennessy could do that for you?"

"That would be great." Cross truly enjoyed his time with Father Cavanaugh. He felt recharged. Cavanaugh had a way of making things feel right, more in perspective, something Cross seemed to have out of balance lately.

"Father, it's becoming difficult working on this investigation, especially with all hell breaking loose while I work."

"That's intentional. Certainly, you don't expect this to be easy, do you?"

Cross had not exactly looked at it that way.

"I guess not. It's just this whole thing is so bizarre that it's becoming a greater challenge everyday."

"You could leave it. Drop what you're doing and move on to something else."

"I thought about it, but my life has changed. My whole reality has been altered. I want to keep going, but I don't know how."

"One foot in front of another, one step at a time, one sentence at a time. God willing, you'll finish your investigation and you can reveal your findings to a grateful world."

"Would anyone listen?"

"Make them listen, Michael. You can do it. If God sees fit, perhaps things will slow down. That's my hope."

"How is your book coming?"

"It is okay, not nearly finished though. I suspect that if I live long enough to finish it, several people will be put on their ears by it."

"You'll finish it, Father."

"As you will finish your work. I'll have Father Hennessy contact you about your house. You are staying close to God, aren't you? Daily mass and confession every two weeks?"

Cross blushed. "I learned my lesson," he smiled.

"You must bring around your work when you've finished. I would like to see it. It doesn't hurt to compare notes."

Chapter Twenty

Cross worked diligently on his investigation. The next few months proved to be fruitful for him. He didn't like his findings, even though he trusted them. His life had taken on the dimensions and dynamics of a spy novel, but it was all very real to him. The most difficult aspect of his work was staying out of the way of the people in power. It was getting harder for him to remain invisible.

His phone was noticeably tapped again and he was followed with regularity. Cross was no longer capable of working undetected. When that became apparent to him, he decided to make himself more visible, taking some lessons from Father Cavanaugh. Cross became a familiar face on television and a fixture as a talking head. People were starting to listen. He made waves and when the tide became too intense, he would back off, waiting for world events to materialize. They always did. With the help of visionaries, Cross was able to keep two steps ahead of the New World Order. His weekly columns reflected incredible insight, totally unappreciated by his enemies.

Cross had become so visible, that killing him had become difficult, just as it had for Father Cavanaugh's enemies. Yet, their common enemies never gave up.

Cavanaugh reached the point where his cane had become unnecessary. He exceeded his physician's expectations and was well on his way to completing his book. His publisher was making plans for its release.

He had also relieved Alicia of most of her demons. There were more days when she was bright and happy than she had been in months. Alicia had grown fond of the priest. She looked forward to their time together. The child had actually seemed so improved, that her mother went shopping with Kiri one afternoon, while Father Cavanaugh met with her.

Alicia's ready smile charmed the old man. He could almost see a light in her eyes now. They talked a bit over milk and cookies. She spoke about her upcoming birthday with great delight. Father Cavanaugh was about to celebrate his birthday too. He didn't mind that another year was upon him. He had great expectations.

At three in the afternoon, the priest got his rosary out of his pocket to say the Divine Mercy Chaplet. He wanted to teach Alicia how to say it. He spoke about the three o'clock hour as the time of great mercy.

Alicia stood still listening to him. Her long black hair glistened in the afternoon sun. The unusual beauty she possessed took on an adult quality to it. Her moist, dark eyes studied Cavanaugh, but when the priest said the name of Jesus, her eyes grew cold.

"You see, Alicia, Jesus is always ready to forgive."

The priest kissed the crucifix and made the sign of the cross. A low, deliberate growl emanated from Alicia. Her pupils appeared blood red as if they were stained. She reached out her hand towards Father Cavanaugh. He paid her no attention, continuing with his prayers. As he knelt facing a crucifix, Alicia walked behind him. She stopped about five feet away from the priest. A rage built up in her small body and she started to say some garbled words in Latin with a voice ten times her size.

She focused on the back of the priest's head and again extended her arm. Cavanaugh instantly keeled over and struck his head on the corner of his desk. He hit the floor with a terrible thud. Blood streamed from a gash on his forehead. Trying to get up, he looked in Alicia's direction, but she was gone. Father Cavanaugh slipped into unconsciousness.

Three hours later, Kiri returned home with Mrs. Hernandez. She found Cavanaugh on the floor and called an ambulance. Mrs. Hernandez went to find Alicia, dreading the worst. Not finding her, she immediately left the apartment.

Cross heard the emergency call go out over the police radio. He waited until the ambulance driver informed dispatch about the hospital where they were headed. Cross heard the priest's condition was critical and wasted no time getting to the hospital.

Father Cavanaugh was already in the emergency room when Cross arrived. He asked the nurse on duty about his condition. She told him that it looked like Father Cavanaugh had another stroke and hit his head. They were prepping him for surgery. He had intracranial bleeding and the doctors were going to try to stop it.

A few minutes before being wheeled to surgery, Father Cavanaugh regained consciousness. Cross was allowed to see him briefly.

"Father, everything's going to be okay."

"Michael, I was pushed."

Cross felt like he had been punched with an anvil.

"Pushed? By whom?"

"When I," Cavanaugh started. He struggled to get the words out.

"When I looked to see, there was no one there."

His eyes lost focus and rolled back in his head. Cross went to find the nurse. Cavanaugh was taken quickly to surgery. No one had to tell Cross that Father Cavanaugh had very little chance of survival. He felt it, but the sadness was chewed alive by anger that someone could do that to his friend.

He didn't know what to think. Cavanaugh seemed lucid, but if no one was in the room with him, perhaps it was just a stroke.

The surgery took three hours. Cavanaugh barely emerged from the ordeal. He regained consciousness, but drifted in and out. The waiting room filled with friends who wondered, as did Cross, about what the priest had said.

Cross chatted and prayed with those friends wondering about how different life would be without their dear friend. They all found out too quickly and they were not prepared for the void.

Not allowing grief to set in, Cross worked hard on his research. Father Cavanaugh's books were an enormous help with which he could put things into the right perspective. Cross also sought out valid visionaries and cultivated new government sources. So many things seemed to be happening at once and the lack of media coverage confirmed Cross' suspicions.

He began to take note of contrails in the sky, not the normal jet trails, but strange ones that formed far below normal altitudes. Cross noticed the contrails were longer lived. People who were exposed to them came down with flu-like symptoms several days later. After asking a few of his government sources, Cross determined the trails, which his friends called chemtrails, were deadly and specifically engineered to attack the human immune system. Some of his sources claimed the chemtrails were intended to cull the population, particularly the elderly and those people suffering from chronic illness.

Visionaries told Cross that heaven called them weapons of the New World Order. Cross studied areas of the country where chemtrails had been spotted. Obituaries began to show larger segments of the elderly population who had died from respiratory problems associated with chemtrails. In fact, elderly deaths were up all over the country, puzzling Cross. He asked actuarial scientists about whether the increase in the elderly deaths seemed normal. They told him that the clusters of elderly deaths indicated that viruses had hit certain areas of the country and those viruses ran rampant through the elderly population. However, they agreed the current numbers were larger than average.

Cross asked a few of his scientific friends about the chemtrails. One medical researcher was building a case against chemtrails and directed him to labs throughout the country responsible for aerosolized vaccinations as the government called them.

The government was not oblivious to what Cross was doing and it did its best to sidetrack and harass him. It was common for hackers to target Cross' computer. Bank accounts again were depleted. Funds would mysteriously disappear. Checks bounced causing an endless stream of check charges. Cross resorted to using only cash. His cell phone conversations were monitored forcing him to swap phones and numbers in order to stay ahead of the surveillance.

Cross did not allow the nuisances to depress him. He stayed focused. He had to stay ahead of the curve. There was a consensus among the visionaries and his government sources indicating that the United States would be attacked.

Klebbans met with Cross frequently to discuss the information he had received from George Hawthorne's friends. The Chinese had amassed thousands of troops in Central America and they were moving northward. Some Chinese soldiers had been spotted as far north as Mexico.

Well acquainted with President Macon's affinity for the Chinese, Cross knew that America was being set up.

Players around the world were strategically positioned to entice the United States into more conflicts than it could handle.

Visionaries told Cross of an invasion coming from the Bering Straits. One visionary had received specific information about a tunnel from the Straits that went through Canada and the United States, ending up in Kentucky. According to the visionaries, America would be invaded by means of this tunnel. Cross checked the information with close government sources and they confirmed the tunnel's existence. When asked if the government was going to do something about it, Cross was told there were not any established plans.

He began to feel desperate. His love for his country was so strong that he couldn't bear anything happening to it. Since the Oklahoma City bombing, there had been rumblings from Macon's administration about gun control. Cross knew that if gun control were implemented, American's would go down the same path as Cubans under Castro. He worked tirelessly accumulating information he hoped to present to a Senate sub-committee exposing the dangers ahead and President Macon's plans. Cross was interrupted from his work by a call from his son.

"Dad, I wanted to let you know that the Vatican is going to release a document on the Third Secret of Fatima. Everyone thinks that the real secret will be released, but I want you to know it's bogus."

Cross was puzzled. "Why would the pope release a false document?"

"He doesn't have anything to do with it. The Holy Father thought it was going to be the real deal, but a few of the cardinals got creative."

"And they don't have Father Cavanaugh to blow the whistle on them."

"Exactly. They waited for his death. Now there isn't anyone to debunk this insanity."

"What about Sister Lucy?"

"She's been silenced by her bishop, and to be honest, I think someone is impersonating her."

"Someone going along with the party line?"

"Yes."

Cross tried to connect the dots. He was having trouble with it all.

"Joe, what does this mean?"

"That's a good question. People are going to think the worst is over and it isn't. Trust me. What's going to be released is a mild statement that has no relationship to the actual Third Secret."

"Okay. But how bad is that?"

"Soul wise, it's very bad. People will be unexpectedly annihilated. We're talking billions. And it's not just that. They'll think Satan has been defeated when in reality, we're rushing towards Hell and World War III."

"Well, I can write about it, Joe. Maybe that will help."

"Do you still have that letter from Sister Lucy?"

"Yeah. I think so. Why?"

"Well, I hope you have it because you're going to need it."

"I'll do what I can. They've got me covering this stinking campaign. Are you doing okay?"

"I'm fine. Pop, I gotta run."

Chapter Twenty-One

Within a few weeks, the Vatican released a sizable document about the Third Secret of Fatima. It didn't resemble anything Father Cavanaugh or Veronica Lueken had told him about the secret's contents. The original secret contained twenty-six lines of handwritten text on one page. In the secret the Vatican released, it was four pages long. Cross noticed something else, the handwriting in Sister Lucy's letter did not match the document attributed to her. Realizing what Joe meant, Cross contacted the premier forensic lab in the country and had them analyze the released letter along with the note Sr. Lucy had given him. The wait for the results seemed like forever, but Cross used the time to study the contrived document and easily agreed it was false. Visionaries called him telling him the documents were a fake. Cross got the lab results proving beyond a doubt the Third Secret of Fatima was still a secret.

He wrote a piece on the hoax. Yet, the Vatican seemed oblivious to the critique and so did much of the world. A few die-hard's clung to the truth and didn't allow the lie to keep them from their watch.

The campaign was heating up and as Election Day approached, sources contacted Cross about possible vote tampering in case Vice President Rose could not pull ahead of J.R. Hawthorne. Knowing the two men were different sides to the same coin, Cross did not hold much hope for the country.

Both men were New World Order boys. The only difference was Rose had a little faster plan for throwing the United States under U.N. control. Hawthorne's plans would take a little longer, giving Cross and his friends more time to stop the machinations of the New World Order.

Just as his sources claimed, the election was a dead heat. A shocked country came to a standstill as votes were counted and recounted. Accusations of fraud were shot from Rose's camp to Hawthorne's and back again. The world watched and hoped that no terrorist or renegade nation would take advantage of the American crisis. Although intelligence sources said there were threats of all kinds, nothing serious happened other than the disillusionment of Americans, which could have been part of the plan.

J.R. Hawthorne was declared the victor by late December, giving way to charges of theft. In the end, Rose bowed out and the country moved forward, a little more divided and a little more tenuous. However, Americans quickly got back to their lives, absorbed by television and schedules that left little time to question anything.

Hawthorne appointed an interesting cabinet heavily occupied by people who had worked for his father. His vice president was a man of questionable health with a heart that looked more like Swiss cheese. Cross was uncomfortable with many of the choices. Many were New World Order cronies who couldn't wait to dissolve American sovereignty. Still, Cross was surprised to see hard line isolationists appointed to the cabinet. He hoped that their influence would help the country.

Wall Street treated the economy like a teenager who had just been given the keys to a Lamborghini. The markets spent the better part of a year in nosedives and in partial recoveries. Global markets began to get shaky. The World Teacher had predicted a global crash and Cross knew it. He watched the financial world teeter, knowing full well strings were being pulled and a chosen few were still reaping enormous profits.

Companies all over the country laid off workers by the thousands, fueling fear and bringing the economy to an abrupt halt.

Islamic extremists reveled in America's woes and looked for an opportunity to settle the score with Hawthorne, whose father had the audacity of bombing a Muslim state.

In the spring of 2001, Hugh Klebbans got in touch with Cross. He told him that the same sources who predicted the 1996 passenger plane would be shot down, were now saying that an attack on American soil was imminent.

Cross asked what the government was doing to thwart the attack and he was told it had not responded with much concern or increase in security measures. Cross was told the attack would happen by the end of summer and definitely before fall.

Through another source, Cross confirmed that an Islamic fundamentalist had been arrested in the Philippines for bombing a Filipino jetliner. Mohammed Murad confessed that there were plans in the making that involved flying a passenger plane into CIA headquarters in Langley, Virginia. Because Murad gave out the information while being tortured, United States officials discounted the plan.

It was decided to concentrate manpower and resources on the possibility of truck bombs or suitcase nukes. Canadian sources told Cross that some plutonium had entered the United States near New York. Cross was able to corroborate that with other sources that said the makings for a dirty bomb had crossed the southern border.

The only thing the feds could agree on was the United States was likely to be hit somewhere and most likely by Muslims. However, Cross did find one source who was quite clear about the government knowing more details and there were men higher up within the government who would not take preventative measures. They even held the position that no counter measures would be launched even if the target materialized.

That disturbed Cross. He thought it sounded too much like Pearl Harbor. Roosevelt knew the attack would happen, but didn't do anything to thwart it. Cross figured the country had learned a lesson from its mistakes and dismissed the likelihood it would happen.

As the months passed, FBI sources had dried up. With summer ending, Cross pushed the possibility of an attack to the back of his mind. He concentrated on having a leisurely Labor Day with Sol and Mitzi Abrams. They wanted him to bring Lori, but Cross could not bring himself to call her. Even though he had a good time with Abrams, Cross felt the need to be alone. Leaving the party early, he went home and headed for bed.

He fell asleep quickly. His dreams were uneventful. Awakening at 5 a.m., Cross was in no hurry to get up. He rolled over and went back to sleep. Within a few minutes, he was dreaming, but the dream seemed so bright and real, he felt as if he were awake.

Cross saw himself watching television. The news was on and the lead story was about a terrorist attack in Washington D.C. He awoke abruptly, certain the dream was his subconscious working with his research and his suspicions.

He got up and put on the coffee and sorted through his thoughts. Cross ran the possibilities through his head and all the what-if's he could conjure. There was a nagging feeling in his stomach that wouldn't leave. By the end of the week, the feeling had become part of him.

Cross called Klebbans to see if he had heard anything new. Klebbans was still sure that America would be attacked. Kicking around a few ideas, Cross decided to hop on a plane and fly to D.C. for the weekend. He made arrangements to speak with a friend at the FBI. Cross told the agent that he had a source that was completely sure of a pending attack. The agent kept a poker face throughout the interview. He wrote down notes and insisted Cross tell him the name of his source. Cross declined. Uncertain if the agent believed him or not, Cross did his best to push the information and to push the agent to see if he could find out anything. He couldn't.

Cross beat the bushes in the District for any information. He was coming up blank. Heading back to New York on a red-eye, he busied himself with his work. He worked through the night and finally went to bed around 7 a.m. He had the dream about Washington being hit. Again, he saw himself sitting in front of the television. This time, the phone rang in his dream. It was Sol Abrams. He asked him if he had heard the news about the missing plane. The phone kept ringing and Cross awoke to the harsh ringing of the phone beside his head.

"Yeah," he mumbled in a fog.

"Mike, did you hear the news? Jesus, it's horrible! The World Trade Center's been hit by two planes."

"What? Was it an accident?"

"Turn on the television, Mike."

Cross hit the remote and the television came on just as the first tower collapsed.

"Oh my God! Sol, I'll call you back." He hastily dressed and left for the scene. The car radio blared the news that the Pentagon had just been hit.

"Where's the freaking Air Force," Cross yelled as he hurried to the site. Then the newscaster mentioned there was a missing plane that was thought to be over Pennsylvania.

"Jesus, Klebbans was right." He hated the feeling he had. Cross thought about the White House and other key sites throughout the country. He contemplated about how many other planes might be involved and didn't like the fear he felt. Cross could not get very close to the Trade Centers. The smoke could be seen for miles. He found a place to park and ran thirty blocks. By the time he got within a couple of blocks, he realized that both towers had collapsed. It was beyond comprehension.

F-16's flew overhead making reality even harder to grasp. Cross went to work getting eyewitness accounts, and trying to piece together the events. The news desk at The Wire informed Cross that the missing plane was found in a field in Pennsylvania. It had augured in and there were no survivors.

The attack held the media's attention for weeks. Although the country pulled together, Cross worried about future attacks from the Russians or the Chinese. The visionaries told him that more attacks were likely, but the country had made great strides in remembering God in their lives.

A new spiritual movement was obvious. Churches and synagogues filled along with the mosques. America had a different look, more patriotic and cohesive than it had been since the short-lived Gulf War. When his boss asked him to go to Afghanistan, Cross agreed without reservation. He had old contacts there and he wanted the opportunity to see what was really happening on the war front.

Upon his arrival, Cross wasted no time in interviewing United States Marines. He learned disturbing details about some members of the Taliban who were successful in terrorizing the entire area without a shot being fired.

One marine was happy to talk with Cross. Strange incidents had bothered most of the Marines there and he wanted Cross to know. Ted Smith was a freckled faced man from Texas. He had baby blue eyes and a good start on a wiry red beard.

"Sergeant Smith, what happened to Mullah Omar? He was being held by the Northern Alliance, right?"

"Yes, sir. He, uh, disappeared, sir, and the search is underway for him now."

"Did he have help in his escape?"

"Not exactly, sir. You see he just disappeared into thin air."

"He couldn't have just evaporated, Sergeant. Did someone help him? Did he overpower the guards?" Cross set his jaw; sure that incompetence was the reason they lost him.

"No, sir. I was there. He just freaking disappeared. It scared the shit out of all of us. There's a lot of that mojo going on here. We're having trouble with the Northern Alliance boys because we've had equipment, planes, helos and jeeps and other shit spontaneously combust."

Cross thought Smith was being straight with him even though it sounded bizarre.

"We've had Alliance guys quitting and heading back to the mountains. Some of the Taliban people are doing crazy stuff. They're creepin' everyone out. I don't know if it is some magic these guys learn or what, but it's some scary shit.

"You can be interrogating them and all of a sudden, flames will come spurting out of their mouths. Omar had a whole bag of tricks that freaked everyone out. The Northern Alliance guys said if he hadn't disappeared, they would have let him go."

"Why? He's second to Bin Laden. Why would they do that?" Cross knew the Afghans were emotional people, but he could not understand this, not after the Taliban abused the whole country.

"People were dropping dead when they got near the guy. I ain't kidding you. If you ask me, Omar should have been killed on the spot, except some of the men thought the bullets would pass right through him, and he'd still be alive. He's got some kind of power."

"I appreciate your talking with me, Sergeant Smith."

"Yes, sir. I just don't want the folks at home to think we just let the guy go. Just don't give out my name. I'd be hosed with the Captain if he found out I said something."

"Understood. Thanks." Cross shook his hand and continued interviewing Marines and Northern Alliance troops and came up with the same story. To him, Omar and the other Taliban officials had similar capabilities as William Mann.

The primary goal of the war effort, at least as far as the Pentagon portrayed, was the destruction of the Taliban and the capture of Bin Laden. For the most part, the end of the Taliban had come quickly, but the capture of Bin Laden and the round up of other Al Qaeda members was slow. After two months in Afghanistan, Cross headed home.

There was something that bothered him about the war. He wasn't sure if it was going to distract us from other attacks. Cross knew the world was on the brink of World War III. For the first time, he understood the third world war would not be caused by a knee jerk reaction resulting in nuclear retaliation, but rather it would have a cancerous effect that would metastasize to every country on the globe. He remembered being shown dozens of mushroom clouds rising above the earth. He also recalled the overwhelming sadness he felt at seeing all out global nuclear annihilation.

The Middle East had grown even more violent with rising casualties. Sooner or later, one rogue country or group would raise the stakes so high; there would be no turning back.

Cross' return to the States drove home the economic impact of the September 11th attacks. The airline industry was nearly asphyxiated. He understood the reluctance of people to fly. His economic sources told him that the United States would be lucky if it pulled out of its downhill spiral. The stock market was more volatile than nitroglycerin. More large companies were calling it quits when they couldn't arrange lifesaving mergers.

One major company in Houston, The Energy for Tomorrow Group, had unraveled, revealing a façade built on shady deals and questionable trading with senators, congressmen and presidents right in the middle. Cross was happy to get off the war beat for a while and sink his teeth into some real Texas barbeque.

Before he got really involved, he was notified about a command performance with the FBI. He had missed their last invitation when he left for Afghanistan. Now the Bureau wanted to question him not only about his sources, but his investigation. The three-hour session produced nothing new for the FBI and gave Cross a headache. His picture was taken and added to the new international database on terror. In a strange way, Cross felt rather honored by it all, but was angry that his own country would bring him in for questioning when the real criminals were still at large.

Cross made it to Texas in time to uncover important financial discrepancies and the revelation of Hawthorne and Macon as partners in overseas operations. Their unlikely partner was Osama Bin Laden's family. Cross felt like he had to pinch himself regularly to make sure he wasn't dreaming, even though at times he wished he were.

From what he could piece together, it appeared that Hawthorne, Macon and Hawthorne's son were all part of the global meltdown. He knew it would take years of investigations and senate committees to get to the bottom of it. The problem for Cross was to anticipate future moves and to uncover plans before they were shoved down people's throats.

Those who opposed the powers-that-be, such as ranking congressmen and senators, found surprises in their mailboxes. Anthrax letters became a weapon of homegrown terrorists. Innocent postal workers died after handling the mail. The media wasn't excluded from harm. Several people at the major networks were placed on high-powered antibiotics after opening letters containing anthrax spores.

Cross was careless opening his mail and ripped open a letter. The telltale powder along with a threatening letter greeted him on a Monday morning, spoiling the rest of the week. He was lucky. The letter contained anthrax, but he acquired only skin anthrax and a couple of lesions appeared on his arm. After surviving flu-like symptoms and a precautionary course of antibiotics, he was fine. Yet the threatening letter failed to silence him. Instead, he made it his business to find out who was behind it. The media fed the public an ever-increasing list of possibilities, trying to force public attention on Iraq as the likely culprit. It had moderate success. Everyone knew that President Hawthorne would move the war to Iraq after he was finished in Afghanistan. The media blitz was used to open the minds of Americans in hopes of having them get behind the expanded war effort.

Cross did some hard-core investigating and discovered the anthrax used in the letters was not the kind of anthrax used by the Iraqis. It was grown in the United States. He thought he found a possible suspect.

A friend of his gave him a lead about a doctor in New England who was instrumental in developing an anthrax vaccine. Doctor Nathan Thomas had a vested interest in an anthrax scare. Not only had Thomas developed the vaccine, but he also had controlling interest in the laboratory that produced it. Curiously, Cross found out that the Bin Laden family also had an interest in it.

The FBI eventually admitted that the letter terrorist was probably an American. But before the investigation produced a suspect, doctors who were involved with BioWarfare projects and contagious diseases, started to disappear. Cross volunteered to follow the story since it was relatively connected with the anthrax letters.

He uncovered a multitude of disappearances. One doctor decided to take a middle of the night plunge off a bridge in Tennessee. Another doctor who was an expert on smallpox had his head beaten in by supposed muggers. Two others died at a Texas Army base. Yet another doctor moved his family in the middle of the night and was never seen again.

Cross anticipated a serious biological attack upon the United States because so many key researchers had been removed. America was now extremely vulnerable and without the best and the brightest, the likelihood of an enormous death toll seemed imminent.

His sources agreed, as did the visionaries with whom he spoke. Cross sorely missed Father Cavanaugh and his great intellect and abilities. His absence made Cross' work all the more difficult. Other problems arose that Cross could not explain.

He found himself sidelined from his work by an immense fatigue. At first he thought he had a reoccurrence of mononucleosis. However, all the lab tests came back negative. There were days when he would try to work but couldn't lift his head from his pillow. He tried vitamins and supplements, but the only impact they had was on his bank account. It wasn't until he received a return email from one of Father Cavanaugh's friends that he understood what was happening to him.

Albert Alphonso was on Cavanaugh's exorcism team and had extraordinary abilities like Father Cavanaugh. After Cross emailed him, Albert was able to detect that something was off with Cross. They set up a meeting to discuss the problem. Cross was not sure he wanted to know what the problem was, but without help, he could not work.

Albert arrived at Cross' home and immediately sensed a problem.

"Come on in and sit down, Albert."

"If you don't mind, Mike, I'd like to walk around a bit, sort of get the feel for the place. You work out of your home a lot, right?"

"Yes. How did you know?"

"I can tell because you've got some really pissed off spirits in your house."

"Great." Cross was not sure about Albert. He knew he had to be all right if he worked with Cavanaugh, but he was not sure about the spirits. He didn't really want to be sure.

"What happens to you when you try to work?"

"If I even think about working, I am suddenly exhausted, so exhausted I have to sleep."

"Uh-huh. Ever get sick to your stomach?"

"Sure. Why?"

"That's part of it." Albert's black eyes twinkled. He walked through the house and then sat down with Cross in the living room.

"I think you got yourself a bit of a demon problem. We can handle it for the most part."

"For the most part?"

"Yeah. Sometimes they change their M.O. If they can't get to you one way, they'll find another. So you gotta cut 'em off at the proverbial pass. Sooner or later they'll give up. Of course, they could always send in the bigger demons."

"Don't even go there, Albert."

"Know what you mean, Mike. But you do want to function, right?"

"Right."

"You don't want to drop what you're doing, right?"

"Right again."

"Well, then let's work at building up your defenses. Got a rosary?"

"Uh, somewhere."

"Find it. Better yet, I'll give you mine. Use it. It's a great defense against the demons."

"Okay."

"Second, I want you to use holy water all around the house and I want you to build a wall around yourself when the fatigue sets in."

"How do I do that?"

Albert wrinkled his forehead, which pushed back a large mop of black curly hair.

"Sprinkle holy water around you and say the St. Michael exorcism prayer. You know that?"

"I've got it written down somewhere. Father Cavanaugh gave it to me."

"Great. That should help."

"Thanks, Albert. I'll try it."

Albert looked at Cross and wondered if Cross would ever try it.

"Let's do it right now."

Albert took out a bottle of holy water, sprinkled the entire house, and then gave it to Cross. They made the sign of the cross. Albert then read the exorcism prayer. Cross felt better immediately.

"Man, I can't believe it. I feel better. Thanks, Albert."

"Hey, no problem. If you ever need help, just give me a call."

"Will do, Albert. So how long have you been involved with exorcisms?"

"About eight years."

"I admire you. I don't have that kind of guts.

"Mike, I'm the most scared guy I know. Hey, one other thing. I think you should buy a dog, maybe a German shepherd."

"Why?"

"Dogs can let you know when the demons surface. They're very helpful. And dogs can't be possessed as easily as cats."

"That's encouraging."

"I was on this case once, when a three pound cat held the entire family captive after it was taken over by a demon. Its eyes got all red and that dinky cat actually cornered the whole family. The guy that this happened to was a cop and he used his pepper spray on the cat, but the cat kept coming."

"I think I'd have shot the damn thing."

"The cat was part of the family and they couldn't bring themselves to do it. So the guy got away from the cat and called me. I went right over and exorcised the whole freaking house. Lemme tell you, that as one bad ass cat."

"Did you kill the cat?"

"Hell no. We slapped a St. Benedict medal on her. That took care of it. If you want some company picking out a dog, I'd be glad to tag along. I got kind of a gift."

"Sure. I'm gonna have to think about it. I travel a lot."

"I could dog sit for you, no problem."

"Okay, thanks. Do you do this stuff full time?" Cross was taking a liking to Albert.

"Well, there's enough need to do it full time. I'm a firefighter though."

"Somehow that seems appropriate."

Chapter Twenty-Two

Cross thought a great deal about getting a dog. Two weeks later, he called Albert and they went looking for a suitable canine.

"You know it can't just be any kind of dog," explained Albert, as he drove Cross to a friend's house.

"Aren't they all pretty much the same?"

"There are dogs and then there are dogs. Some dogs are more spiritual than others."

Now Cross was puzzled and he started to wonder again about Albert.

"How can a dog be spiritual," he asked.

"Some dogs have the ability to see through the veil. They can see what we can't. For instance, ever see something outta the corner of your eye and when you turn you head it's gone?"

"Yeah. Actually I've been seeing more of that lately. I've even seen this cat like shape in the house."

"Not since the exorcism, I hope."

"Come to think of it, no."

"Good. Anyways, certain dogs have gifts, just like people do. My friend, Timmy, has a year old German shepherd who is very in tuned with the spirit world. I thought you could take a look at him. If you guys hit it off, I'm sure he could help you."

They pulled into the driveway of an older two-story stucco house and walked to the back yard. Timothy Ryan was waiting for them. His daughter was playing with a massive dog.

"Hey, Timmy. I brought Mike Cross over to take a look at Buster."

"Mike, nice to meet yous. T.J. Ryan."

"Same here. This the dog?"

Cross looked the dog over. He had a smoky black face and beautiful eyes with an intelligent look out of them. His ears were quite large. The silver and black dog made quite an impression on Cross.

"Yes. He's really a neat dog. Come here, Buster."

The dog ran over to Tim and sat at his feet.

"He's a beaut," said Cross. He patted Buster on his head and the dog took a quick liking to him.

"Why do you want to get rid of such a great dog," asked Cross.

Tim Ryan grinned. "My wife's pregnant with our fourth and Buster's mother is due any day."

Cross fell in love with the overgrown puppy. "How much do you want for him," asked Albert.

"Two hundred. He's papered."

"I don't care about the papers. The dog can't read or can he," Cross quipped.

"Not yet," Tim said.

Cross gladly paid Tim for the dog and got all of his toys and a lead. Albert put a St. Benedict medal on Buster's collar before driving away. Buster sat proudly behind Cross. Within a block, Buster perched his head on Cross' shoulder and licked his face. Cross was surprised at the void the dog filled.

Buster went everywhere with him. They really became inseparable. Albert had become a good friend too. Cross learned a great deal about how spirits work and how they infiltrate people's lives. Albert made the priest's absence much easier to take. He was right about Buster, and that meant a great deal to Cross.

One evening, Cross was home working on a story. Buster seemed quite restless, so Cross grabbed his frisbee and took the dog out for some exercise. Normally, Buster would play catch for hours, chasing the frisbee wherever it was thrown. This evening Buster had something bothering him. Cross brought him back inside and the dog seemed to feel better. A few hours elapsed. Cross was ready for bed. He tried to let Buster out for a few minutes, but the dog wouldn't go. Sensing there might be something in the house bugging the dog, Cross sprayed holy water throughout the home.

He changed and got into bed. Cross patted the bed and Buster willingly go on it and made himself comfortable. Not feeling like reading or watching television, Cross turned out the light. He stroked Buster's head a while and drifted off to sleep.

Buster started whining and jumped down from the bed. He kept it up until Cross awoke.

"I told you. You should have gone outside when you had the chance. You got the bladder of a middle-aged man. I know. I know. I should talk."

The dog whined in earnest. "Okay, pal. Let's go out."

They walked to the front door. Cross opened it and held open the screen. "There you go, Bus." Buster refused to move. "What do you want, boy? You want me to go out with you?"

Cross grabbed the lead and attached it to Buster's collar. He started to go out, but Buster gently took Cross' hand in his mouth and pulled him back inside. Then he started barking incessantly.

It did not take long for Cross to find out the problem. The house started to shake, mildly at first and then violently. Pictures crashed to the floor. Lamps fell over and furniture started to dance around the house. Cross saw his computer jumping all over the top of his desk. He ran for the monitor, but couldn't make it in time. It crashed to the floor and shattered.

"Come on, Buster," he yelled. He ran into the bathroom and Buster willingly followed. Cross picked up the dog and stood in the doorway, hoping they would be safe.

New York had smaller tremors before, but nothing like this. Cross thought about how widespread the damage would be. When the rumbling and shaking subsided, Cross wished he had a cigarette. He put Buster down and went to check on the damage.

The computer was a total loss. The house weathered the quake fairly well, but most of the dishes were in pieces on the kitchen floor.

He went into the bedroom to check on the television. It survived. Flipping on the set, Cross looked out the window. The street was a mess. It looked like a giant can opener had cut a mammoth crack in the pavement.

Water mains were broken and he saw a fire in the middle of the street where a gas line had severed. A tall menacing pillar of flames shot into the night sky.

The television had nothing but white noise covering the screen. Cross shut it off and turned on his radio. Buster came and sat next to him, forcibly putting his head under Cross' hand. He needed reassuring and so did Cross.

Remarkably, WABC was still on the air. The news wasn't good. Early reports estimated the quake at +7.2 on the Richter scale. One reporter said that many of the older buildings in the city had collapsed. Cross remembered a report The Times ran several years ago suggesting the older buildings would never survive a moderate quake due to the lack of proper maintenance and renovations. The

preliminary death toll was high, but more accurate reports
had to wait until daylight.

The morning came and with it the horrifying realization
that the great city was in ruins. Wall Street had serious
damage. It would take some time for the markets to reopen.
Older apartment houses in the city were in piles of
smoldering bricks. Countless people had died. It would be
weeks before city officials would know the true number of
casualties.

The skyline altered by the attack on the World Trade
Center was now completely unrecognizable. President
Hawthorne declared New York City a federal disaster area.
The governor called out the National Guard, which was
quickly dispatched around the Federal Reserve.

Streets were impassible and rescue crews were thwarted
in their attempts to give aid. Cross did what he could to
report on the disaster. The shock of what happened was
etched into the eyes of the survivors. He came across
screaming people desperately digging in the rubble for their
loved ones.

There were also concerns about a tidal wave, but those
concerns were alleviated with the passing of time.
Everyone knew if the wave hit, there would be little or no
hope of survival. Churches filled and endless prayers were
offered.

The Coast Guard and the Navy were dispatched in force
to guard the coastline and the boundary waters. The city
and the outlying areas were in controlled chaos.

Two of the three major networks were down.
Washington Bureau Chiefs took to the air to report the
news. The rest of the country listened in disbelief, much as
it had with the World Trade Center attacks.

The president cautioned Americans not to panic, that
things were under control, especially in the financial

district. He warned America's enemies not to make a move against the country.

Abroad, financial experts speculated about how bad things would get. Although the United States government was doing all that it could to reopen the markets, it did little to eliminate fears overseas.

The Japanese markets crashed. Experts attributed the sell-off to the fact that Japanese investors owned many of Manhattan's buildings. The ripple effect washed over the remainder of the world's markets, drowning them in hysteria and eventually in all out panic.

A global meeting was convened for world leaders to discuss their options, while New Yorkers valiantly cleaned up the city and buried the dead. Observers decided that the quake was far worse than the 1906 shaker, which leveled San Francisco.

Wall Street limped back to life and with the help of the government and patriotic investors, managed to establish some normalcy. Yet, the definition of normalcy was permanently altered.

Even after positive steps were taken in the weeks after the killer quake, Cross began to take seriously the admonitions visionaries had given about New York City. He also paid attention to the messages calling for people to move into more rural areas before the arrival of the Great Warning.

Cross didn't want to abandon New York City, but decided to compromise. He bought some land upstate and spent weekends there with Buster. It took some getting used to before Cross could appreciate the stillness and the peace. The lack of car horns, sirens and mobs of people was quite an adjustment, but one he knew he would come to love. He chastised himself for not doing it sooner. Buster thrived roaming the acreage. Cross was happy to see him run free.

There was a lot of work to do to make the farm truly self-sufficient. Little by little, one acre at a time, Cross managed to turn the place into an efficient refuge. He converted electrical well pumps to hand pumps and added windmills, because he wanted to be sure the horses he acquired would have plenty to drink in case of power outages.

Cross started stocking the farm with extra canned food, but made sure to keep it hidden. The Attorney General had mandated that it was against the law to store more than a thirty-day supply of food. He purchased a year's worth, knowing he would probably need every bit of it after the warning.

He bought two one thousand gallon propane tanks and installed a wood-burning stove in the house. His weekends were spent chopping and stacking wood, and then tending to an extensive herb garden. Annie had always wanted one and he put the garden in for her. He was sorry she couldn't share in it, but he was grateful she didn't live to see all that happened.

Cross kept quiet about his retreat, keeping it all for himself. He had become fairly well known and really needed a place to escape. A place untouched and unvisited.

He cherished his solitary life even more when the rest of the country went into convulsions.

California

On a bright morning, the freeways were clogged with commuters trying to get to work on time. A little after seven, a severe rumbling started and then stopped. Everyone took a deep breath. Then an even sharper tremor struck fear into nearly everyone's heart. Seasoned pros grew pale as they felt the pavement give way under their feet.

Freeway bridges all over Los Angeles crumbled to the ground. Ghastly craters opened in the earth, devouring everything on the surface. It appeared like a monster awoke, angry and hungry after a long slumber. Cars and trucks disappeared into the great expanses that opened as the Big One said good morning.

Studios in Burbank came crashing down, igniting into the worst pyre in history. Stars fell dead, hitting the ground. Their bodies rested next to the nobodies, equal at last. Some people tried to run, but their hearts betrayed them. All the special effects in Hollywood could not prepare them for that morning.

Tens of thousands of homes were lost. The Hollywood hills began to crumble like squashed paper mache. Power lines fell tying up the roadways with sparks and live hissing wires moving with abandon.

As the tremor progressed, the observatory at Griffith Park disintegrated. The seismograph needle went off the chart. Terrified people on Hollywood Boulevard looked at the swaying hills and saw the giant Hollywood sign fall into the canyon.

At Los Angeles International Airport, the runways split in two and some of them were pushed into the ocean by an incredible tremor. There seemed to be one quake right after another. They progressed all the way up the coast to Canada and down to Mexico. By the time the earthquake subsided, two thirds of the Pacific coast was gone.

The captain of a Russian sub watched as the shoreline he knew so well disappeared. The ocean got rough and the submarine had to dive. Massive waves swelled and headed for UCLA, which was now on the waterfront.

At airbases all over southern California, pilots scrambled to get the planes in the air. Most of them never made it. By noon, it was estimated that at least two million people were dead or missing. Police feared the number would triple. People who could travel packed their cars and tried to head east. Nearly every road leading from Los Angeles was heavily damaged. Bumper to bumper traffic snaked out of the valley for a hundred miles.

The waves rolled over the dregs of the coastal area drowning everything. The news the next morning was anchored by beleaguered newscasters who tried to explain to the rest of the nation that the West coast was just about gone.

The president had to deal with the worst disasters in American history. No one had ever dealt with the kind of devastation that was seen. The Coast Guard was put to work immediately checking chunks of land that were taken out to sea in hopes of finding survivors. Only three people were found.

As Cross watched the news with the rest of America, he sat shell-shocked at the enormity of it all. Fears arose about national security. Chinese and Russian ships were swarming within one hundred miles of the coasts. A Pentagon analyst was interviewed about the military's position when a special bulletin cut into the segment.

The New Madrid fault line had a tremendous earthquake ripping through the entire Mississippi River valley. The damage was astronomical. The military stayed at DefCon 7 and Americans started to panic.

Only the dead slept. Grocery stores were mobbed with buyers and gun sales broke every known record. The government established a moratorium on sales, further upsetting the populace.

President Hawthorne was ready to put the country under martial law, but some members of his cabinet persuaded him to wait, not wanting the militias to go on the defensive.

Cross checked with visionaries who confirmed this was merely the beginning of a seemingly endless nightmare. He felt helpless. Somehow he had to prepare people, but he didn't know where to start. Most people had no idea of what was to come.

Darkness descended on Italy. Mount Vesuvius erupted, destroying everything within a four-mile radius. The rest of the country was smothered with ashes.

Violence erupted was well, especially in Rome. The Communist party staged rallies and stormed government offices. There were Muslim demonstrations as well and the two sides would often clash. They had a common enemy, the Church, and eventually they joined forces to go after Christians. Working on a plan, both sides knew that in a few short months the destruction of the Vatican would be possible.

Chapter Twenty-Three

Michael Cross volunteered for the Rome assignment so that he could stay on top of the situation, while keeping an eye on Joe. Even though there was chaos all over Italy, there was still peace inside the Vatican. However, Cross readily detected uneasiness within the corridors. Joe was obviously distracted.

"Joe, how does the Swiss Guard intend to hold back the Muslims and Communists?"

"Through prayer, but eventually all of this well be destroyed."

"Is the pope getting ready to flee?"

"This has to stay between the two of us, Dad."

"Sure."

"We are making plans for the Holy Father to leave. There have been contingency plans in the works for years."

Cross looked at Joe carefully. "Are you going with him?"

"Yes. But I don't want you to worry."

"What, me worry?"

Joe grinned at his father.

"Okay. I'll try not to. Where will you go?"

"We've got a couple of places. One is in France and the other is in Canada. The pope considered going to Poland, but thought against it in the end. We're waiting for the

Great Monarch to take power to fight off the revolutionaries."

"Whoa. The Great Monarch? Seems to me I've read about him in something, but I don't know."

"Yes. He's in a lot of prophecies involving the end times."

"Who is he?"

"I'm not a liberty to say. But he's waiting in the wings and is a major player for our side. All I can say is that he's of royal French descent and his reign is in the near future."

"What's his name?"

"You know I can't tell you that."

"How will I know him?"

"You'll know him by his actions. In time, you won't be able to miss him. Now then, how are things back home?"

Joe watched his father. Cross met his gaze. He was so proud of his son, but he worried about the stress Joe carried with him.

"Unrecognizable in many ways."

"The news reports have been appalling. You do know that there's more to come?"

"Yeah." Cross did not want to deal with it. "Let's not go there. I want to enjoy this time together."

Joe nodded. He understood how much the world had changed. It was all in his father's eyes. The two spent the day together and enjoyed a quiet dinner. They reminisced about their lives and left the future alone.

The rest of Europe seemed to be dancing on a floor just about ready to collapse. Dissidents wreaked havoc and had become the brokers of death. The economy wilted. Countries scurried to build up the European Union Army and increase the number of troops within their own borders.

Russia led the way in military spending and expansion, fueling fears not only on the continent, but in the United States as well. President Hawthorne finally acknowledged that Russia had designs on the free world, and on America in particular. Frequently, relations between the two countries disintegrated to the point of war. Hawthorne wasn't sure how much longer it would be before China or Russia launched a strike.

Intelligence reports indicated that Russia was anything but changed. Hawthorne wondered if he had been double-crossed. The New World Order was something with which he could easily live, but not a Russian domination of freedom as he saw it, especially his.

Makarov tried to calm Hawthorne, instead focusing the president's attention towards what he deemed positive global issues. Some cabinet members were getting uncomfortable. The role-playing constricted their style.

The Secretary of State and some of Hawthorne's people held a late night meeting. Everyone came to the same conclusion. It was time to act. There were enough terrorist problems to provide a fitting scapegoat.

President Hawthorne and his wife were scheduled to appear in Chicago for meetings with business leaders from all over the country. The downtown streets were packed with people who wanted to catch a glimpse of the presidential motorcade and hopefully, the president.

The motorcade turned onto East Monroe and stopped in front of the Palmer House Hilton. The crowd cheered as the president and his wife got out of their limo. The couple waved to the crowd and went over to shake the hands of the people near the hotel entrance.

The Secret Service did their best to scrutinize the crowd. It was a bright, gorgeous day and not too windy. Everyone was upbeat.

Suddenly, several people tossed hand grenades in the president's direction. They all exploded simultaneously. Windows shattered and poured on what was left of the crowd. The president, his wife and scores of others were blown to pieces. The country was on the verge of coming apart.

The vice president was in Washington when he got the news about Hawthorne. The Chief Justice was summoned to swear in Thomas Hart. All eyes were on the next president and his health. While waiting for the Chief Justice, Hart started to perspire heavily. He blotted his head with his handkerchief and did his best to direct the cabinet to find a way to keep order in the country.

By the time the Chief Justice arrived, Hart was looking a little gray. He hurried to the oval office to be sworn in as president. His wife shakily held a bible. Hart placed his left hand on the book and raised his right hand.

The Chief Justice hadn't even begun the oath when Hart hit the floor dead. It was a public relations nightmare. When Michael Cross heard the news, he boarded a flight home.

He wondered if there was a power play in the works. Despite the fact American Muslims were accused of killing Hawthorne, something did not feel right to Cross. Everyone knew how bad Thomas Hart's health was. An assassination was almost a perfect guarantee that Hart would blow a gasket.

Cross began to look at the Speaker of the House for the first time. He had to learn if there were any connections to the New World Order group or the Trilateralists. There were, plenty of them. Speaker Ernest Powers was close friends with George Hawthorne and was on the Trilateral short list for president.

There was a quiet speculation that the hit on President J.R. Hawthorne was a coup d'etat. Cross set out to prove it and in doing so ended up on the government's short list.

He was careful about pointing fingers, but he pointed them anyway. Cross had gotten better at the fine art of criticism, avoiding being too much of a dissenter. The life expectancy of dissenters had decreased sharply in the past few years. It really did not matter to Cross. He had a fatalistic view of life anyway.

After weeks of investigating Hawthorne's assassination, Cross was able to discern that the president was killed in part to push the war against terrorism to another level, a view totally dissimilar to the FBI's explanation of events.

The New World Order faction needed the escalation of wars around the world in order to introduce the World Teacher, the consummate peacemaker.

President Powers wasted no time in intensifying the war in the Middle East. Libya, Iran and Iraq were primary targets, but the Muslims in the Philippines were also targeted. The Secretary of Defense also put North Korea on the hit list supposedly out of fear of their nuclear capabilities and the detestation of the United States.

The Honorable Abdul Mohammed, America's foremost Muslim leader pushed his organization into battle. Unexpectedly, American soldiers were fighting Americans on the streets of Chicago and in other major cities. Battle lines were drawn as Black America awoke and went on the offensive. The riots that ensued were far worse than anything experienced in the 1960's. Unfortunately, the Ku Klux Klan didn't remain in the background for long. Legions of Klansmen were dispatched throughout the country to fight and to kill their enemies.

Soon, it didn't matter whether blacks were Muslims or not. They united as a solid front, a fear-aggressive alliance against white America. The Army National Guard had a terrible time of restoring peace. Once one city gained control, another would explode into violence.

Martial law was imposed. People in the major metropolises were somewhat relieved, at least at first. When the National ID cards were issued, people everywhere began to appreciate their lost freedom. Militia members hurried to recapture their losses.

Checkpoints sprouted throughout the country. It was no longer possible to drive from one city to another without having to stop at security posts. America looked like Nazi Germany. In order to gain control, Congress hurriedly passed gun control laws. Civilians were no longer allowed to own firearms of any kind.

Anyone caught with a weapon was immediately arrested. Many people were killed. Thousands of people protested the gun confiscation and died as a result. People hid as many arms as they could, but random searches harvested a whole new crop of homegrown terrorists. All laws that protected the average citizen were suspended in the name of national security.

All police departments in the country were nationalized. The Federal government governed each department like a queen bee. Local laws were abolished. Cross was shocked by how quickly Americans handed over their lives and what was left of their freedoms. Several members of the press publicly criticized the moves on other parts of the government. They were only allowed to continue to give some semblance of freedom of speech.

Roundups occurred on a daily basis. Some of the detention centers were already in use. The mainstream press sold the New World Order line and Americans swallowed it like ambrosia.

With life disintegrating, many people began to think the rapture would occur at any moment. Each deteriorating condition was seen as the ultimate signal they would be caught up in the rapture and taken away from the turmoil. Rapture enthusiasts began to sell or give away their things fully expecting never to need them.

In some circles, the rapture and its due date were the only things discussed. Cross was puzzled by the concept and tried to find out more about it. He had never been taught about the rapture in Catholic school. He did find that Veronica Lueken had mentioned it, but there wasn't enough information to suit him. After bringing it up to Albert Alphonso, Cross was sent to meet with a Jesuit in Detroit who had been friends with Father Cavanaugh.

Father Tobias Gainer was a pugnacious priest who took his faith very seriously. Gainer was a bit of an oddity in his firm belief in Fatima and other apparitions. He was only too happy to visit with Cross. Gainer and the rapture were the subjects of a piece Cross started. The idea of the rapture wouldn't let go of him.

"Father, what is the real story on the rapture?"

Gainer smiled broadly at Cross and ran his fingers through his long gray beard.

"It is something that has divided Catholics and Protestants for a very long time. Essentially, the Catholic Church dropped the teachings of the rapture. That's why most Catholics have never even heard of it."

"Then it is something that is going to happen for sure?"

"Yes, but I believe it will be different in how it transpires compared to the Protestant viewpoint.

"How so?" It did not take Cross long to get enthused about the prospects of a rapture. Life was becoming unbearable for most people. The idea of the rapture glistened with hope.

"First, Catholics believe we have to die to go to heaven, just as Our Lord died. That is why some theologians discounted the idea of the rapture. You see most of the Protestant world believes they will be taken up to heaven when they hear Jesus' voice. We believe that people will be gathered and taken to paradise, not heaven, to await the Reign of Peace."

"I've heard of the Reign, but I thought paradise was on earth."

"On the contrary. It is near the earth, though. Paradise was believed to have been raised from the surface of the earth because God preserved it from the great flood. Enoch and Elias are there, waiting for their time to fulfill prophecy."

"And they are?" Cross hated to feel stupid.

"Old Testament prophets. Ever hear the story about Elias going up into the heavens in a fiery chariot?"

"Sure."

"Well, he and Enoch are there in paradise."

Now Cross' brain was spinning in place.

"But that would mean they are thousands of years old."

"Yes. But God can preserve anyone's life. Now back to the rapture. It will happen, but not in one giant evacuation."

"How do you see it?"

"I expect the rapture will begin in earnest near the time of the Great Miracle."

"At Garabandal."

"Precisely. As we go through these despicable years, our souls are being cleansed, thus clearing the way for the rapture. The more one offers up, the sooner the person will be raptured."

"Then it's on an individual basis and not on a grand scale."

"More or less. There will be a significant number of people raptured after the Miracle, which will seem like a great harvesting of souls."

"Sounds like it will be hard to explain why so many people disappeared."

"Yes. We'll no doubt hear that they have been snatched away by aliens and carted off in their ships. Don't get me started on that."

Cross laughed. "Okay, Father. Going back to Enoch and Elias. What are they going to be doing when they return?"

"Primarily, their job is to preach to the Jews and to convert them. That won't be an easy task." Father Gainer took a sizable swallow of water and continued to pull on his beard. Cross watched him. Gainer sensed it and folded his arms.

"That's a bad habit, I'm afraid," Gainer chuckled. Cross joined him.

"Where were we? Oh, yes. Enoch and Elias will do battle with the antichrist, but not before they perform many miracles. Ultimately, they will be stoned to death. Their bodies will be left on a Jerusalem street for three days. On the third day, they will rise from the dead, not only confounding the antichrist, but influencing thousands of conversions."

Cross was amazed. "When do you think they will arrive?" Cross felt like a small boy caught up in a marvelous bedtime story.

"I expect they will be here after the warning."

"How long will they be here?"

"About three years, give or take. Time will be shortened because if it weren't, there would be no believers left."

Life was so much of a struggle now, Cross could not imagine how things would be when it got worse.

"Father, do you think the warning is due?"

"Look at what's happening all over, but especially in Rome. The Holy Father is getting ready to abandon the Vatican."

"My son is his aide. He said they'd be leaving quite soon."

"I will pray for him."

"Thanks, Father." Cross had not allowed himself to think about the risks Joe faced with the Holy Father, but he understood how poor Joe's chances were.

"Wouldn't the consecration of Russia stop this?"

"Certainly. But at this point, we can only pray that happens and then there are those who believe we are doomed because it didn't happen in 1960."

The interview with Father Gainer was a popular piece and Cross wrote several follow-up articles. He stayed busy, but longed to see his son. Joe told him not to attempt to travel to Rome. Things were in such an uproar that it was unsafe for anyone. They stayed in touch by phone. The last conversation they had left Cross with a terrible uneasy feeling. Joe sounded like he was saying goodbye. He talked with his dad about every little thing. Joe stayed upbeat until he hung up the phone. Cross was not sure there was a problem.

They hadn't discussed the pope going into exile. Both men limited their conversations to the present. Tomorrow, if it arrived, would be handled.

By that evening, Cross felt sure the pope would leave Rome shortly. Wherever the pope would end up, Cross knew the location would never be disclosed. Joe had promised to remain in exile with the pontiff no matter what the outcome. Cross was proud of his son, but the worry over his future continued to grow.

Back At The Lourdes Gardens At The Vatican

As the fires in Rome burned, Makarov and the Cardinals finished their conversation.

Cardinal Cantore finished his protracted story on Michael Cross' life, pleasing his colleagues.

"Well why don't you write his biography. We have to do something to stop him. He's not the drunk he used to be and unfortunately, people believe what he says," said Cardinal Truman.

"But with his son working at the old man's side, I think we've found our leverage," Truman continued.

"I agree. It is time to make our move. We will get rid of the pope once and for all and Monsignor Cross. That should keep his father from revealing our plans," said Martinelli.

Makarov looked harshly at Martinelli. Although he agreed with the cardinal, he could not tolerate any more failures.

"If you do not succeed this time, you will be retired from College of Cardinals. Permanently."

Martinelli returned the glare. He had no intention of being thwarted.

Cardinal Cantore wiped his hands. The discussion of murder, however necessary, turned his body against him. The stress was unbearable.

The men adjourned to prepare for their move.

Chapter Twenty-Four

Cross tried to spend more of his time upstate enjoying his horses and Buster. Their walks in the woods relaxed him. Just watching Buster chase after rabbits and squirrels kept his mind from focusing on the news.

One weekend, it seemed like all the critters in the woods had moved to another farm. There was an eerie silence, which blanketed the grounds. Cross did not see any wild turkeys, crows or any other birds. He couldn't remember the woods ever being that still. When he got back to the house, the horses seemed on edge. He looked around thinking someone had driven up. Sol Abrams was due to spend the next two weeks with him. He checked the entire area and no on else was there.

An annoying feeling near his solar plexus kept nagging at him the rest of the evening. He went into town for dinner and the people at the café were talking about the inability to shake the sense that something was going to happen. People speculated about another terrorist attack. Some people thought it was something like a pending natural disaster. There were a few who had the unshakeable feeling that something spiritual was about to unfold.

He called Joe when he got home. There was no answer. Cross turned on the television to watch the news, but nothing seemed to be going on, remarkable in itself. They phone rang. It was Sol. They talked for a few minutes. Cross asked him when he was coming for a visit. Sol said he'd be there in a couple of days.

Buster wanted out, so Cross cut short the call. He wandered outside while Buster got some exercise. The horses still seemed upset. Cross tossed them so more hay and then went to bed.

His gut feeling plagued him throughout the night. Buster got peeved at Cross' constant flip-flopping in bed. By 4 a.m., he got up to eat some cereal. Buster stayed by his feet hoping to get any leftovers. Cross turned on the television and flipped through several old movies and infomercials. He landed on the news. The top story ran. He nearly dropped his cereal when he heard it.

"There are concerns in Rome today. Reports about the pope's missing plane have developed in the last several hours. It is not known if the plane has gone down," said the newscaster.

Cross immediately called Joe's cell phone number. He got a message that the cell customer was not available. Buster had little trouble in convincing Cross to give him the cereal. Cross lost his appetite. Changing stations, he desperately tried to find more coverage on the pope.

He remembered a conversation he had with Joe concerning possible news stories indicating the pope was dead. Joe told him not to believe what he heard, but to be aware that the warning would be imminent.

Rome was unraveling into riots. The police had their hands full with unprecedented unrest. Cross was thankful the pope got out while he could.

Unable to go back to sleep, he checked the provisions for the animals. By afternoon, he had more hay delivered and made sure all of the water tanks were full. Just as the sun set, something strange was seen in the sky. A large cross appeared in the Eastern sky and rose until it was about sixty degrees from the horizon. Cross could easily see the body of Jesus upon the cross. The night sky suddenly turned as bright as noon around the incredibly large image. Cross felt like something had punched him in the stomach. He couldn't believe what he saw. Through Jesus' hands and feet, brilliant beams of light streamed from the nail holes and the spiritually dry world soaked it up.

Cross fell to his knees. The sheer beauty and the agony of the image overwhelmed him. Yet the realization of the crucifixion made him profoundly sad. It was as if this was the first time he understood the passion of Jesus.

The cross remained in the sky for twenty-four hours. News reports from all over the world ran continuous coverage. Scientists tried to debunk the image but could not. Arguments from Muslim countries along with Israel were aired complaining the image was a hologram produced by the Vatican to influence the entire world. The pope's plane was still missing, fanning conjecture and anger.

Much of the Christian world spent the day in church. However, violence exploded globally in answer to the spiritual experience. The entire world seemed to have lost control.

Sol Abrams arrived at the farm without Mitzi. They had been having problems again. Cross was glad to see his friend and tried to tell him that the world was in for a major realignment.

"What did you think about the news?"

"Did you see the cross in the sky," he asked Abrams.

"Cross? Forget about that. I'm talking about the freaking asteroid on its way." Cross looked Abrams in the eyes and knew he was telling the truth.

"I've been so busy getting everything ready here that I missed it."

"They just announced it on the radio. It looks like this may be it, Mikey. Experts think it's gonna hit out in the Atlantic. Right now it's orbiting around the earth, actually in orbit. Jesus."

"Don't you think you ought to be home with Mitzi?"

"Serves her right."

"Sol, you don't mean that."

Cross knew better than to argue with Sol. He would have to come around on his own.

"Maybe I won't mean it tomorrow. Right now, I mean it. Have you heard from Joe?"

"Nothing."

"The news also mentioned that they're going to call the conclave in Rome to elect a new pope."

"I expected that. Thing is, the pope isn't dead."

"Oh, yeah? So where is he? No one seems to know."

"I don't know where he is."

"And Joe's with him still?"

"Yes."

"At least he's got good company."

The asteroid was a significant problem for Cross. His boss at The Wire knew Cross' old buddy was in charge of Cheyenne Mountain and asked him to interview General Wolfe to see what measures the military would take against the orbiting rock.

Begrudgingly, Cross agreed. He didn't want to leave the farm with the approach of the warning. However, he hoped the military had plans for the asteroid. He had to know what they were.

Cross flew out that day after Wolfe's aide agreed to the interview.

Cheyenne Mountain

Cross waited to see General Wolfe, and tried to come up with pertinent questions. All he could do was to recall the time he spent with Wolfe in Viet Nam.

Wolfe never played by the rules and that bothered Cross. After one sortie over North Viet Nam, Wolfe had deliberately bombed an innocent village, killing everyone in it. Cross reported him. The brass never took the complaint seriously, but it earned Cross the nickname, "Double-Cross."

It had been years since the two had met. Cross wondered if Wolfe had changed. He doubted it.

Wolfe knew Cross had not changed in his convictions, but right now, it did not matter. The General went against his orders and decided to see Cross, if only to show him his self-righteous behavior had not hurt Wolfe's career. If General Wolfe could have forced his stars down Cross' throat, he would have.

Cross was relieved when Wolfe summoned him. He promised himself he would cut to the chase. Wolfe wasted no time in getting to the point.

"As you know, Mike, we've got a problem."

"What are you going to do about it? Are you at least going to try to shoot that bastard ball down?"

"We've tried, but our guidance systems won't operate properly. Our satellites aren't fully operational. And now it doesn't matter."

"Why? Why doesn't it matter," Cross asked.

"Because it looks that piece of shit is breaking free from its orbit. It seems to be loosing altitude."

Both men buried their hatred towards one another. For once, they were on the same side.

"How long before it drops?" Cross had to know.

"You may as well know, unless our systems are fully operational, it will hit the earth in a few days or less. Even if we could blow it up, the pieces would still hit the earth with catastrophic results."

Wolfe put his cigar down and extended his hand to Cross. "The president and the world leaders have decided not to say anything. I'd appreciate it, Mike, if you kept this under your hat. The panic would be uncontrollable."

Cross took his hand and nodded. He wouldn't know what to say at this point.

Cross wasted no time returning to his farm to finish his preparations.

The world braced itself for the asteroid. Futile attempts to change its course added to the panic. Some people committed suicide, while others partied away the remaining time.

Cross knew the Great Warning was to be seven days from the sighting of the cross. He tried to get Sol ready, but he didn't want any part of it. All Sol could talk about was how glad he was to have left the city.

"Now when this warning starts, you can't leave the house, Sol. The doors and windows will be locked. Don't open them and for God's sake, don't leave. You'll be killed."

"Yeah. Yeah. What are you doing now?"

"I'm putting plastic over the windows to keep out the dust."

"From what?"

"If that ball hits, we're going to be up to the rooftops in dust and debris."

"If that ball hits, we're all dead anyway."

"No, we're not all going to die. I meant what I said about going out."

"You got plenty of food. Where would I go?" Abrams smiled and tried to shrug off Cross' attempts.

Communications began having difficulties due to the asteroid. Satellites lost their signals. Cell phones wouldn't operate properly and radio broadcasts were interrupted.

Stockholders unloaded their stocks until the Exchange put on the brakes, suspending trading. Customers overran banks until the government stepped in and ordered the banks to close. The president addressed the nation calling for calm even though he placed the military on high alert. America responded in hopes that everything would be fine.

People continued to work and to go about their business. Yet a pervasive feeling ate at the hearts and guts of the world.

Seven days from the first appearance of the cross, a white mist formed over the globe. It started at dawn on the International Dateline and enveloped the world, spreading like a foggy growth over the entire planet. The astronauts up in the space station watched the thick substance swallow every bit of Earth. They felt helpless. With their communications down, they could do little else but watch.

Everywhere on earth, people began to feel they were losing control, that they were no longer in charge of their lives. People who were sleeping awoke abruptly, stirred to the core of their souls. Planes stopped in mid-air, suspended by an invisible force. Subways stopped. Car engines died and a fierce quiet filled the world.

Cross was in the corrals with his horses, checking them one last time. He felt a calling in his heart to go inside. It was time. Quickly, he headed for the house. He whistled for Buster who wasted no time in getting to the backdoor. Cross locked the door behind him and checked to see if all of the windows were locked. He met Sol on the stairs. Both men went to the living room to wait. Cross was somewhat unsettled, but remained calm, unlike Sol who perspired uncontrollably.

A presence came over each man. Instantly, Cross found himself kneeling on the floor. The room became powerfully bright, almost blinding him. Then, he saw Jesus on the cross in all His horrific agony. He saw violent lightning and heard deafening thunder. The floor shook beneath him.

Cross could think of nothing else, not even Joe or Sol. The vision of Jesus' suffering brought tears to his eyes and an overpowering heaviness to his heart. He watched as the blood ran from Christ's wounds. It trickled down his arms and legs eventually pooling at the base of the cross. Jesus labored for every breath. Cross wanted to close his eyes, but he could not. He watched as the blood streamed towards him.

Jesus' body grew pale as his agony continued. Slowly he turned his head towards Cross who was struck with great mortification. Their eyes met and instantly Cross knew every sin he had committed. He saw the people who were with him when he sinned. Intense pain and heat seared through him. Cross screamed in agony. Then he felt the pain of the crucifixion and realized better than he could have imagined what Jesus felt because of Cross' sins. As the heat and pain increased, Cross didn't know if he could bear it.

"Look at your sins, Michael. They warrant Hell. Know that I died for you and your sins."

Cross cried, ashamed of what he had done; now fully understanding his position before God.

"See the good things you have done. Look at how you've changed the lives of people around you. Feel the joy of heaven."

Cross saw everything good in his life. He saw a bird he rescued as a small boy. The people he had helped in his life came back to him easing the tremendous pain he felt. People he couldn't remember thanked him for his kindness.

A tremendous joy made his heart feel as though it would burst.

"Know you are loved, Michael. You are loved completely by a perfect and just God. Stay the course. Sin no more or face the eternal sentence of Hell. I love you."

For Cross the warning had ended. But for Sol, and billions of other people, it continued until they accepted their fate before God, until they accepted their sentence, until they came to the knowledge that God did exist, the consummate Judge of all.

Sol screamed in anguish. There was nothing Cross could do for him. Like everyone else, Sol had to accept his fate if he were to die in that hideous moment. Everyone in the world faced his or her personal mini-judgment. Some people found the experience relatively painless, but the majority faced minutes, even hours of the harsh reality that seemed like an eternity.

As the world paused, suspended before God, the earth writhed in a peculiar anguish. Earthquakes carved the ground with a biblical vengeance. Fires erupted all over the globe. No one could respond to them. The justice of God swept the earth in hurricane winds, torrential rains and convulsions that savagely ripped the earth and emptied the oceans.

The predicted asteroid bolted through space and quickly broke through the density of the fog, plummeting into the Atlantic. Tidal waves ensued. England broke into dozens of pieces looking like oyster crackers in the Atlantic soup. The planet lurched.

Nothing was spared. Not one person escaped God's wake up call. For eight long days, the earth and everyone on it felt the wrath their sins had caused. Those venturing outside were killed instantly. God allowed no one to witness His judgment.

Demons attacked people in their homes. People who had crucifixes on their doors were spared the battle, but were not immune to their verbal taunts. Some demons imitated the voices of loved ones. Michael Cross heard Joe's voice quite clearly calling him from outside.

"Let me in, Dad! Please!"

At first, Cross was tempted to open the door, but remembered not to open it. Sol was then pulled by the voice of Mitzi.

"Solly, honey, let me in! It's so terrible out here!"

"Mitzi? I'm coming. Hold on!"

Cross grabbed him and tried to reason with him. When that failed, Cross knocked him out.

Other people were not that fortunate. They hurriedly opened their doors to find grotesque demons waiting for them.

People prayed to die, but death wouldn't come. Millions though did find death. By the end of the eight days, when the thunder had ceased, the upheaval relented; nearly a billion people were dead.

Cross slowly opened his door, fearful of what he would see. Millions of other people found the courage to turn their doorknobs and to open the door. Everyone who bravely ventured outside could not believe their eyes.

End of Part One

About The Author

Kathleen Keating is an investigative journalist and author of the international bestsellers, The Final Warning: Your Survival Guide to The New Millennium and The Gates of Hell. She publishes a monthly newsletter, The Messenger, bringing the world the latest breaking news reports.

Kathleen writes an immensely popular weekly Internet column, The Keating Perspective, and is currently working on her next book.

Kathleen's website
www.kathleenkeating.com

The Messenger
www.materdeipress.com

Did You Enjoy This Book?
You may be interested in some of these titles.

The Final Warning, by Kathleen Keating. The international best selling book that rocked the world. An in-depth look at politics, prophecy and the people behind it all.

The Gates of Hell, by Kathleen Keating. The Gates of Hell puts an end to speculation about the validity of conspiracy theories and where they are taking us. Once and for all, rumors and innuendo are put to rest, permanently knocked out by extraordinary evidence that will leave the perpetrators scurrying for a place to hide.

Noise of the Mourning, by Kathleen Keating. The international best selling author of The Final Warning and The Gates of Hell, takes us back to the book that started it all. Showing she is a master hand at fiction as well as non-fiction, Keating takes you on a non-stop thrill ride. You won't want it to end.

The Messenger, Kathleen's monthly newsletter. Kathleen and her team of experts bring you the best of prophecy, current events, Bible Codes, and much more every month.

Coming Soon…

Torn Sky - Part Two: After a cataclysmic event, the world is decimated. What happens now?

Silence of the Evening: The knockout sequel to Noise of the Mourning, guaranteed to send chills up your spine.

Order Form

	Price	Quantity
The Final Warning	$15.95 US	_____
The Gates of Hell	$15.95 US	_____
Noise of the Mourning	$13.95 US	_____
Israel Betrayed by Barry Chamish	$13.95 US	_____
The Messenger Newsletter – 1yr	$14.95 US	_____
The Broken Election by Scott Gulbransen	$16.95 US	_____
Shipping for books	$5.95 US	_____
Total:		_____

Name: _____

Address: _____

City/State: _____ Zip Code: _____

Phone Number: _____

I've enclosed a:
___ Check   ___ Money order   ___ Credit Card Number

Credit Card Number: _____ Exp. Date: ____

Type of card ___ Visa ___ MC ___ Amex ___ Discover

Please make all checks payable to Counting Coup Press. Thank you!

**Counting Coup Press
PO Box 352
Ainsworth, NE 69210
1-866-394-2665**

Printed in the United States
61423LVS00002BA/5